HI-TECH SHIVA

AND OTHER APOCRYPHAL

STORIES

An Academic Allegory

HI-TECH SHIVA

AND OTHER APOCRYPHAL

STORIES

An Academic Allegory

by

Nazir Ali Jairazbhoy

Apsara Media
Van Nuys, California

Dedicated to all who have suffered anxiety and indignity

in the process of being reviewed

for academic tenure.

Hi-Tech Shiva and Other Apocryphal Stories: An Academic Allegory
by Nazir Ali Jairazbhoy

Copyright © 1991 Apsara Media for Intercultural Education
Printed in the United States of America

Library of Congress Cataloging in Publication Data

Jairazbhoy, Nazir Ali, 1927-
Hi-tech Shiva and other apocryphal stories: an academic allegory
x + 230 p.
I. Title
PS3560.A36H54 1991   813' .54--dc20   91-30406 CIP
      (Note: this supersedes the pre-assigned Library of Congress
      Catalog Card Number 91-075814)

ISBN   1-880519-07-0

Copies of this book, as well as talking book cassette tapes, may be
obtained by writing to

Apsara Media for Intercultural Education
13659 Victory Boulevard, Suite 577
Van Nuys, CA 91401 U.S.A.

Contents

Preface

Since I was having a little bit of trouble with this Preface I decided to go and consult Shiva. He was running late as usual, destination some swami or other on Earth. All he could think of in that fleeting moment when his 'copter was kicking sand everywhere was to reassure me, pat me on the back, and tell me to get cracking with it.

The reader may wonder how it is that I am privileged to communicate with such august beings. I am the Storyteller and travel everywhere without a visa going in and out of the lives of my subjects as I please. I have a vast network of contacts and the sky is no limit to the probes of my imagination. So this book could have been about the Hindu Gods, but it is not, at least not for the most part. It is about myself, not just as the Storyteller, but more particularly, as a professor of ethnomusicology in an academic institution in the U.S. It is also about my profession in which, as in anthropology, folklore, and numerous others, we are expected to carry out fieldwork, preferably in foreign countries whose traditions are remote from ours, return with research data, write up our results, and finally publish them in scholarly articles and books to advance knowledge of mankind. But as we go about our research abroad with substantial grants, state-of-the-art equipment and new-fangled methodologies, the Storyteller sees us as the Gods and me as Shiva, subject to moments of vanity, gullability and perhaps an occasional flash of brilliance loaned to my by the real Shiva's third eye.

It happened one day in New Delhi perhaps ten years ago that I suddenly realized that I had become a Westerner, although my colleagues in the West had long since begun to take me as one of them. I had just arrived from the U.S. on one of my many fieldtrips and walking down Janpath, I was followed by a persistent young boy shouting "Money change! Money change!" I ignored him as long as I could, but his periodic poking me in the back eventually provoked me into turning around and speaking sharply to him in Hindi, "Why are you bothering me? I'm an Indian like you." He was taken aback and gave me a sheepish smile — but as soon as I began to walk away, he resumed his chant, "Money change! Money change!" and followed me for several blocks. If the external signs were so obvious, I finally had to admit to myself that thirty years of living in England, Canada and the U.S. must have taken their toll.

Deep in my heart, however, I still regard myself as an Indian and believe that I have not completely lost my Indian perspective. The Storyteller represents this part of me, using the personal pronoun without quotes and speaking to the listener in asides as he watches with a critical eye the new Gods pursuing their selfish ends under the rubric of scholarship. As the stories progress I feel more and more the necessity of interjecting my Indian views until the Storyteller cannot resist stepping into the final story to interfere actively in its course, as might an applied anthropologist, but fortunately without dire consequences.

Since these stories are concerned with insider-outsider issues, more particularly East and West, and with the shortcomings of Western academia, one might wonder why I have used the Hindu deity framework for them. The whole subject of Hindu mythology is thoroughly fascinating and reveals the most incredible imagination, not to mention nobility of conception. In my many fieldtrips I have enjoyed the tales which are represented everywhere and in virtually all contexts: art, music, dance, literature, and everyday life. The best part of all of this is that the Gods and Goddesses are neither remote nor really frightening or incomprehensible, as in many other religions. Their adventures are real enough for us to empathize with them, and what makes for this feeling of reality is that they not only maintain lofty principles but also have some of our own weaknesses and failings. Storytellers in India, like Harikatha performers, Kirtankars and Das Kathia singers among many others, understand this better than anyone else, and frequently interpose humorous episodes of the Gods' failings during the course of their mythological narratives. The story of the woodcutter embarrassing Shiva in "Hi-Tech Shiva" is, in fact, a story which was related by Das Kathia bards of Orissa in 1963, now of course embellished in my own way.

Humor is part and parcel of storytelling in India and the myths too are "often intentionally hilarious," to quote Wendy O'Flaherty in her Preface to *Sexual Metaphors and Animal Symbols in Indian Mythology* (Delhi: Motilal Banarsidas 1980). She continues, "It seems to me therefore entirely appropriate to write about these subjects in high spirits, without denigrating them . . .." I trust the reader will understand that there is no attempt at mockery in this book, just playfulness; and since it is not about the Hindu Gods per se I have not felt the necessity to follow any source for rendering the myths accurately. In fact the opening sentence of the first story, "Hi-Tech Shiva," is technically incorrect as Mount Kailash is said to be only Shiva's residence, not that of all the Gods, many of whom have their own mountains to live on, e.g., Vishnu's home is said to be Vaikuntha, or Mount Meru. My own perceptions of the Gods and their relations with mankind, not to mention my interpretations of doctrines such as *karma* and *dharma*, should not be taken as the voice of authority, but merely that of a Storyteller and entertainer.

These stories have evolved through many live readings to friends and relatives who have given helpful suggestions along the way. I would especially like to acknowledge the expert editorial assistance and valuable comments given by Jan Steward, Sue DeVale and Wanda Bryant.

It also gives me great pleasure to express my appreciation to my two very good friends S. Raj Choudhury and Sanjay Srivastava who spent many an evening discussing the stories between bouts of ping-pong, making suggestions for new ones and different approaches as well as assisting with problems of layout and formatting. My sincere thanks also go to my daughter, Nish Jairazbhoy, for having taken the time from her busy schedule to do the cover artwork.

While I take responsibility for the ideas expressed in this book, I must acknowledge that it could never have been written without the love and encouragement of my better half, Amy Catlin-Jairazbhoy, who often postponed other projects in order to oversee its production. She helped me to formulate ideas, corrected my English, curbed the excesses of word play, made creative suggestions, and gave practical assistance at every stage, including editing the entire manuscript.

Introduction

Hordes of Aryan tribesmen swept through the mountain passes southward into the lands now called Pakistan and India displacing and destroying many indigenous inhabitants and bringing with them new Gods, new social structures, and a new set of lofty ideals. Even this Storyteller is unable to assign a date to this event, which was actually a series of raids and invasions beginning perhaps 2,000 B.C. It is the Godworld they brought, combined with that which they created in their new homeland through interaction with indigenous God- and Goddess-thoughts, that is referred to in these stories.

The Aryans have preserved their religion and their myths in hymns which were memorized and passed on orally by generations of Brahmin priests into the present. In one of these hymns composed in the language we now refer to as Vedic, the origin of the universe is described as being created by the sacrifice and dismemberment of a primordial man, Purusha, "thousand-headed, thousand-eyed and thousand-footed," who pervaded Earth on all sides and was the lord of immortality. By dividing him they created the four classes of man and other aspects of the universe, loosely translated as follows:

His mouth became the Brahmin priest; from his arms were made the Rajanya or Kshatriya, the kings and warriors; from his thighs were created the Vaishyas, tradespeople; and from his feet the Shudras, the servants.

From his mind they created the Moon and from his eye, the Sun. From his mouth the Gods Indra and Agni were taken in the form of lightning and fire, and from his breath, the God of Wind, Vayu.

*From his navel they created outer space, Heaven from
his head and the Earth from his feet. From his ears they
created the cardinal directions . . .*

This creation hymn provides the general theme underlying
these stories. In the very first story we discover that the sacrifice
of Purusha was not a very sound basis for creating the universe
and that the Gods had tried other bases previously, all of which
had ended in failure and had to be dissolved. Now the signs of
failure are once again evident and dissolution is imminent.
Endlessly ahead are new starts and new ends and a great deal of
hard work for the Gods.

In this twilight of the universe, questions are raised in
heaven: Why did it fail — was it design failure or operator
failure? What can be done to prevent them from repeating the same
mistakes? To find the answers to these and other questions, the
Gods, urged by Shiva, change their lifestyles from indolence to
feverish scholarship, only to discover interference from an
unlikely source — mankind!

ℋℐ·𝒯ℰ𝒞ℋ 𝒮ℋℐ𝒱𝒜

Mount Kailash, where the Gods reside, had seen its share of turbulence in past ages, but now under Shiva's superb helmsmanship even the Demons enjoyed unprecedented prosperity, having finally been recognized as a legitimate minority pressure group in the Heavenly Assembly. Vishnu, the leader of the Opposition Party, was also biding his time, waiting for the right moment to launch his campaign on the eve of the next cataclysm. In short, there had been for the past millennium or two, peace, plenty, and . . . boredom.

It is said that on just such an occasion many aeons ago, the Gods had first created the Earth and all on it, perhaps just as an object of amusement, or perhaps to test their powers of construction for some unknown higher purpose. Their annals record, however, that their earlier creations had always ended in cataclysms, and that Brahma had each time provided the wherewithal for a new start by turning over a new page in his mysterious Book of Creation. There had been great hope that this time would be different, since the Gods had sacrificed the one and only perfect, primeval man, Purusha, the original source of the universe, to be the base of all the elements of this creation, systematically dismembering his parts to create the Heavens, ether, and Earth and all the living species on it. Since Purusha had been perfect, it was argued that all his constituent parts would also be perfect, so that the long-sought-for harmony of creation would be achieved.

It was now becoming apparent, however, that there had been some fault in their reasoning, for an unexpected element had evidently entered the picture. A virus had somehow been introduced into the network and therefore no single element in creation was stable, although each had been derived from the perfect, unchanging Purusha. Processes of degeneration and regeneration were constantly at work — sometimes violently — severely rocking the core of the stable harmony that had been the Gods' goal for the universe. In fact, the intensity of the eruptions sometimes made it impossible for the Gods to enjoy their customary peace, plenty, and . . . boredom.

Some of the younger, junior Gods quite relished this phenomenon, thinking that this could be a heaven-sent opportunity to prove their research capabilities and thus achieve advancement to tenure in the Celestial Assembly. They called the virus by a number of names: evolution, erosion, radiation, instability, or just plain change, and noted that it was present in all matter, reflecting a kind of restlessness on a massive scale that affected equally all elements of the present creation. What single explanation could account for the nature of this virus and the way it had spread its pervasive influence throughout space? Various theories had been put forward. The Big Bang Theory was patently incorrect since the dismemberment of Purusha had been conducted in a precise, controlled manner. The Steady State Theory was obviously based on wishful thinking, since it predicated an endless continuation of the universe. The Gods could see that it had some validity in view of the their past creation failures, but, in fact, Brahma had promised that his book of blank pages was not endless — nor was his patience — and although the state of failures had been steady in the past, all the Gods still believed that they would achieve the perfect, stable creation before Brahma finally closed his book for good.

A new theory had been put forward by one of the bright young Godscholars, which questioned the very basis of this creation. He argued that, although Purusha had been perfect as a whole, his individual parts could not also be perfect, otherwise each part would also be Purusha. Thus Purusha could not be dismembered without the parts losing a fundamental element of perfection, namely the perfect harmony of the whole. He reasoned further that the virus was none other than a search for the ultimate harmony that all things had experienced while being part of Purusha. This, he said, explained why everything was restless, vibrating and changing, blindly seeking that half-forgotten ultimate state of oneness.

It is to the credit of the Gods that such a major theory being proposed by such a junior scholar was not discarded out of hand. In fact, Shiva, the King of the Gods, took it upon himself to explore the validity of the theory. He realized that if it were substantiated, then the Gods would have to find some other basis for the next creation; if not, then it might still be possible to find the clue which would stabilize this one, or at least provide further data for future construction. In either instance, the first order of the day, Shiva realized, was to collect sufficient data about Earth and its inhabitants on which to base a meaningful evaluation.

In their boredom, many of the Gods had, in any case, been taking some interest in the antics on Earth. Now this began to intensify for some into a kind of passion. Shiva had been one of the most avid Earth-watchers, primarily as a recreation, but now the recreation had became a concern for re-creation. He had found himself so fascinated by the 'play'— *lila* — of life, that his wife Parvati was sometimes having, so to speak, a devil of a time distracting him with his favorite curries, and there was growing concern that the urgent matters of state were receiving tardy attention , although admittedly few and far between.

Nothing of the Earthplay really escaped Shiva's all-seeing third eye, but with the proliferation of mankind it was becoming impossible to observe and analyze all the action from his heavenly armchair, so he realized that he would have to carry out fieldwork on Earth. Having made this momentous decision, he was faced with the next problem: what topic was he going to research? Events of everyday human life were far too numerous and repetitive, and much too tedious to suit his flamboyant character. No. It would have to be something out of the ordinary, like some of the strange and wonderful personalities who call themselves *swamis*, or some of the lesser-known rituals and performances whose greatest claim to fame is that they are in the process of dying out. He could imagine himself returning to Heaven from one of these fieldtrips and enrapturing his coterie of young Gods and Goddesses with wondrous tales of his amazing discoveries.

Fortunately, just at that time in the history of man, the video camera had been invented and with it the concepts of audio-visual documentation and time-shifting. This seemed the perfect answer to Shiva, for it would enable him to mull over important events in periods of relative inactivity, and add dramatic effect to his tales. Accordingly, being King of the Gods, he appropriated a significant portion of the annual heavenly budget to purchase video equipment. This did not turn out to be a simple matter for, at the outset, he was faced with a number of decisions regarding formats and technical characteristics, not to mention conflicting advice from dealers promoting their own brands and denigrating others. He went on a buying spree trying out the different formats, 3/4-inch U-Matic, 1/2-inch VHS and S-VHS, Beta and ED Beta, 8mm and Hi8, with all the best cameras, camcorders, palmcorders and steady cams, not to mention analog and digital audio recorders, and all the newest models of each format until the obsolete equipment pile began to clog up the heavenly disposal system. But he ventured with determination into the field again and again with ever-new equipment, returning each time with huge quantities of raw footage in a variety of formats.

As the pile of recorded tapes reached higher and higher in his abode, it became evident that they would have to be properly archived and logged on some computer retrieval system which would enable him to locate particular items without extensive searches. This, once again, was not so simple. Which format was best for preservation, and which computer, with how much memory and which peripherals, not to mention the database, would be most suitable for the heavenly archives? Again he consulted the leading journals and 'experts' and could come to no single conclusive, definitive solution. Since this was the Godworld which ought to have the best of everything, and not being able to decide which was the best, he took the safest course and decided to maintain multiple formats, storing information on IBMs and Apples, AT&Ts and HPs, and numerous others, not giving a second thought to the fact that in the process he was straining the already over-extended heavenly budget even further.

But he achieved phenomenal results, as his colleagues frequently informed him at the weekly showings that he conducted in his favorite cave on Mount Kailash. They were well-attended and favorably received for quite a while. The discussions that followed revealed some of the problems he had faced and endured. When, for instance, he had arrived at an event armed with the most expensive equipment, the participants had not only became self-conscious, but presumed that he represented the BBC, Hollywood, CBC, or CNN and demanded exorbitant rates. His attempts to convince them that his motive was pure scholarship and that he had no commercial goals were usually in vain. He had even argued that his project was eventually for the good of mankind — which was debatable — but they continued to suspect that he would derive personal benefit, if only in terms of recognition, admiration, and advancement in his own world, not knowing, of course, that Shiva was already at the top. Of course, they were right, as Shiva had always planned to show his most spectacular video tapes to his colleagues in the long-term hope that they would be sufficiently impressed to ensure his continuation as the King of the Gods into the next cataclysm.

Seeing the abject condition of many of the performers, Shiva was obliged to agree that they deserved to be compensated, not only for their time and effort, but also for revealing their cultural creations to the outside world, even though copyright laws did not then apply to much of the material which was in the so-called public domain. So he had offered them commensurate value, but they had asked, "Commensurate with whose standards, ours or yours? Since these videotapes are being shown in your world, surely we deserve to be compensated at your union rates."

This had posed a double dilemma for Shiva, since the Godworld had no union and, in fact, did not work for wages. He was thus obliged to fabricate a reality that might have been, and propose a wage rate far in excess of their standards, but considerably less than it could have been, had there been a union in the Godworld. Often this had worked, but there were occasions when astute performers and informants had not been taken in by Shiva's assessment and he was obliged to drop them for fear of what the Budget Committee might say. Needless to say, Shiva did not mention these occasions at his soirées.

The Gods murmured appreciation of Shiva's ingenuity and the consensus feeling was that the added strain on the heavenly budget was probably justified. But some of his older colleagues were beginning to question Shiva's exorbitant expenditures on the project and some of the more precocious, his methodology, which they referred to as the 'quick in-and-out' approach. They questioned whether data collected without an in-depth study of the culture could be used for serious research and were much more in support of a holistic participant-observation technique, whereby the Godscholar went to the culture as a proclaimed student and after a period of good behavior was accepted by the community, and was then made privy to their most secret practices — a process described by one as 'worming one's way into people's confidence to achieve one's own ends.' But it was generally thought that research projects carried out by Gods would never come to the scrutiny of insiders who were, after all, either illiterate or just plain ignorant. Still, just in case their future generations might get with it and discover the dissertations, most of the Gods felt that it would be prudent to conceal the true name of the townships and the identity of the individuals concerned — as if this provided real protection against libel and slander. Other ethical issues were also brought up casually at these soirées in conjunction with Earth research, but just as casually discarded, as the consensus feeling among the Gods was that ethics should not be allowed to interfere with scholarly endeavors.

On one occasion Shiva was challenged on the issue of his 'quick in-and-out' methodology. He explained that he was not at all averse to in-depth studies of culture and, indeed, fully recognized the importance of such studies for the advancement of knowledge. He pointed out, without broaching the subject of ethics, that participant-observation was time-consuming and that all the Gods in the heavens could not possibly cover even a small portion of the events that the restless nature of man was continually devising anew. In view of this, the primary purpose underlying his audio-video documentations had not been to carry out in-depth research, but to enable the time-shifting of events by videotaping them so that they would be available for future research. As events were later to prove, the ambitious junior Gods obviously had little regard for Shiva's goal, for few followed in his footsteps and some were already planning the kind of in-depth research that was designed to further their own advancement in the celestial hierarchy.

In the course of his involvement with the technical world of man, Shiva himself had become quite a technical expert and had several innovations credited to his name. In one of his moments of inventive exhilaration he was flattered into lending his name to a sharp entrepreneur for the production of 'Shiva' computers. On mature deliberation he realized, of course, that this might be interpreted as a conflict of interest — but it was too late. He was locked into a water-tight contract and could no longer withdraw his name from the company. Doubtless he remained supreme in the world of the Gods, but he still had much to learn about the ways of man.

In reviewing the history of this celestial period it is quite evident that the virus of change had already begun to influence the world of the Gods, but it was some time before it was recognized in the heavens. Shiva was definitely infected by it, but the majority of the lay Gods still basked in the eternal light, preferring to regard Shiva's involvement in electronics as the Emperor's whim to be humored — that is, until the Japanese technical genius invented High Definition TV with other added delectables such as surround and holographic sound. When Shiva heard about these new inventions he was hooked, as the expression goes, and was convinced that this was the ultimate and only way to go. How little he knew of man's ingenuity!

"Could the heavenly world hold up its head with less than this?" he argued at the next budget meeting, which he had hastily convened for the express purpose of proposing a switch to HD format. However, despite Shiva's impassioned pleas, the seasoned veterans on the Committee remained unmoved. The annual budget had already been over-extended, leaving only a small contingency fund. All were reluctant to go into deficit funding, but how to say this to the King? Prevarication, as always, was the chosen political ploy. They resorted to it by proposing that a committee be formed to look into this 'very promising' avenue, thinking that this was tantamount to burial of the proposal, as the deliberations of the Committee would lead eventually to a monstrously lengthy report, which no one would read, to be followed by the formation of a Review Committee and its report, which also no one would read, ad infinitum.

But, as it turned out, this was not to be.

Shiva, somewhat discouraged, nevertheless went on with his fieldwork, remaining engrossed in the fascinating cults of man. He had just heard of an extraordinary snake rite being planned in a remote part of India — one that took place only once every thousand years. It was to be incredibly elaborate, with lengthy preliminaries and numerous events simultaneously taking place at different venues. In order to document this satisfactorily, Shiva knew he would need a crew, which was much against his nature since he had always been a loner. Of course, he was still determined to be the first camera(man)-God, chief editor, director, and producer of the project. Although he was not accustomed to this overseer role, he put together a body of compliant crew members to be led by his son, Ganesha, the elephant-God, widely recognized as God of Wisdom and Remover of Obstacles. After numerous hands-on training sessions and meticulous planning, all was ready, and the heavenly crew descended to Earth to take up their shooting stations on the eve of the ritual.

In the meanwhile, in another equally remote part of India a completely unrelated event was taking place, one which was to have a major impact on heaven. Vishvanathan was a poor old blind woodcutter who lived beyond the precincts of a small, little-known village and spent his days outside pottering about in search of firewood. He was the most unfortunate of creatures — helpless, with no offspring, a tiny hut which the legal owner had long since written off as worthless, no annuity or pension and, to top it all, a shrew of a wife. Yet he still had life, and perhaps hope, no matter how hopeless his future seemed. His life had been full of calamities and another one was on the horizon — possibly the ultimate one.

His wife, who had been for several years living in a state of simmering anger, proclaimed one morning, "Husband, you have been less than a husband for many years, nor have you been provider, nor source of any joy. I have had enough of you. Go away and don't come back until you've found all three." With that, she ushered him out into the utterly dark world with just a bowl of dry rice.

Poor Vishvanathan stumbled out without a cane, groping for even a tiny shred of light, but there was none. He would surely have perished, but for some unknown master plan which took him through a series of mishaps to the courtyard of a distant temple. Here he sat in a corner and prepared to waste away into oblivion, but a steady stream of pious pilgrims kept replenishing his bowl, and life refused to leave his tortured body and mind.

So he sat, for hours and hours and days and days. There was nothing to do, no experiences to relive, no dreams for the future — just endless existence in the deepest void. Little by little tiny specks of light began to penetrate the utter darkness, elusive sparks that vanished as soon as he tried to focus on them. Were they real or imaginary? They came with ever-increasing frequency and intensity and he learned to leave them be, to let them wash inside and over his being until they filled him with a glorious inner radiance. Now he found he was free to roam amid the stars and the galaxies, in and out, dancing with the mists of space.

Quite by chance, the Gods noticed this unusual phenomenon, this elusive darting light that flashed through the sky in pirouettes and arabesques amid the stately columns of creation. Of course they were nonplussed, for the light did not follow any of the laws they had created. It was obviously some new form of energy, but what was its source, what its content and what its purpose? As they contemplated and marvelled at its beauty the light flashed around the horizon, below their heaven and over it, and the Godworld began to rock in a disconcerting manner. As though full of joy at this new discovery, the light flashed round and round tossing the celestial abode back and forth and up and down, as though it were caught in some nebulous maelstrom. Emergency sirens — which had been lying dormant for centuries — shrieked their alarms and the fire engines rushed hither and thither seeking stray cats in the trees, for that was the full extent of their experience.

Since Shiva was away, the elders, shaken out of their hammocks, hurriedly scheduled an emergency council meeting at which a hoary one recalled that just such an event had taken place before, a long, long time ago — he called it the 'spark of Buddha' — and it had upset the heavens for quite a while. Unfortunately, he could not remember just how the situation had been resolved, but it had not been easy. So there seemed to be no option but to contact Shiva, even though all the Gods knew that when angered, he could, and would, burn any messenger to a crisp with his third eye. Fortunately, a God mentioned that among Shiva's technical paraphernalia he had noticed a FAX machine, and accordingly, the Gods sent out a memo urging Shiva's immediate return.

When he received the message, Shiva was engrossed in the first extraordinary event of the rite: the propitiation of the snake God, his wife, and all their children, begging their forgiveness for the inadequacy of the incredibly munificent but outlandish offerings which the priests were about to immolate. And just at the moment when the flames sparked into life and embers glowed all around like tiny snake eyes, the FAX arrived.

Shiva's third eye glowed in rage as he fought his immediate impulse to crisp everything around him. As it was, the beam was powerful enough to make the priests' hair stand on end, but all regarded this as a favorable omen for it indicated that the snake God's family had chosen not to do really serious injury to the priests. Although Shiva was still fuming at the interruption, he could not but pause to appreciate the facileness with which humans had converted his momentary lapse to their own advantage, and he was more than ever intrigued to see the succeeding events. But this was the first emergency ever sent out on his new FAX, and he knew that if he disregarded such a desperate call of duty, it would have repercussions on his Hi-Tech aspirations for the heavens.

So he had to go, but he set his camera to wide angle and left it running, just in case his crew bungled all the other angles. As he departed for Kailash, Ganesha saw him off with a cheery wave of his trunk, but his soulful eyes expressed his anxiety, for this was his first experience of fieldwork and he would no longer have any guidance.

And so Shiva floated back to Heaven to rock with his colleagues at the antics of the dazzling dart of light. At the sight, he immediately recalled the 'spark of Buddha' and groaned inwardly at the trouble it had caused before it had finally been appeased, but only by giving Buddha God-status. And here it was again! Who was it this time, another prince, or an ancient with a flowing white beard wise in the ways of the supernatural?

He could hardly have been prepared for what he was about to see!

While Shiva had been returning from Earth, one of the enterprising young Gods had already tracked through a radar beacon the original source of the spark, the courtyard of a small, virtually unknown temple in a remote province in India. Without being told, Shiva knew that it was his job to find the source of this new spark and negotiate with its owner to cease and desist so that the heavens could resume their state of placid benignity. But just as he was about to leave for Earth, the Chair of the Budget Committee gave him a stern reminder that the remaining contingency fund translated to only one wish and that his HD TV set-up could be at stake.

Arriving in the courtyard, Shiva could only see a heap of clothes in a corner. On closer inspection, huddled beneath was a bag of bones surrounded by wizened flesh and remnants of sensory organs. But the spark flashing about in the sightless eyes in a joyous display of impudence convinced him that this was indeed the source of the celestial anxiety. This would not be easy, Shiva warned himself. The utmost diplomacy would be needed. As he debated his next move, the bag of bones stirred, the eyes closed, and suddenly the courtyard was filled with an eerie darkness, as though engulfed in black cotton. Through it he heard Vishvanathan's thin, reedy voice:

"Such fun, such downright fun. I can't remember ever having had such a good time watching them scurrying about and falling over each other! I'm going right back to give them another dose of the same."

Shiva knew that he had to intercept him, so before Vishvanathan could open his eyes to activate the darting light, he stammered, "Uh, uh, your Holiness, uh, I mean Sir, with all due respect and consideration, but uh, I have come a long way to speak to you about the uh, thing with your eyes. Remarkable trick, and er, quite disconcerting to some, but surely, surely of no real substance? I mean, it's clever and, if I might say so, er, quite ingenious, but what can you do with it? Can you levitate? Can you possess another? I mean, what good is it?"

Vishvanathan, not at all disconcerted, replied, "This is supreme bliss, ultimate joy, buzzing the world of the Gods. Surely joy is good, and that's what good it is."

Shiva thought, 'First round to me, at least I have stayed his departure.' Then he responded, "But that's utterly selfish. It might give you a few laughs at the expense of others, and we're good sports and can take a joke or two, but ultimately, where will it get you?"

At this, Vishvanathan began to suspect that he may not be talking with a mortal — but perhaps an emissary of the Gods. So he adopted a more deferential tone of voice.

"I have always heard that the Gods were all-knowing and all-seeing, especially the deeply revered, high and mighty Shiva who has the benefit of the third eye. But have they not known and seen my plight and that of all the other unfortunate ones on Earth? Why have they done nothing to ease our suffering? All I was simply trying to do was to say to them, 'Please look at us, give us your light and guidance' — that is, until I really started enjoying myself with these new powers from the abyss of meditation, and now I don't want to stop. It's just too much fun."

"I now see the true cause and nature of your suffering," said Shiva, projecting himself into the past. "Indeed, you have had a hard life and I extend my fullest sympathies to you. But your life is of your own making. In your last existence you were utterly arrogant and sinful and this is your just reward."

"But surely there must be some other way to atone for one's past sins. Do repentance and forgiveness meaning nothing to the Gods?"

Shiva replied, "Vishvanathan, if they did, Gods would be like mortals and we want none of that. When we set up the laws of this creation, we laid down our ground plan and in it we specified the basic doctrine of *karma:* as you sow now, so shall you reap in your next life. In our considerations, we specifically avoided all human emotions of kindness, forgiveness, turning the other cheek, and the like that might interfere with the dispensation of this justice. We specifically excluded all resources that might have enabled man to plead directly with us to intercede in this process of justice. Man has never believed this and continues to pray, beseech, and to make offerings — sometimes prodigious offerings — but the structure of the universe we created precludes the possibility of our response to these pleas. Think, if it had been otherwise, none of us in heaven would have had a moment of peace and we would all have had to spend endless hours of our precious time adjudicating on human issues."

"I begin to see something of your design for the universe," said Vishvanathan, "but what if your design is faulty, as I think it is? Then who suffers, the designers or us poor humans who have had no say in your master plan?"

Shiva thought for a moment and said, "You raise an interesting point which I shall definitely bring before the next Planning Committee meeting. In the meanwhile, humans are just going to have to live with the conditions of this creation."

Then Vishvanathan responded. "Very well, then I shall continue to buzz Mount Kailash." And with that, he made a show of opening his eyes.

"Wait, wait, wait," Shiva hastily interposed. "I concede your point. Don't go rushing off without thinking. Alright, suppose we were to intercede as a 'one-time' exception — just in your case, mind you. For your information alone, there is a clause in the bylaws which does permit us this kind of flexibility, but I want you to know that it must be exercised with the greatest restraint and when it happens there is always an elaborate hearing — and who knows what other issues might be raised? But suppose for the sake of argument we were to intervene on your behalf. I must tell you that we are now down to contingency level and that translates to a single, last final wish left in this year's budget. It is within my emergency powers to grant you this one wish, much as I would personally have preferred to use it for another purpose" — thinking of his HD TV. But, in the tradition of all God-Kings who put the common good above their own predilections, he pronounced, in a grandiloquent tone: "As a matter of fact, I now give you this one last wish."

Vishvanathan deliberated. Just one wish. How to make it most effective? What did he really want? He recalled his miserable life and his wife's parting words. True, she was now a shrew, but it had not always been so. Once he had loved her, and she him. Those were the only pleasant memories of his adult life he could recall. Suddenly, he knew what he wanted.

While he was waiting, Shiva began to realize the full implications of his thoughtless commitment, and concern washed over his face. What if Vishvanathan asked for something impossible, like the moon, or even worse, if he asked for the Gods to bow down to him? Would they be prepared to stoop just to save his face, or would they compel him to go back on his word? And what would that do to his reputation on Earth and in the celestial sphere? He now knew that he should have laid down some ground rules and placed some restrictions on the wish he had granted. But it was too late — he had given his word.

Imagine his relief when Vishvanathan said, "My wish is simple. I just want to see my son eating out of a gold plate."

'Of all things!' Shiva thought. 'The trouble I could have been in!' But outwardly he showed no sign of his relief and merely stated, "Your wish is granted."

As he soared off to Mount Kailash, he mentally patted himself on the back and thought about the ways he could embellish the story to enhance his role in the matter. Surely the Gods would be impressed. Approaching the Mount, he could see a reception committee had collected with his wife, Parvati, in the forefront. But as he drew nearer, he began to sense that something was wrong. Perhaps this was not going to be the expected hero's welcome. What could have gone awry? He saw Parvati, breasts heaving and seething inwardly, was valiantly trying to keep her composure in front of the others. She beckoned him aside as he landed and in a tight-lipped, restrained tone, she whispered, "They are mad at you. Now what will you do, you feckless King of the Gods! I shouldn't be surprised if you're impeached."

Shiva could not believe his ears. He had expected to be showered with flowers and the episode to go down in the annals of his accomplishments. Instead, talk of impeachment! "What have I done?" he blurted. Parvati told him, "You have been hoodwinked by that bundle of rags. You have really granted him five wishes, not one. Firstly, you have granted him his sight. Didn't you know he was blind? Secondly, you have granted him a son. You know what that means. His days of virility are long gone. You are going to have to make him virile again. And what about his wife who is long past bearing? You are going to have to give her back her youth. Then you are going to have to give them a son — a son that they could not have when they were young, no matter how often they tried. Admittedly the gold plate is easy enough and you can take one from one of our sets, but the budget committee is distraught at your indiscretion over the other wishes and the Gods are actually questioning your qualifications to remain King."

Shiva was mortified. Perhaps it would have been easier to give Vishvanathan the moon! What was to be done?

Actually, it was not as bad as all that. The members of the Committee greeted him with their usual courtesy and the Chair, an old friend, reprimanded him rather mildly, saying, "Sir Shiva, I've known you to do some great and wonderful things in your days, but also some foolhardy ones. All great Gods have to blunder sometimes and you seem to have done it here. There will, of course, have to be a hearing, but I think it will turn out all right in the end. After all, your past record speaks for itself except for one or two indiscretions which we can gloss over. Don't worry, I'll speak up for you."

Shiva was somewhat relieved but knew that he was in a delicate situation. With the help of one of the most brilliant attorneys in Heaven he planned his brief very carefully, and at the hearing he presented his opening statement.

"Members of the Budget Committee and colleagues present, this is a moment to be remembered in our annals. We have seen in this little episode an event which illustrates par excellence that we have not utterly failed in this creation. On the contrary, I would say that we have had phenomenal success in some areas which we must try to emulate in our future creations — if, indeed, we need more than one. It is an event that must be documented carefully and studied in detail by all of us. It is one of the extremely rare, if not unique, occasions when one of the created has bested his creators. Just think of it! Can there be any greater joy for us than to know that we have created something that is capable of challenging and contesting our own limitless powers? This has never happened in any previous creation. How did we achieve it here? Was it by giving man free will and the ability to shape his own destiny? In any case, we created man and especially Vishvanathan; we should be proud and be prepared to take the responsibility for it. If it means that we have to create a deficit budget at this time, then I say we must do it, for this moment is of fundamental importance to our vision of the future.

"Our scholars will have to research this in great depth and they will need all the help we can give them. And so I plead with you to approve this deficit budget to include, not only the extra wishes of Vishvanathan but also the HD TV system I have been advocating, to document this momentous event and others that I anticipate, as they deserve to be, with the best visual definition and sound that money can buy. I rest in defense of my case with the classic expression: You get out only what you have seen fit to put in."

The conclusion was foregone, and yet it was new. The deficit budget was approved, Vishvanathan lived to live again, and Shiva lived to face another big battle when SUPER High Definition TV was introduced.

And what of the snake rite? Maybe Ganesha should have trodden more warily, for the blatant cameras, lights, and crew members suddenly came to the notice of the devout. Objections were raised and rumours ricocheted from every wall — the interlopers were interested only in sensationalism and the event would be exploited in every way imaginable — not to mention some unimaginable ones. Lurid newspaper headlines incensed the general public who descended on the scene in droves to watch, secretly hoping to participate in some hysterical manner. Religious extremists and fanatics of all kinds, including students, embarked on fasts to the death and threats flew fast and furiously.

What a first field experience for poor Ganesha! He had no recourse but to order a hasty retreat. And was Shiva disappointed? Well, not really. He knew that mankind doesn't give up its traditions easily, and that the rite would be performed again. And this time, he would be armed with his brand new Hi-Definition recording system.

DRAMA AND DEVI'S DREAM

Once, long before the advent of television, when the Gods had to provide their own entertainment, Indra, past King of the Gods, approached the great father Brahma, requesting him to produce an audio-visual object of diversion. He specified further that it should not be in obscure language and be suited to a general audience, with ratings no higher than PG. This meant, of course, that some of the most interesting but lurid events of the Godworld would have to be omitted. Brahma, after going into a state of supreme concentration, came up with an enormously elaborate system, which he named *natya* — loosely translated as drama. It was a grand scheme, drawing from the four previous sources of knowledge called the Vedas, and designed to entertain and educate viewers, principally about the mythological and semi-historical tales in which the Gods regularly vanquish the demons.

Indra was delighted. 'What a marvellous idea!' he thought. 'What a wonderful way to glory in my past successes!' — until Brahma handed him a massive tome of 36,000 couplets on the science of drama and said, "My part is done. It is now up to you to audition the Gods for the different roles. Make sure that none of them suffers from stage fright and that all are accustomed to hard work."

At this Indra's spirits plummeted, for he knew that none of the Gods cared for any kind of work, and he could not think of a single God who would be bothered to remember the lines or come to rehearsals. Looking at the volume in his hands, it suddenly occurred to him that someone would have to direct the performance, which would mean not only reading the whole work but memorizing huge chunks of it, if not all. It then occurred to him that Brahma might have presumed that Indra would himself be prepared to direct the performances since he had proposed its invention, and paled at the very thought of it. Sure enough, that was exactly what Brahma had presumed, for he continued:

"I have every confidence in your ability to follow my injunctions which are clearly laid down throughout the work, and I am sure that you will produce one masterpiece after another."

'Horrors,' Indra thought, 'I'm a warrior, not a pansy poet, a God of my word, prepared to defend right against all odds. What does Brahma expect of me? To change my whole nature? And who's going to give me the kind of respect that I, Chief Warrior of the Gods, must have? This is an utterly ridiculous situation and somehow I must let Brahma know that it was just a casual request of mine to dally away the hours, reclining pleasantly on the heavenly sod and watching the re-enactment of my glorious deeds. The thought of sweating away behind the stage, hour after hour, prompting Shiva and Vishnu through their lines is enough to give me the chills.'

Palms joined in the deeply respectful pose, Indra said with all the humility he could muster, "O Nearly Eternal One, no doubt you have done a truly wondrous job in producing this work. One as humble as I hardly deserves it. I had not intended to put you to such great trouble — In fact, it was just an idle thought on my part . . ."

"What do you mean, 'idle thought'?" interrupted Brahma impatiently. "Idle thought indeed! Do you realize just how many hours I have spent in creating this work of perfection? Even the Greeks don't have such an elaborate and effective dramatic tradition! And all for nothing, you say! Just an idle thought! I can only hope that you are not serious."

"No, no, O Holy One," Indra chimed in. "Of course I didn't mean that in the way it sounded, and for that my deepest apologies. It's just that I have responsibilities of state which prevent me from undertaking such an important venture. There are budgets and things that constantly need my attention. And I didn't want to start anything on such a grand scale that I could not do full justice to . . . that is, with my other commitments and all . . . No, no, I certainly did not mean to denigrate in any way your wonderful, utterly new form of expression that even the Greeks and Romans will envy. I am absolutely sure that when it comes to their attention, the Endowment for the Heavenly Arts will provide a substantial subvention. And as past King, I shall make absolutely sure that they leave no stone unturned in seeking all the funds we might need to ensure the success of the productions. It's just that Gods have their virtues, and indolence is one of them. As it is, virtues are scarce in the Godworld and we shouldn't really approve any weakening in this area. So I was thinking, what about giving drama to the sages, the *rishis*, the wise ones on Earth? They have mastered the mysteries of the Vedas and now understand them better than we do, what with all the interpretive commentaries and linguistic studies they have subjected them to. They already have prodigious feats of memory on their records and would have no trouble in memorizing all your injunctions and guidelines. Yes, the more I think of it, they are the right beings to produce these dramas," Indra bubbled on. "Mankind would, of course, make the perfect puppets to enact the plays. They're capable of intense concentration and they're incredible workaholics, especially the Nats — you know, the acrobats, balancers, and storytellers. Did you know that they're also genealogists and jongleurs? But, of course, you know all things. The more I think about it, yes, that is the answer. Get them to do the dirty work — er, I mean, put on the show."

Brahma, knowing all things, knew that Indra was right. For a moment he had hoped that the Gods might have taken to *natya* in such a big way that they would have changed their life styles. But then he imagined the flop on opening night, as the prima donnas of the heavenly world, primped and puckered, meandered through their lines, and he knew that it could never be.

Then he considered Indra's solution. Yes, it might well work. Humans had great respect for their *rishis*, and if he just infected an important sage, such as Bharata, with the *natya* bug, then the epidemic was bound to spread through the populace.

And so it came to be. Thus ordered and infected, Bharata introduced *natya* on Earth to his hundred sons, and through them to the whole populace. But it was not without its problems. The program Natya™ 1.0, as communicated by Brahma to Bharata, had not been thoroughly debugged. While the human actors learned their parts reasonably well, the early rehearsals indicated to Bharata that some vital spark was missing and that the actors seemed to be going through their lines almost mechanically — This was, of course, long before 'method acting.' Bharata tried everything he could think of. If an actor was supposed to depict pain, Bharata even tried jabbing him with a hatpin, but when he came in front of the lights, he would become so self-conscious that he would forget the prick of the pin and resume mouthing his words. The actors just could not communicate with conviction, perhaps because the plays were all about the Gods and the Demons and none of them about humans. Yet Bharata had been commissioned to produce these plays which depicted the victories of the Gods over the Demons, a commission which was one of the greatest opportunities of his life and one that he could not afford to pass up. What to do?

Bharata finally went back to Brahma and pleaded with him to provide an update of the program, and although Brahma didn't relish all the extra effort, he promised to work on it in his spare moments. The truth of the matter was that he couldn't think of a solution to the problem. Bharata, in the meanwhile, was becoming more and more desperate. The opening had been announced and the invitations sent out. It was too late to back out of it and he was deeply concerned that his reputation was at stake.

So he continued to bug Brahma for a debugged update. In desperation, Brahma, who was becoming thoroughly fed up with these tiresome interruptions, reluctantly brought the matter up at a meeting of the Heavenly Entertainment Committee, which he had constituted as an afterthought. He told them about Bharata's concern and, even more reluctantly, his inability to produce an update. Actually, he didn't quite put it that way. He pointed out that his program was utterly perfect. The fault, he said, was not in its design, but could be ascribed to consumer error. Any changes he might introduce would make the program less than perfect, and that he was not prepared to do.

At first, the Gods felt no need to heed Bharata's plea; after all, drama had only been invented to satisfy their vanity. Besides, they knew all the stories. It did not matter greatly to them that the actors were just going through the motions; they could add the conviction themselves as needed. They just delighted in seeing themselves thrashing their traditional enemies, the Demons and the 'noseless, phallus-worshipping aborigines,' as they called them. Their consensus view was, 'On with the show.' It wasn't drama they were interested in, but exhibitionism and a chance to indulge in nostalgia over their glorious past.

It was obvious, however, that Bharata was truly concerned, as he continued to plead: "It is clearly stated in my guidelines that *natya* was not created just for the Gods, but also for the edification of the common man. Surely general audiences, even with parental guidance, can't be expected to know the exploits of the Aryan Gods as you do, since many of them have their own myths and legends involving Gods and Goddesses from a pre-Aryan period. How will they adopt your world and adventures as part of their own heritage if our actors are not convincing? I am afraid that without the empathy from the audiences, your wars and battles may seem vicious and bloody to them — not that they are, of course — but if we can't convince the audience of the necessity for them and get them on your side, sympathizing with your cause, I am afraid they may turn the other way. Being Gods you must know that I have tried my best with the actors, and they have worked hard, very hard — I can certainly vouch for that — but to make theater work, some divine spark is necessary, and that is missing. So I plead with you to help me in this matter."

The Gods were finally more or less convinced by Bharata's words, but looked at each other in dismay, because most of them knew very little about human experience. How does one provide the divine spark in an actor to make his performance come to life? So there was a long silence, and the matter was deferred, and referred to the next meeting of the General Assembly which Shiva called soon after, especially to consider this particular issue.

As often happens, the meeting began quietly since few of the tenured Gods were ever eager to draw undue attention to themselves in meetings lest this involve them in new committee work. But not all the Gods in the Assembly had tenure and some were eager to get recognition. Among them was Ayappan, a Dravidian deity, not young, but one who had not yet achieved acceptance among the Aryan Gods. While he did not dare propose an update to the program which would have offended Brahma, he came up with another kind of solution:

"We can hardly expect human actors to put emotion into stories about our experiences and adventures," he said. "They can't possibly know our value systems or our feelings. Either we have to become actors ourselves . . ." — which was greeted with boos — "or at least help them in some way. I suggest that we take possession of their innermost worlds at the most passionate moments of the play and speak our feelings through them, thus providing the divine spark of conviction which seems to be an essential part of theater. This way we won't have to remember lines, arrange stage sets, or provide the very elaborate music and dance Brahma has invented for this purpose. Most of the time we can relax, watch, and enjoy, just using our mental powers at critical moments."

Needless to say, no one was really happy with this proposal, although it seemed utterly logical. In creating *natya* they had wanted to bask in the euphoria of their own exploits, but now they would have to follow the action and make sure they didn't miss their cues. Of course, it was not nearly as bad as being asked to memorize lines and physically cavort about the stage, but possessing humans was not all that easy either. It took a great deal of energy and concentration and that meant work, something the Gods had learned to live without eons ago.

"I presume that this is a motion. Before we take a vote on it, there must be a second," said Shiva, hoping secretly that no one would volunteer, but he was to be disappointed as several hands went up, principally from the non-tenured faculty (who had only recently been accepted as voting members in the Assembly, except on personnel issues). "Very well then," announced Shiva, "Any discussion?"

"A point of clarification, Mr. Chairman. Precisely how does our Honorable Mr. Ayappan propose we should go about this?" asked Indra, the seasoned veteran of many campaigns, somewhat sarcastically. "We can't all go down to Earth willy-nilly, possessing actors right and left. After all, some of us have more important things to do." "That's true," said Skanda, another warrior God, who was also seeking a new vocation in these non-martial times. "I can envision complete chaos."

All eyes turned to Ayappan as though to intimidate him, but Ayappan remained unperturbed. "Mr. Chairman, sir. With all humility I suggest that this is not so complicated. We are here dealing with the artistic experience of man, and since I have spent many years studying humanity, the myriad human emotions of real life can, for artistic purposes, be symbolized by just eight essences, or *rasas*, as Brahma has already pointed out in his Natya™ program. These are:

Erotic (*sringara*)

Comic (*hasya*)   Pathetic (*karuna*)

Heroic (*vira*)   Furious (*raudra*)

Terrible (*bhayanaka*)

Odious (*bibhatsa*)   Wonderful (*adbhuta*)

(. . . ? . . .)

"With just these eight — we might call them sentiments —
all human emotions can be portrayed in theater. But you will notice
that the infinitely wise Brahma has chosen not to complete the
symmetry by adding the ninth at this time. That one will be

Peace (*shanti*).

But the time is not yet — and besides, peace is much too boring for
the theater."

"I wish he would get to the point," mumbled the Chair, as
Ayappan continued. "We need not possess the whole body and
spirit of the actors, which I recognize is extremely demanding, but
just enough to imbue them with the divine counterparts of these
emotions, and only at those moments when they are at their height
in the play. And we need not bother about minor characters, just
the leading players."

This was still not going to be easy, but perhaps
manageable. Nevertheless, Skanda, who was eager to impress the
august personages present, continued to be picky. "This can lead
to chaos if we all try to assert our individual interpretations of the
emotions on the actors at the same time. I can see them getting so
confused that they'll look as if they have the seven-year itch!"

"I quite see your point," said Ayappan, as though he hadn't thought of it before. "You're probably right in drawing our attention to the different views that are held on virtually everything in the Godworld, and when it comes to the human sentiments, I am sure it would be no different. Without debating the matter of correct interpretations, which I believe would be counter-productive, I propose that we select the best God to represent each emotion on the strength of his dossier in the areas concerned. It would then be the responsibility of the chosen God to inject his divine spark into the actors' and actresses' veins at appropriate moments."

This led to mutter and chatter, but since no one articulated an objection, the vote was called for and the motion approved, albeit with a large number of abstentions.

The tricky business of choosing the most appropriate God for each emotion was now at hand, but there was an awkward silence as no one wanted to seem pushy and make the first nomination. Finally Vishnu, who was leader of the Opposition Party, spoke up. He had reasoned that all the choice emotions might be doled out to the members of the dominant party, and to obviate this he volunteered to take over the Erotic sentiment, citing his vast experiences in this area, especially in his incarnation as the dark, romantic Krishna. None could gainsay this since his renown in this area was not only known widely on Earth, but had also caused occasional distress to husbands in heaven.

The appointment was approved with acclamation. One of the other Gods from the Opposition then moved that Vishnu represent the other sentiments as well, since in his many incarnations he had embodied them all. Not unexpectedly, this was not well-received by the members of the dominant party, who had little difficulty in persuading the Chair that the motion was out of order.

Indra was the next to volunteer, naturally choosing the Heroic sentiment. Had he not led the heavenly Aryan armies

against the Dravidian *dasa*s and *dasyu*s who infested the Earth,
and had he not slaughtered them in large numbers without fear for
his own safety? Could his bravery be questioned? This, too, was
approved by acclamation — indeed, who would dare to challenge
this awesome wielder of the thunderbolt? Obviously no one,
otherwise Indra's infamous loss at the hands of the demon
Ravana's son and other small misadventures might well have been
brought up.

Skanda, the disputed son of Shiva who also fancied
himself as a hero-type, had hoped to have been nominated to
represent the Heroic sentiment on account of his destruction of the
Demoness, Taraka, and was extremely disappointed. But he was
determined that his family should be represented on this roster,
and without embarrassment, perhaps recalling some childhood
experience, proposed that his father represent Anger. After all —
he hardly needed to remind the Assembly — the wrath of Shiva's
third eye was legendary, and did not his fiery temper frequently
break beyond control, such as when he had cut off his own son
Ganesha's head merely for disturbing him during his meditation?
Of course, he had replaced the head with one taken off an elephant
that happened to be passing by, but Skanda argued that his father
was so great precisely because his violent temper was tempered by
forgiveness. Skanda's motion was immediately seconded by
Agni, the God of Fire; but the wise Buddha, who was one of the
constitutional experts on the Senate, pointed out that according to
the bylaws, the Chair of the Senate could not also be a voting
member of a Senate Committee, so that this disadvantage would
render Shiva's participation on the *Rasa* Roster ineffective.

This caused no little consternation until Surya, the Sun
God, dispelled the uncertainty with a ray of his luminous clarity,
pointing out that this was not an officially constituted committee
— more a gentlemen's agreement to convene — and that if the
leader of the opposition were to be represented, surely the leader
of the dominant party should also find representation. He then

called for a consensus vote that Shiva in his most terrible aspect as Rudra 'the howler or roarer' represent the Furious sentiment, *raudra*. And so it was acclaimed.

One could see that the Opposition Party was not entirely happy with this, even though it was inevitable. One of the members thought of a ploy that might help to counterbalance the impact of the family by proposing that Shiva's elephant-headed son, Ganesha, represent the Comic sentiment. "After all," he argued, "what could be funnier than seeing a half-elephant with one tusk, the other half a pudgy human, zipping about on a rat, as Ganesha loves to do?" But Ganesha himself objected to what he called stereotyping and pointed out that he had many other facets to his character, and was widely worshipped as the God of Wisdom and Remover of Obstacles. He was also regarded as the Lord of Beginnings, whose propitiation was considered by all to be auspicious. If his name were to be associated with the Comic sentiment, it would certainly have a negative impact on his other duties and responsibilities.

The Gods, nevertheless, felt that the Comic would be most appropriate for Ganesha and attempted to convince him, one pointing out that the Comic did not only mean laughing at, but also laughing with, and that he might be even more effective if fun could be added to his normal duties, which were otherwise rather stuffy. If the truth be known, Ganesha was already aware of the humorous aspect of his appearance, and rather liked it. He loved tooling about mounted on the rat and careening around corners on just two of its tiny feet. But he wasn't about to accept so easily and found himself saying that he would only do so on one condition — but promptly forgot what it was.

Fortunately his father, who had felt that it would not be seemly for the son of the Chairman of the Senate to be regarded as a Comic, came to his rescue. "I can't deny that some might regard Ganesha's antics as being humorous, but you all know that the very sight of him lightens our burdens — few as they are in

Heaven. I also can't deny that humans might well find him funny, but you are overlooking one thing. The sight of an elephant riding on a rat is not only funny, but it is also a source of wonderment that such a phenomenon could have come into being and, ultimately, reflects on the imagination and miraculous powers of his creator." (Modesty prevented him from mentioning his own name.) "If indeed," he continued, "the august members continue to feel that Ganesha should represent the Comic — and frankly I can't think of any alternative in Heaven — then I say, contrary to our earlier practice of limiting Gods to just one sentiment, that he should also represent Wonderment. I do not think this will be too much of an imposition on him since he is not presently overburdened by committee work."

As usual, Shiva had turned the opposition's proposal to his advantage, and although there was some concern that this would mean over-representation of the dominant party's views, Shiva's argument was irrefutable and the Gods gave their approval. Ganesha, glowing in the recognition he had finally received from the Heavenly Assembly, accepted the dual responsibility, with the modesty becoming a tenured assemblyman.

There still remained three sentiments to be assigned: the Pathetic, the Terrible, and the Odious. Vishnu, who had been sitting quietly and contemplating his new appointment as Chief of Erotica — although no one had called it that — now realized that his party was looking for him to do something positive in his role of Opposition leader, and he rose to the occasion.

"It hurts me greatly that the Supreme Spirit and Creator of the Universe, our revered Brahma, has not been considered in our discussions. I think it is symptomatic of the way we continually bypass him in all our considerations. And on Earth, too, insufficient credit is given to him. Did you know that there are only two modest temples dedicated to him in India, whereas there are hundreds to the Chair and the Opposition leader? His is the ultimate power of creation and dissolution, and yet we have relegated him to the role of an ordinary assemblyman!" A murmur of acknowledgment greeted Vishnu's words as he continued. "In my mind, there is no God in the heavens or on Earth who has been so undeservedly ignored, and I thus propose that he be our representative for the Pathetic sentiment."

Vishnu had surely raised a good point, although some felt that Brahma might have brought it on himself by having an incestuous relationship with his own daughter, Vach. Nevertheless, Brahma was one of the Celestial Trinity and there could be no denying that he deserved the recognition. The Gods were silent for a long time, recognizing the truth of what Vishnu had said, but not wanting to admit that they were ultimately responsible for having reduced the once-supreme Lord to his present state. Shiva had been carrying guilty feelings for a long time. He had adopted high- and many-handed tactics in wresting power away from Brahma many creations ago, and yet Brahma had never given any sign of discomfiture nor had he ever resorted to accusation or back-biting. Surely, he felt, this would be a harmless way to honor him without endangering his hold on the Assembly, and would also show himself in a favorable light as an impartial leader. Shiva thus urged the Assembly to approve the appointment, which it did with acclamation.

Brahma, with characteristic modesty which hid his true power, then finally spoke, thanking the Chair, the leader of the Opposition, and the members of the Assembly for thinking of him, and humbly accepted the position. Some now say that it is because the Pathetic sentiment was given over to the Supreme Lord that the people of India are so engrossed by it.

There still remained two sentiments to be assigned, but there were no volunteers and no nominations were forthcoming. Shiva could easily have been responsible for Fear, for Gods and man were terrified of his third eye and his image of Bhairava, the terrible destroyer, was ever-present. But he was already overburdened and his family overrepresented. Besides, this was not the image he wanted to convey as Chair of the Senate. As a matter of fact, all the Gods had, at one time or another, terrified their constituencies and behaved in odious ways; thus any of them could have represented these sentiments admirably, but times had changed and it was no longer fashionable to terrify, bully, and disgust others. Democratic ways had set in and one now had to be much more subtle in achieving one's ends, enlisting the support of BBC, CNN, and the rest of the media.

Sitting quietly in a remote corner of the assembly hall were the minorities — the black Gods (waiting to be whitewashed), the Demons (waiting for their moment to come), and above all (and yet below), the female Deities. Among them was the charming, beautiful and demure Devi, who could be all things and yet was none in this male-dominated society. Surely she knew as much as Vishnu about romantic love — after all, even Vishnu had been obliged to disguise himself as a woman, Mohini, to tempt Shiva in order to beget progeny for the preservation of the universe; whereas Devi had had absolutely no difficulty seducing males without resort to disguise. And in her mother mode — what mother had not experienced pathos or laughter and the wonderment of giving birth? And was not every son a hero? She could have made a convincing case for representing all these sentiments and more, but the male ego, she knew, would have brooked no competition from one of her sex. So she had been still. But the bile in her had been welling from years of discrimination and she could no longer keep it in. Women had to find representation on the *Rasa* Roster.

And so she spoke, thereby causing a ripple in Ripley's book of records, for no one of her gender had ever spoken at a Heavenly Assembly meeting — let alone achieving tenure.

"If you superior beings should see fit," she said with seeming diffidence, "I could handle the other two sentiments, if it would not cause any offense. I do have a few credentials to support my case — not nearly comparable to yours, I am sure, but if it is not beneath your dignity to glance at my dossier you will perhaps notice one or two items which might be worthy of your consideration," and with that she offered her dossier to the Chair.

The Chair accepted the dossier and without looking at it passed it to the closest member of the Assembly who, also without looking at it, passed it on to the next, who also passed it on until it had achieved its rounds without anyone looking at it. In the meantime, the enormity of Devi's gall and her suggestion that she could handle the sentiments of Terror and Odiousness set the hall to tittering with amusement. Such a sweet, pretty and demure woman! Her place was surely in the home waiting to comfort and console weary Gods returning from their exhausting and trying day at the golf links!

Devi began to seethe at the mockery being made of her kind. She might perhaps have withdrawn her offer had they reasoned with her; indeed, these sentiments were not particularly those for which she wished to be known any more than did the Gods. But Heaven, too, hath no fury like a woman scorned, and so she fumed. Nevertheless, in a quiet, controlled voice with little more than the slightest hint of the anger rising within her, she said, "Some of you may recall that I did not have a vicious streak in me until that business about Mahishasura — the buffalo demon. Then you came to me with a plea to save the universe because you had unthinkingly granted Mahishasura the boon that he would be invincible against all males. When things got really ugly and you were defeated time and again in battle against him, you had the audacity to approach me and plead with me to come to your rescue by destroying him in battle. I put myself out and did exactly that for you, remember?"

Then summoning up all her latent energies she produced a vision, the realism and power of which made the Gods gasp in awe. The demure Devi was no longer. In her place stood a veritable demoness, the likes of which could not be envisioned even by the best sci-fi animators. There she stood, with twisted fangs and matted hair, blood dripping out of her mouth, dancing triumphantly over her hapless victim, ripping out his entrails with her bare hands. And the vision was not without the audition of hellish sounds in super hi-fi and surround sound, screamingly musical and yet not born of melody and rhythm.

Many of the Gods related afterwards that they could feel the rising tide of bile before they managed to turn their heads away in horror. And just then the sounds died in mid-scream and the apparition dissolved into a close-up of the demure Devi, shaking slightly, as much from her audacity at exhibiting herself in front of the Gods as from the strenuous exertion of focusing energy into such a molten stream of intensity.

But prejudice has roots deeper than mine shafts, and moved as they were by the savage display, they were still reluctant to offer such an important position on the *Rasa* Roster to a mere female. They whispered in asides seeking to find fault with her demonic demonstration, and they might have succeeded, but the overriding consideration was that none of the male Gods wanted to be associated with such horrible sentiments. This was a stalemate, and might have remained as such had not Shiva given his comforting words. "Relax," he said, "she can never be a threat to our hegemony as long as we give her no chance to display her charms. Let her be violent and vicious. That way, people will begin to hate her, and in contrast, to love and respect us even more." The logic of his argument could not be denied and the Gods reluctantly muttered their agreement, but one could sense that some were still suspicious — one foot in the door and even the Gods didn't know where it might lead!

In his proclamation, Shiva made doubly sure that there could be no possible misunderstanding. "The Assembly has decreed," he said, "that Devi be permitted to represent the two sentiments of Odiousness and Terribleness purely on a trial basis. The Assembly will countenance no interference from her in the performance of their duties and any meddling in other sentiments will immediately and irrevocably render her ineligible to continue to serve the cause of *natya*."

Devi flinched inwardly at the continuing affront to her sex, but acting prudently, she meekly agreed to abide by the conditions. Nevertheless, one can imagine the torment in her mind — subservience had never come easily to her or her kind, but for ages it had been like this. One put-down after another. When was it to end? When would women stop being regarded as hearth-sitters? She resolved that notwithstanding the dastardly limitations imposed on her activities, through this tiny opening she would leave her imprint in the everlasting struggle for e(wo)mancipation in the Godworld.

Bharata was delighted to find that the Gods had agreed to imbue the actors with their divine essences. Now, surely, theater would become convincing. Of course, he would have preferred to have them possess the actors throughout the play, not just at the most heightened moments of experience, for he knew just how important the lead-up was to the denouement. But still, this would be terrific. Who would resist succumbing to scenes of divine possession? Of course, he was concerned about Devi's role (as he hadn't seen her satanic display), but he was secretly glad that she was on the roster. He accepted the situation without complaint, but underneath he could not help but think just how vibrant his barebreasted but emotionless actresses would have been under Devi's tutelage in matters of love — enough to warm the cockles of even an old sage's heart!

So rehearsals began. The Gods were just about as conscientious as indolent Gods can be expected to be. They came and they went, moved by their own cycles of perambulation. But theater, even then began to carry conviction — one could sense the spirit of inspiration, and somehow the actors and actresses were speaking to the heart. Even the musicians sensed this new vitality and began adding vivid colors, *raga*s, into their modes, and the dancers began moving to some primordial rhythm of the universe, no doubt inspired by Shiva's invention of the 'frantic' *tandava* dance and its female counterpart, *lasya*.

Devi bided her time, knowing that the Gods could neither outlast her patience nor did they have the conviction of her gender. And sure enough, when all was going well the Gods sloughed off during rehearsals — Vishnu went off on another of Krishna's escapades, Shiva was too tied up with administration, Indra went off to Korea, Vietnam, or the Middle East, and Ganesha found a coterie of admirers and stayed wrapped in their attention. Only Devi remained true to her purpose and continued to inspire the players with intensity.

Opening night was fast approaching and Bharata had every reason to be optimistic. He could already see and hear the standing ovation as the final curtain came down. Surely his earthly king would reward him handsomely and forever ensure the well-being of his troupe. He wondered if there might also be a knighthood in the offing!

But even Brahma had not anticipated the problems that lay ahead. He had suggested that the opening night be on the occasion of the banner festival celebrating Indra's victory over the enemy hordes of Asuras and Danavas. So Bharata's first production began with a benediction followed by a skit depicting the Gods chopping off the enemies' limbs. However, in the audience, uninvited, were the same Asuras and Danavas who were being maligned and chastised on the stage. Brahma's Natya™ version 1.0 had not given a single thought to their feelings. Naturally, they took umbrage at this flagrant distortion of the worst moment in their history and using all their supernatural powers, they made the actors forget their lines and paralyzed their speech and movements, caused the sets to fall and the curtain to go up and down at utterly inappropriate moments. To add to the chaos, they made the musicians play false notes and forget cues, and the dancers miss beats and lose balance. The audience, in high anticipation, had come to shower the players with flowers, but seeing this debacle, they turned them into rotten eggs and soft tomatoes. And the enemies laughed and laughed. This, too, they felt, should go down in the history books.

Indra was mortified and fit to be tied — but there was no one with the courage to do it. In his anger, he resorted to his only recourse: violence. So he took up his staff and beat about him until the enemy was routed once again. Even this did not end the problems, for the enemy had pride and did not give up easily, resorting to subversion and sabotage. And the troubles continued.

The Gods now realized the seriousness of the situation and that no solution would be found out of hand. They went into a series of high-powered meetings and a number of practical solutions were proposed. Brahma, with the help of the chief architect of the universe, Vishvakarma, was asked to design a new kind of maximum security playhouse with the most modern electronic surveillance system. Just in case it failed, the best and most powerful Gods were positioned at strategic points in and around it, with specific instructions to leave no stone unturned and no shadow unquestioned in the quest for security. But the enemy was endlessly resourceful, bypassing and jamming electronic beams and sneaking past the heavenly guards, and continued to make life miserable for Bharata and his troupe.

This kind of guerilla warfare was too much for the Gods. They began mumbling and muttering in the ranks and finally sent a delegation to Brahma pleading with him to try a conciliatory approach. After all, this was just supposed to be entertainment, and although they quite enjoyed bashing enemy heads, it was becoming too much of a muchness. And so, with the sentiment of the hoi polloi Gods going against him, Brahma finally agreed to modify the program.

Now the Gods, bearing appropriate gifts carried by charming heavenly nymphs, set out to placate the evil enemy. They delivered formal invitations with R.S.V.P. (Reserved Seats Very Probable) tickets to all the home drama games and agreed to make numerous concessions, like letting them win occasional small battles and not constantly showing them in such a monstrous light. But they found their enemy implacable. No concession without representation, they insisted. And after much backing and forthing, not to mention frothing at the mouth, the Gods reluctantly agreed to admit two of their representatives to the Heavenly Assembly, albeit only as non-voting members. But what actually swung their vote was the offer of ten front-row tickets (side aisles only) for opening night.

So drama kicked off on a rocky field. The bounce of the ball was not always true, but the games had finally begun and for quite a while they flourished. Admittedly, they were not exactly as Indra had envisaged nor as Brahma had conceived, but attendance was high and numerous performances sold out long in advance. There were some marvellous playwrights, wonderful plays, and many stage successes. Although the Gods began to tire of this diversion after awhile, they continued to put in just enough of themselves so that their presence was felt at critical moments.

Devi, on the other hand, had an age-long gender axe to grind, and put substantially more of herself into the sentiments than did the male Gods, so that gradually the Terrible and the Odious began to steal the shows. Among her many talents, Devi was also a consummate actress, and began to portray much more than those two sentiments, arguing, when questioned by the Gods, that she merely used the other sentiments to highlight the Odious and the Terrible and had no intention whatever of interfering with the Gods' roles. And so they let her be.

In the course of time, one began to notice, if one looked ' carefully, that a counterculture seemed to be spreading — a Devi cult — as segments of the audience began applauding her every entrance, knowing that, as long as she was on stage, they would get their full money's worth. Devi temples began to sprout all over the country. True, they were modest in appearance and were usually attended by the lowest of the low. But in terms of numbers, the low were high — in fact, the largest segment of the populace. And their passions were even higher when Devi possessed them, for she cared conscientiously for all her subjects. The Demons, too, bathed in the wash of these new sentiments rising in support of the disadvantaged minorities, began spreading subversive propaganda which showed their activities in a new light. They argued that they were not evil, just the opposite of good. "After all," they reasoned, "good would lose its meaning if everything were good without any opposition, and besides, what would the Gods do without us, loll about on the beach all day and soak up the sun's rays?"

Slowly the message was being heard on Mount Kailash. Brahma's revised program, Natya™ 1.01, for masterpiece theater was, after all, not quite so perfect. He had forgotten to take into account the fact that, in the wrong hands, it was equally as powerful a weapon for propaganda as it had been in the hands of the Gods, and now it had somehow surely fallen into the wrong hands. In the tempestuous Heavenly Assembly meeting that followed, recriminations flew — barely short of libel — and Devi came in for a bad time; but secretly, she laughed her way to the spirit bank and continued saving lost souls. There seemed to be no solution save to call for the final curtain. And so classical Sanskrit drama came to an end sometime before the 10th century A.D.

And what of Devi's dream for equality of the sexes? Some say that she inadvertently created a counterculture which was just as sexist in its own way. Instead of giving woman her equal and rightful place in the Heavenly Assembly and integrating the sexes, she succeeded in creating just another pressure group which only enhanced divisiveness in the Godworld, causing the male Gods to view their female counterparts with ever-increasing suspicion. Perhaps they are right, but I, the Storyteller, say it was a noble vision that still remains to be realized.

THE TEMPLE OF SHIT

In his documentation of Earth, Shiva had focused mostly on ritual and performance because he felt they encapsulated those aspects of human life which would be most promising in terms of data for the next creation. But as the heavenly archives began to fill up with audio-visual documents, Shiva began to be more selective in his choice of subject matter, looking for unusual events and locations. On one occasion he was told about a small temple lying in a remote place on the outskirts of civilization. No one seemed to know much about it and even his principal informant, a wise man with vast experience in the ways of the world — whose name is here protected in case some of the information he provided might incriminate him — had only the vaguest knowledge of it; and yet, all seemed to have heard about it, even though no one seemed to know why it was important or unusual. Shiva was intrigued enough to investigate it himself. Accordingly, he transported himself to this remote place with just a small, unobtrusive, low-light camcorder, figuring that he didn't want to alarm the natives unduly. As he entered the precincts, he set his camera up and let it run.

On this videotape (which your Storyteller watched at one of Shiva's weekly soirées) we see Shiva the scholar entering the precincts of the temple, vastly overgrown with bushes and weeds. On the periphery of what looks like a rectangular courtyard, there are a number of rooms — presumably where priests and perhaps also respected visitors might once have stayed. They are now in a truly decrepit condition and show little sign of habitation. In fact, there is no sign of life anywhere. We see Shiva surveying this scene, then hesitantly walking toward one of the rooms which, on closer inspection, is in slightly better condition than the others. As he approaches, an old man with a magnificent flowing white beard emerges wearing a simple yellow (or yellowed) robe and a motley assortment of unusual necklaces — each of which must have had a fascinating story to tell. Apart from the immaculate condition of his beard, he is totally unkempt in appearance.

Shiva greets him. "Maharajji, I have come a very long way and I would be most grateful for a drink of water and a few words with you."

Maharajji hesitates, then seemingly reluctantly, points to a well. "The water is rather cruddy, I am afraid. I am used to it, of course, but a city person like yourself could find it disagreeable. In any case, that's all there is around here." We then see Shiva in some uncertainty, evidently debating with himself whether or not to take a chance with the water. Finally deciding against it, he addresses Maharajji. "Have you lived here long?"

Maharajji replies, "Longer than I or anyone can remember, and I hope to continue to do so until the end of time."

Evidently resisting the impulse to pursue this further, Shiva says, "I see. Then you must, of course, know the whole history of this temple and why it is now deserted. And yet, people know about it in many parts of India, but don't know what they know or why. I am a scholar and find this most intriguing. Could you please enlighten me?"

Shiva must then have changed the camera angle, for we now see a closeup of the two sitting in the shade of an immensely overgrown banyan tree. We can only guess at what might have taken place in the interim. Then Maharajji begins to talk.

"It's a long story. There used to be a temple here many ages ago dedicated to the Goddess Banodokri which was once extremely popular and people would come here from all over the country to worship. Her story is very interesting because she was once a beautiful princess who was subjected to the most cruel vagaries of fate. It was due to her extraordinary steadfastness of purpose and her rectitude that she was made into a Goddess after her life was ended. But that story took place long ago and it would take too long to tell in this first meeting between us — perhaps later. Such are fate's vagaries that the Goddess began to lose popularity in the succeeding hundreds of years, largely because she was a Goddess of such high moral standards that it was beneath her dignity to grant small personal favors. People were always making selfish requests: one would ask for protection from smallpox and another would ask for a male child. There are appropriate deities for such requests, but not our Mother, Banodokri. They would sacrifice the lives of chickens, goats, and even buffalos, in the desperate hope that they could bribe her into granting their wishes.

"You see, the world was degenerating and lofty values meant less and less as time went on," Maharajji explains. "This temple became a complete ruin. I was caretaker even then, waiting as I had been instructed to do, and keeping her memory alive."

After a pause to light a little squib of tobacco in his homemade pipe, Maharajji continues. "I don't know how much of the recent events you want to hear, but I will tell you about its most recent history. If it becomes too tiresome for you, please let me know and we can talk about whatever frivolities you wish."

Shiva assures him that he has enormous patience and interest, but it is clear that Maharajji is not fully convinced (nor are those viewing the tape, for Shiva is not generally known for being a good listener, notwithstanding his many other virtues).

"Very well then," Maharajji continues, "a few centuries ago this part of the country was flourishing with commerce and industry, and the nearby town of Pukar was an important port of world trade. I used to see visitors from all foreign lands walking by, from Greece and Rome and Algiers and Shanghai and places that I had never heard of. No one looked my way because the old temple had long since fallen down and all one could see were piles of broken brick and stone. There was hustle and bustle everywhere and no one had the time of day to pause and reflect. This too has disappeared since — such is fate's endless sport!

"At that time our country was governed by a Prime Minister, Jaisinghji, because the King was still too young to take over the reins. Jaisinghji was also of royal blood, but was descended from a succession of younger sons and therefore was denied most of the privileges given to the oldest sons of the royal family. It was only by dint of hard work, diplomacy, and deception that he had achieved his standing, but in the process he often had to resort to what we might call underhanded tactics, which included lying, cheating, and worse. He became immensely rich and had businesses in many foreign lands; and yet to look at him, he seemed a most unfortunate creature, bent and crooked, his appearance reflecting his ugly way of life.

"But he had lived with it, convinced that the rewards more than compensated for his growing physical deformity — that is, until he began to get monstrous backaches, neckaches, and headaches. These got steadily worse as he became richer. He tried many patent remedies, but nothing seemed to help. Then he began visiting temples and praying to Gods and Goddesses for relief and tempting (or should one say bribing?) them by offering to construct a magnificent temple to whichever one would alleviate his suffering. But evidently the heavenly spirits had better things to do — and besides, the final word on psychosomatic disorders had yet to be written."

Pausing for another deep puff, and perhaps for dramatic effect, Maharajji continues. "And so the situation grew from bad to worse. All the known deities had failed to respond, with Jaisinghji truly in a desperate strait, when he heard about Mother's temple and came to visit me, explaining his problem. You must understand, Sir, that her temple had long since fallen down and the place was covered by vegetation, so that it was a wonder that he found it — but desperation knows no bounds. Mother had been in a long, long sleep, with no devotees except myself, and I had learned to leave her in peace unless she were truly needed, which hadn't happened for ages. Now Jaisinghji was pleading with me to intercede on his behalf, and I hesitated, for my world could topple at one stroke. I had not spoken to Mother for some time — what if she had gone away and I was tending an empty crib? My whole life would have been a farce. So with trepidation one evening, I lit the appropriate fires and made the usual offerings — it was so long ago that I had last done so, I was beginning to forget the precise ritual incantations that would request her presence."

At this point we can see Shiva's eyes light up, and sure enough, he speaks. "Maharajji, you mustn't let such a thing happen, at least not until it has been properly documented on videotape for future generations, and by chance, I have my camcorder with me."

Maharajji then looks at him in a curious way, ignores his statement and continues with the story. "But Mother was kind and she came, quietly, without any fanfare, as was her wont — not like others who resort to thunder-and-lightning entrances to impress their devotees. She stood there in a simple white gown billowing in the still night air. Jaisinghji fell on his knees and began to plead, 'Mother, Mother. Thank you, O thank you for responding to my suffering. I am indeed an unfortunate man, although I have everything that money can buy. If you could only ease my pain a little, just a little, so that I can live with it, I will build you the most lavish temple you can imagine. I have contacts in many different countries and I shall get the best architects from Italy and France to help design it. And have you seen the Italian marble they have been quarrying recently? It is truly magnificent. And the diamonds they are mining in South Africa? I shall stud your temple with them, if only you can ease my pain even a bit.' As Mother stood there unmoved, Jaisinghji went on in an even more desperate tone, pleading and exhorting and offering ever more extravagant details of the temple he would build — not realizing that Mother never cared for such things.

"I fully expected Mother to leave as unceremoniously as she had come. I knew that she could not be bribed, and Jaisinghji was being so obvious it was embarrassing. I half expected Mother to go into a rage — but of course, she would never do that. To my surprise she stayed and listened, silently, unmovingly, and I could not believe my ears when she finally spoke after so many years of silence! I felt my love come gushing out with more intensity than ever before. Then it dawned on me that she said she would grant his wish!

"I couldn't believe it. 'Oh, Goddess Mother,' I thought, 'have you also succumbed to vanity and pride? Have you been so lonely in your solitude that your high moral principles have become numbed? Have I been devoting my being to an empty dream?' She turned to me and looked at me deeply for what seemed an eternity and I, poor fool, had no idea what she was trying to say! It's true that I had much to learn in those days, as I still do, but I had thought that I knew my own Mother and her every glance — but I was wrong, very wrong."

After another pause and another deep drag on his pipe, Maharajji goes on. "Mother gave me no explanations and turned to Jaisinghji. She said in an impersonal tone, 'The way the Gods have constructed this universe, no deity may actively interfere with man's destiny. And yet, in their infinite wisdom, they have provided you with all the clues for your own salvation. You are luckier than most others, who can only see the results of their actions in the next life when they can no longer remember their previous sins. In your case they have placed the mirror of that future life right in front of you here and now.' That was all Mother said and faded back into her secret world.

"Jaisinghji was thoroughly nonplussed, although I knew what she was saying — but why? I could not believe that she

really wanted this magnificent temple that was being promised —
it was so completely against her principles as I knew them.

"Of course, I explained to Jaisinghji the meaning of her
message. His life of lies and deceit had manifest itself in this life
as a twisted and bent body. The pains he had been suffering,
which should have been reserved for his next life, were being
inflicted on him here and now. To rid himself of them, he merely
had to change his lifestyle: instead of lies, truth; instead of
hypocrisy, sincerity; instead of diplomacy, forthrightness. And
Jaisinghji went away determined to mend his ways."

Shiva was becoming restless. It was a nice story, but
there was nothing special about it. Everyone knew that Gods are
not supposed to interfere with man's destiny, but there were
occasions when they all did. As a matter of fact, no one found
fault with Banodokri, who was a minor Goddess, and the general
feeling was that she had been quite circumspect in her handling of
the case. But now Maharajji was speaking again.

"So Jaisinghji began telling the truth and stopped all his
shady dealings, and Lo! He began to hold his head up high and
his spine began to straighten. Soon his aches and pains began to
fall away like leaves in autumn. He was so grateful to Mother that
he began to build this temple. It was to be so grand, but," with a
sweeping hand gesture, "just look at it. It was never completed
and it wasn't entirely Jaisinghji's fault — it was Mother's intent.

"As he had promised, Jaisinghji sent for the foreign
architects and they created a magnificent design which won many
international awards and made the architects famous. Then with
much fanfare the construction work began. First they started with
the outside rooms, there . . ." Maharajji points, "and then worked
around to where we are sitting. It was all going very splendidly,
but I could never imagine myself living and meditating in such
elegant surroundings. I could not help but feel that Mother had
lost faith in her ideals. I could believe that this might be another of
the wonders of the world and that tourists would be flocking from

all over the Earth and trampling all our values into the dust. Then, when my morale was at its lowest, she appeared to me with the words, 'Just wait and see.' And I could see that the inner light had never left her. So I waited, all my doubts behind me."

Once again Shiva's interest in the story is reviving, as Maharajji continues after another puff of smoke. "All Jaisinghji's ailments were now gone, but I began to see occasional clouds of concern on his face and his brow periodically wrinkling in a most unbecoming manner. I could see that he wanted to confide in me but just could not find the courage to do so. Finally I prompted him. 'Not long ago,' I said, 'you would have given anything to be rid of those aches and pains. Now that they are gone, you should be in rapture, but still something is troubling you.'

"Hesitantly, Jaisinghji confided: 'Yes, Maharajji,' he said, 'I am in very serious trouble. I no longer have any illegal black money to pay the architects — and the marble and the diamonds are held up in Aden. Since I became honest, no one wants to do business with me. They don't trust me anymore and no one is prepared to extend me any credit. Rumors are floating around that there will soon be a run on my bank and if that happens I shall be ruined. Like everyone else around me, I loaned money to my family members and friends without proper collateral — but it would have been alright if I could have continued prevaricating, cajoling and being devious. I promised Mother that I would build her a magnificent temple, but if I continue to be forthright and honest, I won't have the money with which to do it. My promise to Mother is binding. I have no choice — I must resume my old ways. At least then Mother will have her temple.' There was nothing I could say. Jaisinghji was in an impossible dilemma and my experience did not encompass problems of high finance. And so, heeding Mother's advice, I waited silently to see what would transpire."

After another dramatic pause and a cloud of smoke, Maharajji continues. "Jaisinghji gradually resumed his old ways, and his body began to bend and twist again, and the old pains began to return. They were just as painful as before, but now he comforted himself with the knowledge that he was fulfilling his vow to Mother, and soon she would take her rightful place in the most resplendent temple that money could buy — so he thought.

"Now the construction workers had started on the main structure. It was to have such a glorious *vimana* tower, bedecked with the finest marble and encrusted with diamonds and rubies, emeralds and sapphires. The materials were all finally there and with an inaugural prayer the workers began their task. They were so enthusiastic that they made remarkable progress on the very first day, eliciting predictions that the work would be completed long before the penalty clause in the contract could be invoked.

"When they returned to the site on the next day, they were horrified to find that all their work had been undone and the raw materials stacked neatly in piles as though they had never been used. Jaisinghji was beside himself, wondering what evil spirit could be strong enough to defy the great Mother. He called together the greatest soothsayers of the land and the best Brahmin chanters to exorcise the demon that was causing the trouble, but to no avail. Everything they built was taken down in the night — and so the temple has never been completed and never will, unless Mother has a change of heart."

It is obvious from the video that Shiva now knows the whole story, but not wanting to reveal his divinity just at this stage, he asks in seeming innocence, "But who was the demon that was deconstructing the building work in the dead of night, and why?"

Maharajji looks as though he is enjoying himself at having confounded his interviewer. "Why of course, it was Mother. I knew it all along. She would not allow her temple to be built from ill-gotten gains. That's why I call this the temple of SHIT, which stands for Sincerity, Honesty, Integrity, and Truth. And it will never be built because these values are dead in this world, and rightly so, because they have had no meaning for ages — perhaps since the first day of creation."

Maharajji paused and puffed. Shiva waited, giving an admirable display of patience and sensitivity. Finally Maharajji resumed. "I am proud of SHIT because it is a true element of Mother's being, and as her spokesperson, of mine. I will never give up these values, come what may. But I don't expect anyone else to care about SHIT because it has nothing going for it, I mean no tangible rewards. Can one become the President of the U.S.A. by practising SHIT? No way! He (she?) would, as Pogo would have put it in the 'fifties, be 'drummed out of the lodge' in no time! So where would the SHIT practitioners go? To Ojai, California? There's already competition there. And what would they gain? Can one imagine an important contract being given to a company that had SHIT as a Logo?

"I admit that people following the principles of SHIT could get something out of it, an inner smugness that comes from believing that they were better than others. But, hey, that 'better than others' bit has already been appropriated by so many others — from Christians to Quakers, Muslims to Jews — and all believers, no matter what their beliefs. So what makes SHIT different or better? Nothing."

Pausing for the puff that refreshes, Maharajji continues — but not before Shiva's soirée viewers can appreciate Shiva's tact in not interfering with the flow of Maharajji's rhetoric, even though Shiva mutters that the camcorder battery is sending CHARGE signals.

"Nothing is precisely where I am at, as I sit from day to day waiting for the end of recorded time — no reference intended to your camcorder, which incidentally, needs attention."

We see Shiva get up, presumably to change batteries, followed by video noise for a few moments, and then the picture returns. One can see that Shiva has altered the angle of the camera and adjusted the zoom just a hair, perhaps to alleviate the monotony of having only a single camera view, but the angle now accentuates the prominence of Maharajji's nose.

Maharajji continues, "There are many causes that righteous people befriend, sometimes volunteering their life-hours, or life-hours-earned money (not necessarily their own). SHIT is not one of them. It has no concrete goal, like cleaning up the environment or saving an endangered species, because it in itself is an endangered species — or should I say dead, except in this decrepit haven. But we have no cause, no program, and no need for funding because we don't plan to go anywhere or do anything. I just plan to sit and contemplate SHIT."

Now Maharajji's pipe is re-stoked and smoke billows forth as he puffs and puffs. Shiva still waits discreetly until the silence becomes oppressive, and he evidently begins to feel concern over the lack of action on camera which might turn off his viewers, so he finally speaks.

"Maharajji," he says, "I admire your conviction and your dedication to it. I cannot say that I am a follower of SHIT; yet I feel that you have a point to make — but to whom, I am not sure. Mankind perhaps, or the Gods? But would either of them care? Sincerity, Honesty, Integrity, and Truth. What a noble set of words! But they are only words that man has created which have no relevance to the universe. Can one require a star to be sincere? Or, for that matter, the Gods to be honest?"

"Precisely the point," said Maharajji. "SHIT values are obscure, subjective, and not easy to live up to. It is virtually impossible to make a convincing commercial to sell the idea because it has no reward, unless one is masochistically inclined and derives pleasure from the suffering and hardship that the practice of SHIT invariably entails. Even the temptation of reward in the afterlife is insufficient to motivate mankind — and the proof of that is right here, in this deserted, dilapidated shrine. So SHIT is usually put on the dung heap or down some invisible drain to be engulfed by the endless, swirling waters of the undiscriminating seas. But Mother doesn't mind, nor do I. We have our commitment and our purpose, and we shall fulfill it."

"And what is this purpose?" Shiva asks.

Another deep puff and Maharajji resumes. "O King of Gods — I have known who you were since you arrived."

Shiva seems to be taken aback at this. "How in Heav ..., er, Earth did you know?"

Maharajji responds, "Even Watson would have guessed. You came without any conveyance — no jeep, no rickshaw, no helicopter. So I guessed it must have been a heavenlicopter. Elementary, no?

"In any case, the purpose of this shrine is to keep SHIT alive until the end of this universe so that when the Gods take their end-of-season inventory they will note its presence — even in such a remote place — and perhaps see fit to include it in the next creation. If this should come to be, I plead with you in all humility, to design some tangible reward for the dedicated practice of SHIT, at least equal to those the Gods offer for lying and deception which are obvious for man to see."

Evidently having learned his lesson in the episode of the blind woodcutter, Shiva makes no hasty commitment and merely says, "We shall see."

The unedited tape ends to ringing applause, especially from the sycophant Gods that tended to cluster at Shiva's soirées, and there was general agreement that Shiva had collected valuable data for the next creation. Even the Opposition members conceded that Shiva had handled himself impeccably, and that this was one up for him at the polls in his quest for re-election as King of the Gods after the cataclysm.

MEENAKSHI'S THIRD BREAST

The Goddess Sarasvati, universally regarded as the 'pure one,' looked in dismay at the mounting piles of manuscripts on one side of her study. It had begun in a small way not long ago when the Gods' pastimes had changed to research and scholarship, in preparation for the transition to the next creation. Since then, most of the young Gods, as well as a few of the senior ones, had been writing up the results of their research projects in the hope of reaching the attention of the Committee on Heavenly Personnel. Since Sarasvati was the recognized Goddess of education, scholarship, the arts, culture, and other such esoteric subjects that no male God had wished to claim, it was understandable that all these reports were dedicated to her, and a copy invariably ended up in her study. There was no established mechanism then to ensure that the manuscripts reached CHP, who would have, in any case, thrown up their hands in despair if they had seen the huge pile.

Since no one else did, the Goddess felt a little bit responsible for the situation. Even her husband Brahma, the creator of the universe and other odd things, seemed not to notice the pile when he came into her study. You see, it wasn't yet fashionable for husbands to take any interest in their wives' activities, and when it came to anything other than housework, it was easier to ignore it than to create a ruckus.

The only one who showed any interest was Shiva, but he was always busy chasing off to earth after some swami or other in between Senate and Assembly meetings and what not. When Sarasvati did finally catch up with him and explained her predicament, he promised to give the matter some thought, and a day or two later he visited her and said:

"I've got it. When you brought up the issue of the manuscripts, I suddenly realized that it had been bothering me too — but, of course, I had no idea that there were now so many! How is CHP going to go through all of these in the review process, and how are they going to evaluate them, seeing that they represent state-of-the-art research? Our committee members were chosen for their ability to assess the usual Godly achievements, like killing demons and assuring the victory of good over evil, not reviewing scholarly papers. Now I'm not trying to denigrate them in any way. After all, we chose them because they were good solid traditionalists and would not be swayed by new-fangled ideas. Who could have predicted that our ways would change so drastically? Needless to say, we now have a big problem, especially as most of them are senior Gods and may not take kindly to interference of any sort."

The Goddess was somewhat taken aback by these revelations which had always been reserved for the male of the species, and Shiva also realized that he was being indiscreet and attempted to gloss over the issues.

"These are matters which concern heads of state and need not concern your, er . . ." (he was going to say 'your pretty little head', but realized that it would not have been appropriate in application to the wise and highly respected Sarasvati) " . . . august being," causing modest Sarasvati further embarrassment at being described so by the King of the Gods. But Shiva continued, only slightly ruffled by his near faux pas:

"I suddenly got the answer while I was watching my wife Parvati doing the laundry. You're in a wonderful position to help us. Why don't you start a publication company? With the new developments in desktop publishing they say anyone can do it. If you can take the best of the manuscripts, get them edited into a readable form and publish them, it will not only help CHP in making their review decisions, but also let Gods know about the research that's already been conducted so that they won't rush off on the same projects. Yes, the more I think of it, the more I like it. And I'm pretty sure that we can find you a substantial subvention to get the ball rolling. It would be most appropriate for the Goddess of learning and scholarship, and the only one in Heaven who understands what the terms really mean, to take such a giant step forward. What do you think?"

Poor Sarasvati! All her life had been dedicated to refinement and finesse. When she had accepted the role of Goddess of the arts and sciences and such like, she had thought that it was an honorary position, with no responsibilities other than playing the *vina* lute in gorgeous gardens, attended by peacocks and delicate deer. There had been no mention of any responsibilities. She had her gentle Brahma to take care of and that was quite demanding sometimes, especially when he went into fits of depression at the state of the universe. Everything else had to be a hobby reserved for her spare time. But now Shiva was suggesting that she become a businesswoman. What did that mean? Would she have to give up her white sari to wear austere business suits? She wondered why deadlines seemed more important in the business world than lifelines. Didn't they also need to be met? And what if Brahma needed her just when a deadline was approaching and some calamity of the business lifeline came along at the same time? Would she be torn between duty and duty?

Shiva waited patiently for her response, although he was already distracted by the thought of documenting a strange swamystic he had recently heard about, who groped about in the unseen world of non-being. Sarasvati was still thinking about the ramifications of being a businesswoman, and now it was beginning to seem not quite so formidable. After all, she wouldn't have financial problems with the resources of the heavenly budget behind her; but being a female she was not privy to budgetary matters and not unnaturally thought the heavens had a bottomless purse. So she thought she could hire all the help she needed. The only problem was that no one in the Godworld knew anything about publishing, so whom would she hire? Shiva was disturbed out of his swamystic reverie as Sarasvati spoke:

"Goddesses were created only to do Gods' biddings and thus shall I be bidden. But first, I must clear it with my gentle consort."

Shiva responded with confidence, "That will be no problem, I am sure. I shall speak with him. Dear Brahma never refuses me anything."

So Shiva obtained the clearance for the project. We all know that Brahma is not mercenary; still it is always understood that obtaining clearance for anything must be accompanied by some palm-greasing and one presumes that this was no exception.

When next they met, both Sarasvati and Brahma were somewhat embarrassed; she, because she had agreed to a proposition which would take her away from being a full-time housewife, and he because he had agreed to her agreement. But they were still very much in love and got over their initial hang-ups in the agreeable manner that lovers have.

Later — considerably later — their concerns surfaced once again. Brahma broke the silence:

"I must confess that I'm worried for you. I remember hearing somewhere that one has to have a head on one's shoulders to succeed in business. We all have heads on our shoulders and some of us more than one," modestly exhibiting his four, "so I don't quite know what that expression means. Who can advise you how to operate a business? To the best of my knowledge, there are only one or two such heads in the whole of the heavens, but I don't even know which Gods own them."

"Dear Lord," responded Sarasvati, "You mustn't worry so. This is uncle Shiva's baby . . . er, so to speak, and I am sure he'll advise me if I run into any problems. I think the first step is to put together a team — isn't that what they call it? Then we can have some solid rap sessions and come up with an agenda."

Brahma was, to put it mildly, taken aback. He had forgotten that Sarasvati was more than a pretty face. Of course, he knew that she was Goddess of Learning and the Arts — but where on heaven did she find out about rap sessions and the like — things that he had not even heard of? But he was not going to admit his ignorance.

"That's exactly what I was going to suggest too. We need a rap team.I'm going to pass the word around to see if anyone's interested in joining it."

"Dear One," said Sarasvati hastily, "we don't really want to call it a rap team, or who knows what they'll want to rap about. No, no. We have to say something about publishing. Let's call it, um . . . I know, let's call it a Publications . . . Group? Service? Committee? Which do you like?"

Brahma was quite out of his depth and was frankly beginning to get bored. Sarasvati, hearing his thoughts, chimed in, "Board. Yes, let's call it a Publications Board. Then we can have an oak-panelled boardroom with plush leather chairs and a shiny round table.Yes, I like it."

And so the word went out that Board members were being sought for Sarasvati's publishing firm. Not long ago, the response would have been zilch, but now, in this new climate of exploration, it was overwhelming. Admittedly everyone applying was grossly under-qualified but there were some fascinating cases. Among them was Vayu, the God of Wind, who had started one of the few businesses in heaven, a diaper service, and used the slogan "Breeze-dried for Perfect Biodegradability." Sarasvati immediately snapped him up, impressed by the range of his imagination. And Bali, monkey King and son of Indra, who had invented the Bali-point pen and was rollering it over the stylus. He too was brought on board, as was Soma, God of the intoxicating drink of the Brahmin priests, who had been lost for centuries and was just beginning to find himself.

The most interesting and probably the most qualified was Meenakshi, a beautiful and extremely talented young maid, destined to be worshipped in one of the most glorious temples on Earth. She was close to being perfect in every respect, save one. She had beauty and intellect, imagination, and flair, not to mention that her typing speed was well over 150 words per minute, but lodged between her two perfectly rounded breasts was a third one, equally matching in shape and size. Now some might argue that a deformity of this nature could be converted to one's advantage, but one must always keep in mind the reactionary force of tradition, and tradition had fixed itself on two, not three.

Right from the beginning she was destined to follow a tortuous path. Even her birth was abnormal as she is said to have emerged from a sacrificial fire already aged three. Her royal father ignored this little oddity, just as he did her third breast which was obvious for all to see. His reaction was curious, for he refused to accept that a girl had been born to his wife and treated her as a dearly cherished first son, instilling in her the royal credo of conquest: the ability to defend herself at all times, with its corollary: the skill to destroy others under the pretense of defense.

But as a son she was also exposed to other aspects of royal male etiquette, among them a knowledge of the martial arts and the sciences as they were then known. This explains why she knew nothing about cooking and homemaking, but instead excelled in sports and other manly exercises which developed her coordination, leading eventually to her remarkable dexterity at the typewriter.

And so, in the course of time, she had ascended to the throne and had been — for a short while — warrior supreme, acting as king and indulging her deceased father in the successful game of conquest, cruelty, and bloodshed. There was no question that she was good at it, but in time it began to pall on her and she gradually became convinced that it was obviously not her true metier. She had just given up being king and had made up her mind that it was now time to find her true self and the meaning of her third breast when the openings on Sarasvati's Publication Board were announced. Of course she knew nothing about the world of publication and didn't seriously think of it as a career, but, at least, it would be different; so she sent in her application and to her surprise found herself shortlisted.

She arrived at the initial interview wearing a smart business suit especially crafted to the fit of her body, looking efficient and self-possessed, as well as charming and irresistible. It was difficult to keep from staring at her only deformity, but Gods and Goddesses have had considerable practice in self-control and they managed it. Sarasvati was thoroughly impressed by her professional appearance and immediately appointed her to the Board, even before she found out about her typing speed.

We need not go into the personalities of the other Board members selected since they are not pertinent to this story. Suffice it to say that it was now a somewhat motley gang of ten that filed into the oak-panelled boardroom and sank into the plush leather chairs for their first meeting. After the God Ganesha who had been invited to consecrate the opening had done his bit, Sarasvati, who naturally chaired the meeting, welcomed the members in her inimitably gracious way and introduced the reasons underlying the publications venture. She then continued:

"I am sure you all know that I have no experience running a business, but I do know enough to assure you that it will not work unless we are thoroughly professional about it." She was looking at Meenakshi, who somehow epitomized professionalism in her mind, and then continued, "I am not yet sure exactly what that means, but that is exactly what I mean to achieve, that is, when I find out the full implication of the term. I want our publication firm to be able to hold its head up high in the company of the most scholarly publishers of the universe, I mean the Harvards, the Oxfords, the Cambridges, and the Californias. I don't expect it to be too difficult, since we're Gods, and they're only mortals, but we may have to learn a few tricks from them to begin with. Before long, I am sure, they will be looking to us for leadership."

With this preamble, Sarasvati turned the meeting open to the members for their comments.

Vayu was the first to speak. "I am the only experienced businessGod in this group and my experience of running the HDS — the Heavenly Diaper Service — should be perfectly applicable to publishing because they both involve, so to speak, soiled linen. Ha! Ha!"

No one seemed to get it, so Vayu continued, slightly miffed: "Well, the two businesses are a bit alike, as I see it. Firstly someone has to soil the diaper — that's like someone putting marks on paper. Then it has to be processed; instead of breeze-drying, we'll be using desktop publishing, same difference. And finally we have to distribute the cleaned-up product. The packaging may be different — the diapers go out in soft covers, but I guess our books will go out in hard covers — everything else seems about the same to me."

Whether or not he had a point, all the members seemed relieved that he hadn't been as windy as usual in trying to make it. Meenakshi, seeing that no one was about to refute this coarse comparison, felt obliged to speak.

"The Honorable member has certainly drawn an interesting parallel between the two ventures. But in all humility, I'd like to suggest there are a few little differences. For one thing, the HDS does not have to examine each diaper to see whether or not it should be breeze-dried, whereas we have to examine each manuscript closely to determine whether or not it is worthy of being published. This is, in my opinion, our biggest problem. How do we decide which of the manuscripts to publish?"

The Chair then broke in. "You are absolutely right, Meenakshi. That is our biggest problem. We can't publish all the manuscripts at once, in any case; and I can see authors who get left out accusing us of discrimination, nepotism, and what not. How do other publishers handle it? I mean, what criteria do they use? Obviously they can't publish every manuscript that comes to them — or can they? If they have to be selective, how do they do it? Does anyone know?"

Of course, no one knew. There were a few wild guesses offered, but it hardly seems necessary to relate them in view of what followed, and Meenakshi spoke again. "There is only one way to find out and that is by one of us going down to Earth to carry out research on the methods used by some of the major publishing companies there. Then we can make educated decisions on the policies we should follow."

No one saw fault with this reasoning, but it was obvious that no one wanted to leave his or her comfortable celestial abode for a stint of rough Earthly fieldwork. (Vayu tentatively offered to see if anything in the wind might provide some clues, but was not prepared to go further than that.) Somehow, all eyes began turning to Meenakshi who was in any case well worth looking at.

"Well, Meenakshi?" said Sarasvati. "It looks like you're It. Think you can do it?"

It was not so much a question of whether she could do it, but whether she wanted to. Of course she could do it — hadn't she already proved that she could out-man men? That was on battlefields, of course, but why should business offices be any different? No, the question was really not whether she could, but whether she would. And after a brief moment of consideration she decided she would.

So the meeting was adjourned on an optimistic note, with the promise that the next one would be scheduled in due course to consider Meenakshi's eagerly anticipated report.

Meenakshi was quite elated at the turn of events. She had been singled out to perform an important role in the cause of scholarship which would undoubtedly be recognized in the Heavenly Assembly. This might be the opening to the tenure track to which all novice Gods and Goddesses aspired, although no one could quite recall when one of the latter had made it. Being a Dravidian Goddess, the path was going to be doubly difficult since the Assembly was dominated by male-oriented Aryan Gods, but if she acquitted herself with distinction, this would certainly be a move in the right direction. Tenure, however, was not her only consideration; she fervently hoped that this field experience might expose the real significance of her third breast.

Shots and inoculations for this and that and multiple-entry visas and travellers' checks, packing and concern about baggage overweight, kept our heroine out of sight for weeks until her departure for Earth was imminent. Then, when flight time finally arrived, she was given a handsome sendoff, with all important Gods, Goddesses, and friends attending. "Good-bye, dear Goddess. Our best wishes for a safe journey, happy landing, and successful trip. When you return we will receive you with flags waving, cheering your every step to the boardroom."

But, of course, it was not like that — not the return, at least. True, we did send her off in grand style, but . . . perhaps I should not jump the gun and give away the ending prematurely.

Thanks to the blessings, no doubt, Meenakshi arrived safely and became apprenticed to a publishing house chosen at random, and she got to learn the ropes, starting from the bottom and moving up at such a rapid pace that she could have been an Indian magician doing the old rope trick. But the way up was not without its male chauvinistic resistance couched in derogatory asides addressing her only deformity: "Who's on third base?" and "Here comes the third front!" and innumerable other silly, fractious, insulting comments that males spew forth without the slightest thought. These are so deeply embedded into our languages and into our perceptions of masculinity that they slip out inadvertently and, sometimes, advertently. But Meenakshi endured them all and proved that she was more person than they were men.

What a way to have to go! Not only must one do what needs to be done, but one must also overcome the suspicion raised by the fact that the doing is done by a doer that is other than the gender of those recognized as the true doers! And yet, Meenakshi did it. Never once in all this time did anyone suggest that her third breast was a symbol of the male phallus and that Meenakshi was, in fact, a he. Had it been so, her rise to the top would have undoubtedly been more acceptable. To them — I mean the male, white colleagues who abound in all the professional areas — Meenakshi was still regarded as a 'she,' notwithstanding the fact that she could out-do them in both areas of he and she.

Still, this discussion has raised an essential consideration. Was Meenakshi a he, or a Meenak-she? No doubt, this must have entered her consciousness more than once, and certainly when Shiva came into her life. Let me backtrack for a moment.

The Lord Shiva visited Sarasvati after Meenakshi had left for Earth, to find out how the publication project was faring. "All is progressing better than expected," said Sarasvati. "We have sent our best research scholar to report on publication procedures and methodologies on Earth. I am confident that when she returns we will be able to go ahead at full steam. Her name is Meenakshi, and she's a fascinating person. Incidentally, on your next visit to Earth, please look her up, for she must be homesick and would like to meet someone from her homeland."

Shiva, who was always looking for fieldworkers to assist in his grand projects, was excited by this news and on his very next trip looked up Meenakshi, who was then living in an elegant penthouse in Old York, or some such place. Let me say that what happened next must have been ordained a long time ago. He was smitten and she was smitten, and before long they were being seen together in all the top spots in the city. Then, she accompanied Shiva on one of his rough field trips, acquitting herself fearlessly but with efficiency and charm that Shiva found utterly irresistible.

I must now take a moment to remind you that Shiva has been around and has seen and done more unusual things than most Gods. In one of his forms he is called *Ardhanarisvara,* where one half of his body is that of a female. Thus he understands both the sexes in an intimate way and can see in Meenakshi the two elements deliciously intertwined. But what did he fall in love with: Meenakshi-he, Meenak-she or the delicate combination? I am afraid that the story that is passed on to me, leaves this fascinating question, in no doubt whatever. Shiva offered to marry her but made it quite plain that if she accepted him, she would lose her third breast and become a traditional Hindu wife and housewife, serving her master! It would have given me great pleasure to have been able to tell you that Meenakshi, being a liberated woman, laughed in scorn at this absurd proposal of marriage, but that is not how this story goes, as we shall see.

On hearing Shiva's proposal, Meenakshi finally understood the significance of the third breast: it was indeed a symbol of the phallus which she would have to dispense with if she married Shiva. This meant that she was actually neither wholly male nor female and perhaps had the best aspects of both sexes. But she was in love and in order to consummate it she would have to renounce half of her being. So she was torn between her love for Shiva and her love for her whole self. Vacillating this way and that, she agonized and finally replied to Shiva, "Dearest one, please give me time to weigh all the pros and cons." And of course Shiva knew the nature of her dilemma and waited.

In the meanwhile the magic moments of their endearment to each other had to be left aside as mundane responsibilities impinged on their consciousnesses. Shiva had received a stack of FAXes calling for his return to attend to yet another heavenly emergency, with P.S.'s from Sarasvati asking for Meenakshi to report in on her project. Since the essential aspects of her research had been completed, Meenakshi tendered her resignation on the earthly editorial board, and returned to submit her report to the heavenly counterpart.

The Heavens were high with anticipation and the Gods and Goddesses collected to cheer her arrival at the appropriate arrivals platform. But rumor of Meenakshi's entanglement with Shiva had reached ahead and also in the crowds were gossip columnists and reporters, especially from the more lurid papers, dying to get a scoop on the amorous details. There was no way Meenakshi could face that, so she overshot the heavens, and descended by the down service elevator in a remote part of Kailash. Naturally, everyone went home disappointed, but when her presentation at the Board meeting was announced, they lined all the avenues and gave a rousing cheer as she drove up in her limo. Clearly she had something of no little importance to tell.

Meenakshi was steered into the boardroom amid jostling crowds, popping flash bulbs, and endless camera crews. Then the doors closed and Sarasvati embraced her and took her aside. "This must be a trying time for you — let me offer you some herbal tea." Meenakshi gratefully accepted, although she was now accustomed to much more potent stuff. After this refreshing pause and another while she powdered her nose, she announced herself ready for the presentation, and handed Sarasvati her report, huge, but not excessively so, considering its contents. "Of course," she said, "I'll only summarize some of the main points."

This document, I am pleased to say, is preserved in the heavenly archives and is well worth reading in full, although there are a few rather boring sections which could be omitted without detriment to the whole. But the story continues:

The chairGoddess, without mincing her words, introduced Meenakshi: "Members, I will not open the proceedings today with the usual joke that is expected of Chairs on such occasions. Our dear research scholar, Meenakshi, is finally here to present her report which I am sure will open the door to our first bookshop."

Meenakshi rose, steadied herself for a moment, then reached down into a briefcase and pulled out a manuscript and a handsomely leather-bound volume with embossed letters in gold, placed them on the table and began:

"The whole business of academic publishing on Earth is, for want of more elegant words, just plain screwed up. I collected a mass of data on Earth — far too much to present at this meeting. I am sure that you will all read my full report."

This must have been with tongue in cheek, since everyone knows that few Gods or Goddesses have that kind of persistence. Meenakshi continued:

"Today I'm going to focus on just one issue which is of immediate concern to us — how to decide which manuscripts to publish. I have in front of me two exhibits for your perusal," as she passed them around. "Exhibit One is a brilliant piece of research as it was originally submitted to the publishing firm with which I worked. If you open it up, you'll see that it has already been cruelly defaced by the editors. Exhibit Two is this elegant publication of the manuscript in its final form, leather-bound to simulate the kind of classic editions of the works of Shakespeare and Dickens."

After a brief pause, Meenakshi continued. "There is no doubt which of the two exhibits is more elegant, but in my opinion, the manuscript is far more important because it embodies the author's original thoughts before it was molded into its more elegant shape. The editors started out by asking the author what kind of readership he had in mind. Well, of course, like a typical scholar, he hadn't given a single thought to the readers. He had made a discovery and he was putting it down on paper. This was not good enough for the editors — not by a long shot. 'Before we can publish this work we must be sure of adequate sales and therefore, we are afraid you are going to have to rewrite it with a specific reader in mind — and we would much prefer it if you could write it in such a manner that it will communicate to the largest possible audience.'

"The manuscript went through numerous editions until finally it became the merest shadow of the original, and this is what you see in Exhibit Two — glossy and glamorous, but with only the smallest sherd of its original content."

Meenakshi continued after a suitable pause. "Most of the scholarly publications on Earth are written by academics striving to live up to the oft-quoted adage, 'Publish or Perish' — mind you, not 'Write or Perish' and not 'Research or Perish,' but 'Publish or Perish.' Publication is merely the marketing of a written manuscript — why should scholars have to be able to market their research in order to continue in the academic world? Is the marketing more important than the research? In the present system, the answer would have to be yes. One can write a lousy book and somehow convince a publisher, and in no time, we have a glamor-ready copy on the market. And that constitutes material for advancement in the academic world!

"Fear of perishing pressures scholars into committing themselves in print before they have anything to say — but say, they must, or die. More and more are doing it, of course, and there is already more published in virtually every field than can possibly be read by a conscientious scholar. One striving for tenure is faced with an impossible decision, read and therefore perish, since there won't be enough time for research and writing; or write and take a chance of being shown up as an ill- or nil-read scholar and, so to speak, die of embarrassment.

"So, who is upholding the Publish or Perish dogma? I say it is the universities, and specifically, the committees which review the work of scholars for tenure and advancement. We have an important lesson to learn from this. The members of these committees are either too lazy, or feel incompetent to judge the work of their colleagues, so they give greater credence to a published work over one that has not been published. Their justification is that publishers would not have published it without first having it approved by reviewers. But who are these reviewers and what are their criteria for approving a manuscript? What is being kept under the table here is that publishers do not have the same goals as universities and that a perfectly good piece of research could well be rejected by a publisher because the subject matter and approach are thought to be too esoteric to make its publication economically viable.

"I am sure you all know what I am leading up to," continued Meenakshi — but seeing the blank looks facing her she could probably have been more sure of the reverse. "I mean, of course, the matter of our publishing concern. The mandate passed on to us by Lord Shiva was that the prime reason for going into the publishing business would be to simplify the Committee on Heavenly Personnel's review process. In other words, we would do their dirty work for them: go through the manuscripts, decide which ones we think are worthy of publication, and publish them. Then when it comes time for their review, all they need to do is to see whether or not a deity-scholar has a sufficient quantity of publications, without having to assess the quality of the research and writings themselves. I find this utterly objectionable, even though the mandate comes from the King of the Gods."

This really set the boardroom buzzing. Meenakshi's affair with Shiva was the talk of the town, and it was hard to believe that she was being critical of him in public! How would he react when he heard of it, as he was bound to, notwithstanding the confidentiality that supposedly accompanies such meetings?

Chair Sarasvati rapped for order and spoke as the muttering subsided: "The Chair feels obliged to point out that the Publications Board as a whole takes no responsibility for our speaker's views." Turning to Meenakshi she said, "You know as well as I do that our Senate members could never review these manuscripts on their own; they are dear old things and not accustomed to work. Besides, it takes a great deal of specialized expertise to review some of these esoteric studies. How do they handle it on Earth?"

"I wouldn't want to recommend Earth university practices to CHP," Meenakshi responded. "They send out review copies of writings to leading external scholars requesting them to evaluate them as a favor to the university. What is utterly shameful is that even if all the reviews are favorable, the review committee still can, and does sometimes, turn down a tenure request for whatever reason or non-reason by which they are motivated. Ignoring the content of these reviews by recognized experts, they insult them and say in effect that they don't think too highly of their intelligence or expertise. In such instances the only reason they get external letters is because they want it to appear that they are carrying out an objective review, but they have already condemned the tenure applicant."

By her fervid oratory it was clear that she was talking from personal experience and the Board members felt embarrassed to interrupt her recall. Finally, Sarasvati prompted Meenakshi to continue. "I am convinced that we have to have a better system for CHP. Part of the problem is that the academic world is utterly unprofessional. What other profession would expect their specialists to spend hours reviewing materials and giving their considered opinions without any remuneration? The answer is none, of course. Why don't professors just stop doing it? If they did, universities would have a choice: either make all their reviews in-house, thereby giving up the pretence of calling them objective, as there is no way that colleagues can be objective in assessing each other's accomplishments, or make them really objective by appointing review committees of independent, external experts."

"There is no doubt that Meenakshi has made an important point," Sarasvati interposed, "and I will certainly pass this on to the CHP Chair in my report. It remains now to hear her recommendation on how we should proceed with our publications."

"I must point out," Meenakshi said, "that we have not been legally constituted to provide judgement on the fates of young Gods and Goddesses. That is a task CHP has reserved for itself. It is thus their duty, not ours, to decide which manuscripts deserve to be published, whether they like it or not, and I suspect they won't enjoy wading through that pile in our Chair's study. But they have to do it, and conscientiously, or else face the prospect of a vote of no confidence in the future. How they do it is up to them, but I hope they see fit to appoint an impartial external committee consisting of experts from Earth. Once they send us a prioritized publications list, we can go ahead with our publications program, but I would strongly advise that we take no action until then."

This put the onus squarely on CHP, but knowing the Gods' predilection for procrastination, all the Board members realized that this meant another long period of inaction, at the very least. Although no one liked Meenakshi's proposal, her point had been well made and no alternative proposal was forthcoming. After some discussion, Sarasvati concluded:

"Meenakshi is right in her assessment of the situation, and we should give due acknowledgment to her, particularly for the hardships and privations she has endured on behalf of this Board. All is not lost, however. In due course, CHP will come up with their decisions and then we must be ready to publish at a moment's notice. So, this Board will continue to prepare for that moment, learning all that is to be known about publishing, and, if there is no pressing business at hand, we can occasionally repair to a pleasure garden to have a picnic."

This was received with a huge round of applause; finally, we were talking the kind of language the Gods appreciate!

Sarasvati continued: "I can see one positive advantage of Meenakshi's proposal. Now I have every justification for sending off that pile of manuscripts to CHP quarters so that I can have my study back to myself again."

I suppose that I can't really end this story without resolving the matter of the two lovers. How did Shiva react when he heard about the proceedings at this meeting and Meenakshi's accusation? He laughed and laughed, knowing that this was her last gesture of independence.

Meenakshi now understood the true significance of her third breast. She was what she was, and that third breast was an essential part of it. The things she had done and the things she had seen could never have been had she had only two, no matter how perfect. But love was love and that meant sacrifice and as she moved into Shiva's arms her third breast was immolated by the fiery ardor blazing in Shiva's chest.

Personally, I truly don't believe that Shiva would have been so insensitive as to want to take away her third breast and make the glorious Meenakshi into a dutiful housewife. And even if he did, I can't believe that she would have accepted no matter how much she loved him. But they say he did, and they say she did, and to prove it they built a magnificent temple in Madurai to commemorate her capitulation. But I still wonder . . .

PAIN

Of all his fieldwork experiences, Shiva cherished most of all his interview with Maharajji. As a matter of fact, he was particularly partial to swamis — those half-naked, disheveled beings with matted locks who seemed to spend all their time dreaming up interesting ways to look at the universe. This is not surprising since Shiva is known to have spent much of his life being one himself. In fact, in those days he easily out-disheveled all swamis in terms of the profuseness of hair-matting and the wild application of body ashes. He was then so ill-kempt and outrageous looking that his father-in-law refused to invite his own daughter, Sati, to any of his parties just in case Shiva should turn up with her; the embarrassment of being excluded from all these events — not to mention missing out on all the fun and festivity — eventually caused her to take her own life in a dramatic display of pyrotechnics. But this did not deter Shiva from asceticism. If anything, he became even more of a fundamentalist swami and might have remained as such, if he hadn't somehow decided to go into politics and wound up becoming King of the Gods.

So it is not entirely unexpected that when Shiva heard of an unusual swami in another remote part of India, it was a case of *deja vu,* and off he went with his video camcorder, this time making sure he arrived by conventional transport, rather than the heavenlicopter which had given away his identity to Maharajji.

This particular swami, without a trace of dishevelment, looked more like a prosperous landowner. He was perfectly groomed and seated on a rather comfortable padded swing, with an attractive young girl keeping it in perpetual motion by gracefully nudging it every second swing period. And what's more, Shiva's arrival seemed to cause him no surprise. As he walked into the courtyard, the swami greeted him with "Welcome. We've been waiting for you. Do sit down," pointing to a swing opposite his. "By the way, you can place your camcorder on that tripod. You'll find that it's in exactly the right spot."

"What on earth!" wondered Shiva. "Is this some kind of a set-up? How did he know I was coming and does he know who I really am?"

"Yes," said the swami, as though reading Shiva's mind. "I received word from your paper, the *Sentinel,* that you would be coming today to interview me. Would you care for a drink?"

'Is this truly a coincidence or had some grapevine tendril sneaked up into the *Heavenly Sentinel* office?' Shiva wondered as he mulled over the possibility, reaching for the drink he was being offered by another young attractive girl. Without taking a sip he placed it on a table, set up his camcorder, then picked up his drink and seated himself on the swing which began oscillating in perfect rhythm with swami's swing, aided by the ministrations of this second charmer.

The swami continued, "I don't generally give interviews to newspaper reporters, but this time it seemed like the right thing to do. By the way, my name used to be Dhundhun — hard to pronounce because both the D's are retroflex and the N's nasals. My guru said it meant 'one who is seeking.' Anyway, it is no longer that. I am no longer seeking and I expect I'll get a new name when I see my guru next. For your article it would be just as well if you would refer to me simply as Swami, at least for the time being."

Shiva decided to be honest — up to a point, that is. "My name is Shiva," he said, it not being unusual for Hindus to be named after Gods. "I'm not exactly a reporter, but perhaps in this case I am," thinking that he might possibly put in a brief report in the *Heavenly Sentinel*, if the interview were to be newsworthy. "You see Swamiji," he said, adding the appropriate honorific, "I work freelance and they may or may not like my story."

"You see Swamiji," he said, adding the appropriate honorific, "I work freelance and they may or may not like my story."

"Oh they will," responded Swami. "This story will knock their socks off, I assure you. Shall I begin?"

Later Shiva, in telling of this experience, always describes the dizzy sensation of being swung in synchrony with Swamiji's swing opposite him remaining equidistant and stationary, while the rest of the environment kept swinging back and forth . . . back and forth . . .

Soon Swami's voice began to sound hollow and distant, as he said, "I gave up seeking for moral reasons. It was only a few months ago that I saw the light. Before that, I was the usual dishevelled bag o' bones swami that one sees everywhere. Look at me now — prosperous, huh? You'd never guess that I'm ninety-two, but I looked beyond the measure of time then. Seeking is the way to keep looking young, but once you find, it's all over. Now that I've given up seeking, I expect my age will catch up with me one of these days. But, I'm digressing — you young reporters have no time for old fools like me."

And indeed, Shiva was now looking and feeling young. He was temporarily away from affairs of state, swinging in peace and listening to the rise and fall of the hypnotic voice, which undulated on . . .

"For what seems like forever, I practised penance and self-mortification and concentration and meditation, and finally I thought the Gods were beginning to notice my presence. I was elated at getting through. In those days I just sat and sat — right there, on the straw — until my body was more than numb and the sap had flowed out of my bones. And still I sat and looked within myself, ever deeper, to find the power to reach out beyond myself in order to shake the universe. Now I ask myself, why did I want this power? The usual answer to this question is insecurity. But as a child, I had little occasion to be insecure. My father was rich, so rich that we had five automobiles in our stables, led by the two thoroughbreds, Rolls Royce and Daimler. And in the planting season we employed sixty gardeners — I know, because my mother persuaded me to keep accounts of their wages, just to make me aware of the privileged position in which I had been born. I don't think I was impressed in the right way, because I escaped as soon as I could and chose quite a different path.

"I suppose there must have been a reason for my insecurity — perhaps something I experienced in a past life, or something in my childhood. I remember one episode when I was about six and was showing off how great I was to my friends. I picked up a stone and pointed to a bird sitting on the ground and said, 'See, I'll knock off that bird with one stone,' and with that I let fly, not believing that I had a ghost of a chance to hit it. But I did — and killed it just like that. Tore its head off. My first reaction was elation at my own accuracy, but then I felt intense pain, as though I was the bird, twitching lifelessly on the ground and yet feeling the pain of life after death. Could it be that I was doing penance for that heedless and needless act?"

At this point Swami looked intensely at Shiva, who felt pressured to respond. "It must have been a terrible experience! But still, as I understand it, yours was not a truly wicked act. You didn't really think you would kill it — you were still young and full of life and just feeling your oats, in a manner of speaking. Even I have done things like that, I mean, when I was young. I still remember the time . . ." Shiva stopped abruptly in mid-sentence, not so much because he was interrupting Swami's story, which he had momentarily forgotten in his own reveries, but because he was about to divulge his intimate recollections of the divine world.

Fortunately, Swami picked up the thread on his own. "There is no question that your story is no less fascinating than mine, but since we are moving down one stream, maybe we should keep going for just a while longer to see where it reaches. You see, that pain I experienced, I suppose one would say

vicariously — although I don't really know whether the bird
would have felt anything after it was dead — that pain has been
with me all my life — that is, until just a few months ago. Well
maybe it wasn't that pain. It could have been another, quite
unrelated pain. How can one tell? Pain is pain and sometimes it's
difficult to tell its source. Mind you, it's not as though my life has
been full of pain. On the contrary, I've had a lot of fun. In my
time I was quite a ladies' man and now I'm resuming those old
habits once again. I bet you've had your share of escapades too,
huh? Anyway, I've had lots of pleasure at one time or another.
Pleasure is a lot like pain and I could have been talking about
pleasure, except that pain is, I think, more . . . grabbing?
Anyway, I think people are more interested in hearing about other
people's pain — especially if there are gory details involved —
than about their pleasures, don't you?"

Shiva was now beginning to feel ill. Maybe it was
because he was stroboscoping with the Swami on their swings, or
the drink he'd had, or just the time-lagging of conventional travel,
but something was getting to him. He knew that he was supposed
to respond, but couldn't get his tongue detached from his palate,
where, quite inadvertently, it had found itself. Besides, he
couldn't think of what to say. Actually, had he known that this
was going to lead to a discourse on pain he'd probably have
stayed at home. Then the Swami turned around to his charming
companion and conducted her to an accelerated swing pace, with
Shiva's companion following suit, and now Shiva could feel
various parts of his innards vying with others to occupy the same
space. Through the bilious haze in which he was being enveloped,
he suddenly saw an image of himself at one of his weekly soirées
attended by many-splendored Gods and Goddesses, trying to
communicate what he was experiencing, and their expressions of
disbelief, for Gods are theoretically beyond such susceptibilities.
Now he wished that man had invented some kind of device that

could capture not just audio-visual images, but also the inner feelings of the fieldworker and his subjects.

As it turned out, Shiva did show this video extract at one of his soirées, but to his viewers he merely seemed to be waiting for Swami to continue. In fact, Shiva missed out on some of the Swami's most profound thoughts on pain while he was still in his reverie, and as he faded back into the present scene, the Swami was still going on:

"Pain, sublime pain, beautiful pain, the transformation of pain, the painlessness of pain, the pleasure of pain, the painful necessity of pain, pain as a moral deterrent and pain as a non-deterrent, pain as proof of reality and the fiction of pain — all jumbled into a fortune-pot and each one is forced to reach down through its narrow neck and take a pick. And I, Dhundhun, was seeking and seeking to find the mystery behind all this, and finally I have finally found it. What do you say to that?"

Shiva's momentary mental excursion to his mountain retreat had righted some of his bearings and he was finally able to respond. "I thought you said that this would be a story, if I remember rightly, which would knock their socks off. So far, the only socks it might knock off are their bed socks. Can't you liven it up somewhat? I think it might even put the Gods to sleep!"

"I'm glad you mentioned the Gods," said Swami. "In fact, this is all to do with them — I mean pain and all. Of course, I'm also hoping that we can publicize it on Earth in a big way and make them look like they have Tinker-Toy mentalities. But if we can only put the Gods to shame, maybe they'll let us be responsible for designing the next creation — and we'll do a darn sight better job of it!"

Shiva knew that he had missed something important, but consoled himself with the comforting thought that he had had the foresight to bring his camcorder so he could review the whole conversation later. But this belittling of the Gods had to be stopped, or at least discouraged. He certainly could not let it go unchallenged. What would his Assembly members think?

So he spoke, not quite sure what he was going to say but saying it anyway, knowing it was important to say something. "Hold on, hold on. Take your time about all this. Well, uh . . . I mean, time is meant for fools to go rushing into treadmills of . . ." Shiva tapered off as he couldn't think of any cogent metaphor. "Well anyway, er . . . You have some good thoughts and you should keep thinking, at least, it'll keep you young." This last was said with a slight smirk which went right by Swami, who continued: "What's left to think? I've thought and thought and thought and now I have the answer. So what's left, except to stop seeking and have a good time?"

"Well, uh, let me see," said Shiva (later he would apologize to the Gods for his excessive use of 'well' and 'uh'). "Let me see if I really understand you. Please correct me if I go wrong because I'm not very good at recapping arguments. Ah, you were talking about pain, and I remember it was getting to be painfully long. Then, just a moment — or was it many moments later? . . . Time seems to be so relative here, I can't really put it into any kind of perspective. Anyway, uh, you suggested that the Gods had left a grab-bag of pain which people dipped into. For what? Fun? Because the Gods got them to do it? Is that what you are trying to suggest? That the Gods made them delve haphazardly into the bag?"

"Well, I can't really blame you for not understanding — after all you're only a journalist, not a God." Naturally, Shiva cringed inwardly, and if one looks closely at the videotape, one can see his shoulders hunch slightly and, looking at it in slo-mo — which is dangerous without holding a black negative in front of one's eyes — one can glimpse a one-hundred-thousandth-of-a-second flash of his third eye.

"Yes, pain was the clue," continued Swami, "to the incompetence of the Gods. And when I found it, why did I need to bother with pain any more? So I gave it up and am now into pleasure, which may not have the same kind of gut intensity, but I like it. All the same, the pain was pretty good too; that is, after I'd learned to live with it. Looking back on things, it's all been good. Some better than others, but all good. So now you see me swinging — but if you want to see me really swing, there's this joint just around the corner, which is something else! I've been going there every night since my, shall I call it, emancipation? You're invited tonight — and the drinks will be on me."

Going to the occasional joint is not regarded as moral turpitude among the Gods, so I suppose Shiva went, but it's a pity that there's no record of the evening in Shiva's documentation. I'm sure many of us would've been interested in seeing the joint, not to mention seeing the Swami swing.

Shiva replied: "You're extremely generous, for which I thank you. My paper would like, I think, a little more meat on the bones, so would you kindly expand your thesis? Not overly much of course, but just enough to give the story some filling, if you know what I mean."

"Yes, I suppose I must get on with my story. I know what would add a little more pepper. Let's go and visit Auntie. She lives close by and boy, does she know about pain!" And with that, Swami orchestrated the halt of the swings, leaving Shiva in a reverse mode — still, but with the earth still swinging.

"Come," said Swami, "this will be something to remember, for Auntie knows it all." And with that, he hopped off the swing (while Shiva gingerly eased off) and purposefully strode forth out of the temple grounds, down a narrow dusty lane to a tenement house only a block or two away. Shiva followed, testing his muscles and his reactions as he walked. Fortunately, one of the swing-pushers followed with his camcorder.

Looking at the videotape at Shiva's evening soirée, we now see an amateur's view of stairs being climbed, and notwithstanding the steady-cam feature, the camera perspective continually shifting from the worm's eye view to a view of the worm, had there been one. The stairs are negotiated and Swami raps on the door. Actually the camera misses that dramatic moment, but one can hear the raps quite distinctly. The door is answered by . . . Well, it's difficult to describe her. Her, she is, quite clearly, with ample buxom proof, but what else? Teeth she clearly has, and I suppose most of the appendages one expects. But the total combination exceeds the sum of my imagination. In short, thank Man for the video camera which spares me the necessity of trying to describe her.

Her greeting is hearty, to say the least. "Dhundhun," she shrieks. "I never thought to see you again — at least, not after your emancipation." And he gently enfolds her in his arms and caresses her for a long moment. "How could I not come back to you? — You who have been my salvation and my release from the eternal scourge of pain."

Then, after they slowly disentangle, Shiva is introduced as a sincere but naïve journalist who might be able to foster the cause of pain. Shiva winces, but follows Swami inside. It is dark and bleak. No furniture except a 'four-leg' string cot on which he is motioned to sit. As Shiva sits, the camera shifts over to Auntie who is still bubbling over with joy at the sight of Swami:

"I'm all choked up. I can't speak. My joy, my bliss. You've come back. I've waited and waited, not daring to dream of this moment. You look so handsome and daring. My darling . . . My darling . . . My darling . . . I can see that pain has left you forever, but forever it will be with me. Still I can take joy in your joy and enjoin others to join me in sharing such moments of bliss even in the sea of pain which is, alas, my destiny. Such is the wisdom of the Gods."

"My true beloved," says Swami, "my true heart of pain. It is not the wisdom of the Gods that brings us together now, but the idiocy of the Gods. You have been the succorer of those in pain nearly all your life, and you have relieved others' misery by your kind ministrations time and time again. No one has seen fit to award you a Nobel Prize or any kind of international award; and you still sit in this tenement without any furniture! Not only have you been carrying their pains all these years but also the pain of your own deprivations."

"Deprivations," says Auntie, "deprivations are part of one's lot; they may be painful or not. When my husband died prematurely, deprivation became my lot; helping to alleviate pain was of my own choosing. It was I who decided that others' pains should supersede my own. And, of course, I suffered in the beginning. When I saw women scream desperately for help or any kind of relief from the excruciating pain they were subjected to — yes, I suffered. And all I could offer for consolation was to remind them of the warm, squirming, glistening newborn child that would be theirs soon — so soon, I said, that the pain would be just a distant memory engulfed by the joy of creation. I don't know if they believed it, but they went on to have more children and more children and more children. And I, I went on with the pains of birth, one after another, never having an opportunity to share the joys and mortifications of bringing up a child, or guiding it through moments of impishness, exuberance and distress. Such has been my lot, and a lot it has truly been. Would that it would end on a happy note somewhere, somewhen. But that, too, is in the hands of the Gods."

Tears begin to fall, not only from her eyes but also from those of Swami. The video footage shows that Shiva too is moved by this midwife's story, as would be all Gods and Goddesses if they but had the time and patience to hear about the terrible anxieties faced by their creations. But why should they bother? To them, mankind was just an experiment which wasn't too successful. At most they might say, 'Well, next time if we can create something that doesn't have to go through all of this pain stuff, so much the better. That's what we're carrying out research for, isn't it? That proves that we're conscientious and not just space- and time-trotters, caring only for the beaches of Hawaii and Acapulco.'

Then, Swami reaches out to Auntie. Shiva, still in a state of swinging synchrony, is also seen moving his hand toward her but restrains himself, as Swami speaks:

"Beloved, I hate to disappoint you, but disappoint you I must. There are no Gods. Those that created us were young children of some unknown superior beings just exploring their own capabilities. Even the God Shiva, wise and old beyond our reckoning, is still a youth. He has seen much and done much — but he's still young by the ultimate Gods' reckonings and there is so much more for him to learn ahead. And pain will surely be part of that education. Please tell our young friend like it is . . . I mean, about pain."

"When I grew up," began Auntie, "my mother always told me that pain was punishment for having done something wrong, and every time I did anything wrong, she would punish me, sometimes very painfully. She also told me that pleasure was reward for doing the right things, and she would buy me sweets to prove it, that is when I did the right things. It took me a long time to find out that she was wrong. Pain and pleasure are not connected with right and wrong. One just has to look around to know that it isn't true. Take Mukund Lal, that rich bastard who lives across the street. Every time a girl walks past he has an insulting comment for her. Why, I have seen him entice young girls to come closer just so he can slip his hand under their skirts! I don't know how many girls he has seduced, but I have helped at least three to give birth. He must be the most wicked man I've ever seen. But he's rich and he's always laughing. I keep thinking that one day his sins will catch up with him, but it's been going on for twenty years and more and he still doesn't seem to have a single ailment. Then I think, well, his sins will catch up with him in the next life, and try to imagine how miserable he'll be, but I can't do it. I still see him smiling and laughing and bullying and having a good time.

"You see, I lost faith in a crime and punishment type of *karma* a long time ago. In my work, I see all women having to go through pain, but what have they done wrong? Why should childbirth be so painful? Do the Gods not want us to have children? Is that it? If that's the case, then Gods should learn that pain doesn't stop women. What makes me really angry is that men don't suffer in the same way. They have all the fun of making love — which they do like pigs wallowing in a trough — and have no painful consequences. All I can say is that the designers of our world must have been male Gods and that this is another example of their discrimination against us."

"Now, now," said Swami, patting her on the shoulder, "don't take on so. We must look at this matter of pain dispassionately and prove to the Gods that their universe design is full of inconsistencies. Once we have convinced them of that, then we must demand that they take full responsibility for the state we are in and make full reparation."

Somehow, some third sense had made the cameraperson turn just then to a closeup of Shiva's face over which flashed a series of enigmatic expressions in lightning succession. Needless to say, the storyteller can hardly be expected to read the mind of the King of the Gods, but, there's nothing to stop him from making a guess or two to account for them.

Shiva obviously felt the need to respond — after all, this was a deadly serious accusation, but he did not want to say anything that might incriminate him or the Gods as a whole. If only he had had his attorney with him, a hurried consultation, he could have made a brilliant, but noncommittal, rebuttal. He knew that he himself was not with it when it came to legal matters, and without the attorney, anything he said might put him in hot water. Then it occurred to him that he was, after all, here in the guise of a reporter and that anything he said would incriminate the newspaper, not the Gods — unless of course they discovered that he was a God posing as a journalist. How would he stand then? He needed his attorney to give him the answer to that one. Then he thought, 'What if I make a clean breast of it and admit that we Gods did make a few mistakes, but we were well meaning and humans are bound to understand that?' But no sooner did he think it than warning bells began to sound in his ears — which accounts for at least one of the inscrutable expressions that crossed his face at a millionth of a second, but which one, I would not presume to say. What would the Gods say to that? Gods are the greatest. The slayers of demons and other undesirables. They bow to no being born or unborn, except temporarily. Admitting that Gods had been wrong was tantamount to acknowledging defeat. No. This would never be condoned. Better to bluster it out to the end, even if it be bitter. No quarter asked and no quarter received. Yes, that must be his motto. Fight on . . .

In the meanwhile, Swami was getting up to leave, having given up waiting for Shiva's response. "Auntie, I am sorry to have raked up all those coals that burn deeply within your being. I thought it would be good for our young journalist to feel the intensity of injustice through your eyes. And his speechlessness tells me that we made our point. But now, my dear one, you must come and share the fruits of my emancipation from pain. Let's go to the old Horseshoe Tavern and kick up our heels in mockery of the Gods. I'll be in touch very soon." With that, he steers Shiva out the door, down the stairs, into the street and, pausing briefly to point out Mukund Lal who was just then pawing a young girl, leads Shiva back to the temple swings. When they had settled and the swings were synchronized, he says:

"That was probably not a very good thing for me to do, I mean to expose a raw journalist to the fervidity of pain-livers. But it could be good for you in the long run. You see, my painful research into pain ended when I discovered that pain was painful, but only until it is transcended — and I didn't even need to lie on a bed of nails to do it! It was the nature of the beast that I discovered that saved me.

"While I was looking for answers to the question 'why?' I was floundering. I had hoped to find a logical explanation. Maybe, I thought, it was inflicted on one because of something in one's past life. But then Auntie awakened me to the pain all women feel going through childbirth. Surely, all women couldn't have sinned in their past lives and were only now getting their just deserts? It didn't stand to reason. This would have meant that being a woman was itself a punishment of some sort, and I couldn't really believe that. Say, for the sake of argument, that womanhood was a punishment, then in their past lives they would have had to have been men who transgressed in some fashion or another and were thus made into women in this one, to suffer pain and indignities of one sort or another. I admit that this notion has some semblance of validity in view of the way man tends to treat them, particularly in some repressive societies. But then I said to myself. 'This can't be.' About half the population of this world consists of women. If they were men in their past lives, how would mankind have propagated to the present state, unless males were able to give birth sometime in the past — and there's no evidence of that. It didn't make any sense, and still doesn't.

"After having spent many years trying to find the whys of pain, I suddenly hit upon the notion that pain was perhaps the result of woolly thinking on the part of the creators. Believe me, I didn't want to admit this possibility and kept brushing it aside for a long time while I continued my meditations on pain. But it kept gnawing at the fringes of my consciousness, until I could no longer keep it out. Then finally I invited it in and gave it a chance to speak its mind. And it spoke like this:

"'In your reveries on pain you have often thought about a fortune pot of pain with everyone being obliged to reach down its narrow neck to take a pick — Did you ever think about what that really meant? You picked a number that called for an excess of pain, just as did Auntie. Did the Gods cheat in making you pick that number? Sure, they stacked the pile with pain Chance cards and pain Community Chest cards, but do you think they cared who picked which one, as long as they were all picked at some time or another?'

"And I thought to myself, that has to be the answer. Gods don't care what happens to any particular person. Their only concern is to keep the world in balance, and they need to have pain as a counter to pleasure. For everyone that gets an overdose of one, there has to be another that gets an overdose of the other. Who gets what is irrelevant to the Gods. But it means that the rich sometimes get richer, the poor sometimes get poorer, the sufferers add to their sufferings and the Mukund Lals of the world get away scot-free and even add to their lechery. We would call it an inhuman way to be. But the Gods sit in their pleasure palaces without a jot of consideration for the individual, for that is the Godly way, and a mighty poor way for it to be!"

Shiva finally spoke. "You have an interesting way of looking at things, and I can see something of your rationale. If you had your druthers, how would you have treated pain and pleasure in your universe?"

"O.K.," said Swami, "the Gods have created a living chain of misery. Eat or be eaten — a universe of predators and victims. Every living creature has to eat a living creature in order to live — sometimes of its own species! How would the Gods feel if they had to eat each other or die? I'm sure that doesn't happen in Heaven. So how do the Gods keep alive? Do they eat? And what do they eat? I've wondered about that a lot, but I guess I'll never find out."

Shiva was momentarily tempted to enlighten him, but prudence gave him the wisdom to refrain, as Swami continued:

"What if one were to create a food chain of joy in which each species was responsible, not only for feeding its young, but also was provided with the wherewithal and the desire to feed at least one other species? One could do away with the predatory instincts altogether. Each living creature would not only have parents, but also Godparents. See what I mean — GODparents. Gods that cared enough for us all, as groups and as individuals, to provide us with sustenance and rid us of the need to kill."

Shiva is silent and Swami is silent. The videotape runs on, the cameraperson switching in uncertainty from one swing to the other, and back again and again and again, finally ending in video noise.

KANNAKI AND THE SECRET SERVICE

Why on Earth would they want to deify her — a princess who destroyed herself, not to mention thousands of others, by tearing her left breast off in a fit of anger and using it to set fire to Madurai city! Admittedly she spared Brahmins and other righteous men, chaste women, children, and the aged, as my colleague Prince Ilango Adigal reports in his story, *Silappadikaram;* but that still left a whole bunch of others innocent of any crime against her who got snuffed out like birthday candles on an ageless being's birthday cake. In one sudden stroke, a living, breathing city, with its share of iniquity and excitement, not to mention courtesans with their sixty-four arts, all gone in a furious, discriminatory blaze, to be replaced by a bunch of good guys and chaste women faced with a lot of reconstruction work ahead. Not much fun for anyone, I'd say. She may as well have destroyed the whole lot!

Maybe I should start from the beginning of the story.

Princess Kannaki was beautiful and desirable, and by previous arrangement had married Prince Kovalan who was equally beautiful and desirable. One might call it a match made in Heaven, except that it didn't fare quite so well on Earth. After living and loving with Kannaki, Kovalan fell in love with a ravishing courtesan, Madhavi, and they lived it up while Kannaki languished patiently. She might have languished indefinitely, except that one day Kovalan took umbrage at the text of one of Madhavi's poignant songs and decided to return to his first love, Kannaki. Madhavi, though a supposedly heartless courtesan who had extracted every ounce of Kovalan's wealth in exchange for giving him a good time, was shattered and eventually sought refuge in a Buddhist nunnery with their daughter.

One must acknowledge that at this point Kannaki was an ideal wife and a kindly woman, patient and forgiving — it was only later that she became deranged. Kovalan returned to her broke, and she without hesitation forgave him his indiscretions and went even further, offering him her two ankle bracelets filled with precious stones with which they could make a new start. So they hiked from the international port of Pukar where they lived, to faraway Madurai to set up a new business. Crossing mountains and forests on foot is not fun, but they endured the hardships with courage and fortitude, especially on Kannaki's part since she insisted on wearing her heavy ankle bracelets all through the journey. Kovalan, however, never got the business off the ground, which may have been just as well since he hadn't a clue about making money. As he went to the nearest pawnshop to hock one of the bracelets, he met a wicked goldsmith who just happened to have stolen the Queen's ankle bracelet which just happened to look like Kannaki's, except that it was filled with pearls. Then one after another, events flashed by at a furious rate: Kovalan was accused of robbery, apprehended by soldiers, and unceremoniously separated from his vital organs.

Not surprisingly, Kannaki was made distraught by the news, but after proving her husband's innocence which only seemed to double her anger, she decided to take matters into her own hands — more precisely, her left breast which she wrenched off with an excruciating tweak to throw at the city in revenge. The searing pain of her drastic action set the place on fire, destroying all the non-righteous. Kannaki did not live long after this self-mutilation and was last seen on Earth in far away Kerala, being escorted to Heaven by Kovalan and the Gods.

I suppose it was because of this unique form of revenge that temples erected in her name sprang up here and there and she received rounds of dedicated worship and thus became a Goddess. How Kovalan became a God is more clearly explained by Adigal: he saved the life of a Brahmin who was about to be gored by a rambunctious elephant — which not everyone might recognize as a powerful reason for deification, but that's the way Adigal tells it. In any case, Kovalan and Kannaki found a modest little mansion in a YUM (Young, Unpretentious, Middlers) district of Mount Kailash and lived peacefully until the Gods switched on to research and scholarship.

I was lucky to meet Kannaki — long after the breast-tearing episode which curiously had left no physical blemish on the bodily perfection Adigal ages ago had compared with that of the Goddess Lakshmi. I was bowled over by her breathtaking beauty and found myself returning to her mansion at every excuse. I suppose I got to know her pretty well and could finally understand why she had been deified. There was now nothing left of that elemental breast-tearing passion that had motivated her in the past; instead, there was the serenity and dignity of three dimensional still life that all deities envy.

I once asked her why she'd spared only the righteous on that distant day in Madurai, and of course, she said that there was no way she could have done it, even if it had occurred to her to do so. A raging fire, she said, was a raging fire and fires of that intensity are just not selective — and besides, she'd had other preoccupations at that moment, like trying to stanch the gushing of blood! That 'saving the righteous' bit was obviously Adigal's addition to make Kannaki's violent act seem less immoral. I still couldn't condone the wholesale slaughter, but I did feel better knowing that she hadn't discriminated against the less-than-perfect, and especially the upholders of the arts, the courtesans.

But those days were long gone; Kannaki had served her time and mellowed a great deal. I was sure that she'd have held a grudge against Madhavi the courtesan who had precipitated all their Earthly problems. But no. She told me that on the contrary, she'd been having recurring dreams of Madhavi dancing and singing and that she'd always appeared innocent of any guile. Over the years Kannaki said that she had, in fact, become extremely fond of her and had yearned to meet her — but of course Madhavi not being a Goddess, would long since have shrivelled into dust. Still her yearning to meet Madhavi continued, and was becoming ever more intense.

I suppose I put her up to it. One day I suggested, casually at first, that Madhavi was a product of her environment and her hereditary profession which had required her to devote her life to the study of the sixty-four arts. That was why she'd been so elegant, graceful, and refined. Perhaps, I suggested, warming to the idea myself, that there were others like her on Earth and it wouldn't hurt her to pay a quick visit down there. After all, she'd been away for a long time. But then I got a better idea. Why not, I suggested, get on the research bandwagon and apply for a grant from the Nominal Endowment for the Humanities to examine the courtesan cult and its impact on the development of human civilization? I knew that Kannaki liked the idea of returning to Earth, but she was hesitant since she'd had no training in research or scholarship. It took me quite a while to convince her that she didn't need extensive training, and it was only after I'd assured her that most field researchers were inadequately prepared when they first set out that she began to give it serious consideration.

She was also worried about how Kovalan would react to the idea and the separation it would entail. But I pointed out that it wouldn't be all that difficult to convince him, if she emphasized the fact that she'd be learning more about the sixty-four arts just so that she could titillate him with the courtesan's coquetry, and could rejuvenate, among other things, their beginning-to-get-humdrum sex life. And that's the way it turned out. He just put up a feeble objection or two, but I could see that secretly he was thrilled at the prospect of Kannaki the courtesan.

Now things moved apace. We struggled over the proposal a bit, but the NEH was eagerly looking for research scholars, particularly those belonging to minorities, i.e., females, to make their annual report seem affirmative action-oriented, and so glossed over weaknesses in the proposal and came up with a pretty decent sum. Everyone was cooperative, especially Shiva, who showered her with the latest in field equipment.

So Kannaki moved down to Earth and found a flat in a large city. I had advised her to feel her way into the project, rather than to jump in, so she wisely spent the first few weeks just settling in. She had the usual problems with food, cooks and servants, drinking water, 'Earth belly,' and the like, but gradually she began to adjust.

Two thousand years is a long time to have been away from any place. There is of course the adaptation to technological advancements which one must face, and no doubt Kannaki went through some awkward as well as humorous experiences in the process. But there were also so many other differences; even people didn't seem to be quite the same. She noticed that everything was now highly organized and there was little room for spontaneity. People no longer sang and played music when they felt like it — or if they did, they felt embarrassed. Now when they wanted music, they turned on the radio or the television; or they went to concerts, which usually meant buying tickets in advance, arranging for baby-sitters, dog-sitters, and house-sitters, rushing through dinner, driving through jam-packed streets, hunting for a parking space, arriving embarrassingly late and waiting outside the auditorium for a suitable moment to be ushered in, stumbling in the dark through the aisles and rows, past excessively perfumed men and women, joggling knees and excuse me's, to locate the only vacant seats which always seemed to lie furthest from the aisle. Having successfully negotiated all these hazards, one would certainly be forgiven for letting out a rousing cheer or two. But no such fate awaits the concert-goer. Now they have to sit silently and still in a darkened seat, surrounded on all sides by others doing the same, and listen interminably; until finally, as one, all start applauding and fidget and wriggle to get comfortable. But by then it's intermission time, and everyone is on the go, back to

jostling and stumbling, pushing and mumbling, to get out into the
foyer for a quick widdle or a piddle or a smoke or a diddle, before
the bell signals the jostle back again into one's silent seat.

It's no wonder Kannaki grew to dislike concerts
intensely, as she recalled the pleasure gardens of her youth when
music was unrestrained and free, like the songs of the birds that
filled her memories. And the birds that sang with the utmost
unrestrained beauty and controlled passion, were the *ganikas*, the
courtesans whose songs and dances could, and did, extract the
most ardent ascetics from the depths of their meditations. Where
were they now?

Little did Kannaki realize that courtesans were now being
regarded as common prostitutes. Their services to mankind all
over the world as creators and preservers of the most delicate
artistic traditions — which did not exclude the sensory delights of
sexual interplay, but were in no way limited to them — have been
belittled into nothingness. Where, indeed, were they now? Still
there, but in tenement buildings and chawls, in the ghettos of
every city, hiding from the police and the Victorian morality that
finds only shame and embarrassment in everything they do. Once
royalty and nobility sent their sons to them so that they could
acquire the sophistications of artistic living which was impossible
for them to find in their home lives. But now that courtesans were
associated only with wanton and depraved sex, the new standards
of morality would never dream of exposing respectable manhood
to their vicious wiles. More fools they, for their sons had lost the
freedom of the birds and the joys of Madhavi's artistic world that
Kannaki remembered so vividly.

In all innocence, Kannaki one day felt she was ready to
begin and set out to find the courtesans. How does one locate
courtesans in a big city? Not knowing the ill-repute with which
they were now associated, she went to the National Tourist Office
and spoke to the clerk at the desk.

"I'm working on a research project on *ganikas* — you know, courtesans. Can you please tell me where to find them?"

The clerk couldn't believe his ears, although he must have known they existed. To emphasize his innocence, he further Indianized his accent, as though to suggest that he was only a country bumpkin. "*Ganika*! Courtesans? Vat are they? Ve have not such trade registering in this country. Ve have many fine people and everyone is following trade vinds, but I am not finding courtesanship among them."

Kannaki was a bit surprised at this seeming ignorance, or was it something else? *Ganikas* were the greatest potential export that the country could offer the rest of the world, and here a clerk in the Tourist Office was claiming that he didn't even know of their existence!

"Now wait, do I understand you to say that you don't know who *ganikas* are? Are you telling me that the National Tourist Office doesn't know the traditional carriers of the sixty-four arts which are so clearly described in Vatsyayana's *Kamasutra*? Do you people have no regard for your own traditional values?"

Now the poor clerk was clearly out of his depth, especially as he was befuddled by the classic beauty confronting him. All he could think of to say, and that after a rather long, stuporous, blank look into eternity, was, "Vait, one moment please, in seated position, please," pointing to the chair opposite him, as he disappeared in 'beyond-my-jurisdiction' manner.

Kannaki waited patiently, her mind wandering to the good old days, while clerk conferred with senior clerk who conferred with most senior clerk who finally disappeared to confer with presumably some non-clerks, and possibly also higher-ups, whoever they may be.

Eventually, first clerk returned, with a 'solution-found' smile, and with an extra beam, accompanied by rubbing hands, said, "Madam, er . . . Young lady. The Tourist Office is just an

underling of an overling. Please to go and see them. Ve have
arranged to have our Vite House open their doors to your presence
at 10 o'clock of the a.m. in the morning, tomorrow, 11th January
of the augustus year of the Christian calendar, 1992, in case you
are able to render your presence. Should this case not be open for
you, ve have scheduled a second possibility for meeting Dr. Ram
Charan on Christian calendar 1992, date 17th February, time 2
p.m., in the afternoon, in case Dr. Ram Charan is still in office on
that date. But vith Indian politics in such a fluxory state of
uncertainty, ve recommend highly the first. It maybe will be too
late even; here today and gone tomorrow has been our peoples'
mandate for the last one-two years, or so approximately,
considering all possibilities."

So we move on to the next face-off, this time with the
clerk in the monsoon-greyed White House, as Kannaki presents
her credentials, a fabricated passport, establishing her as being of
royal 'Andowoman-Nicobar' descent, good enough to impress
officialdom and most others. Bowing and scraping is a special
technique underlings have developed in this part of the world, and
this 'White' House clerk had to be seen to be believed. In fact, I
would say that he'd added a new dimension to the ritual! "Yes,
Yes. Of course. No doubt about it. Absolutely. No question.
Highest consideration. No comparable proposition. Transcendent.
Exclusive. Permanent. No reconfiguration. Sublimity itself.
Perfect. Thrilled with joy!"

As he went on and on, Kannaki mercifully broke in. "I'm
here to research the 'sixty-four-art courtesans' who have
preserved India's artistic heritage for thousands of years. Please
tell me where to find them."

A simple enough request, but it set the White House into
consternation. Governments do not distinguish between
courtesans and prostitutes and, in any case, avoid admitting the
existence of either in their fair land, notwithstanding the streaky
monsoon greys of their edifices. And so the first clerk excused

himself, with the usual, 'One moment please,' and vanished to confer with leagues of colleagues and higher ups.

Let it not be said that Government employees are all buck-passers, although at a certain stage in their careers it is a highly recommended form of action. Even so, there are exceptions, and one was now found; a small, youngish lady with unusually delicate features, looking elegant, in spite of the fact that she was wearing a khaki uniform-style of sari. It was precisely because she was not afraid to confront unusual situations that some had predicted that she would go far, and she seemed to know it, as she introduced herself:

"Good morning, Ms. Kannaki. Let me introduce myself. I'm Sita Ramani. I'm the Third Undersecretary in the Home Office and I've been delegated to render you whatever assistance you may need, provided it lies within the bounds of my duties. Fortunately, the definition of my duties leave me considerable flexibility." This was spoken with the casual sophistication that comes with an exclusive boarding school education. "I'm told," she continued, "that you're carrying out research on courtesans, a fascinating subject, but not one which is high on our research priority list, I'm afraid. Still, it's a topic which interests me personally, and I was able to persuade my superiors to let me help you with the project. Well . . . that's not exactly the truth. They wanted someone to divert your studies into something that they consider to be more constructive, as they put it, and I volunteered. Now I suggest we go to this quiet little restaurant just around the corner where we can chat more comfortably."

So, seated in a quiet corner, over mugs of steaming South Indian coffee, Kannaki was about to explain her project, when Sita interrupted her:

"Let me first tell you why your subject interests me. When I was young, about seven or eight, I desperately wanted to learn to sing and dance. My father was a railroad engineer and he always wanted me to take up a profession, as they called it, which meant becoming a lawyer, a medical doctor or an engineer. At the same time my parents wanted me to acquire some knowledge of the arts, so that they could advertise me as a sophisticated young lady with a university education, which would enable them to find a suitable husband for me. By suitable, they meant a rich, influential or affluent type, without regard for age or beauty, so long as he came from a respectable ancestry which would enhance the reputation of our family. So they let me indulge my whim — for a while. And I had a few wonderful years dancing and singing, without a care in the world. But then when they saw that I was so involved in music and dance — and, with due modesty, I must admit I was good at both — they started worrying. What if I wanted to become a professional *ganewali* (singer) or *nachnewali* (dancer)? Horror of horrors! The family reputation built over generations, would have been destroyed in one debut recital!

"You see," explained Sita, "This is where we're at. The arts are approved as mate-finding sophistications and even dalliances for young girls. But at the first sign of any real proficiency in them, the elders invoke the image of prostitution, and I am sorry to say, even courtesanship, and summarily cut off the music and dance lessons.

"Yes, I'm one of those who care for the sixty-four arts, but I had a terrible time growing up, and my involvement with the performing arts was crushed like a cockroach trapped in a meat grinder. But throughout my school and college years, I dreamt of myself wearing diaphanous robes, singing and dancing in the presence of Shiva, Vishnu, and Brahma, and even noblemen — not the gross males one sees all around. I've always been too embarrassed to admit these secret fantasies until you came into the picture with your concern for courtesans. Instead, I made myself all tough, and believe it or not, I became a policewoman, confronting religious riots until I became blue in the face! Then, just as I was getting really good at it, having honed my heart into steel, I was transferred to the Home Office. When I first heard of the transfer, I immediately tendered my resignation. That was it. I would go back to my true love, singing and dancing. But you see, it didn't work out that way."

Kannaki was so taken by Sita's life story that she placed her eagerness to talk about her own research on hold, as Sita continued: "My Uncle was a dreamer and a singer of devotional and mystic songs. He had a lot of trouble with his parents too, when he decided to go 'professional.' But I guess it wasn't so bad for him, although males also face the same anti-professional-music syndrome. Anyway, males can hide a lot of their profligacies under the rubric of mysticism, but when a woman tries to do the same, it's always associated with her flesh. And even though my Uncle was renowned for his broadmindedness, he saw fit to take me to the street where the prostitutes and courtesans make their livelihood, just to show me where I was headed. It's a bad scene, but I'll take you there, if you wish . . .

"So that's my whole story up to now, but who knows? I'm still young and my dreams are not yet buried."

Kannaki looked at Sita's perfectly proportioned facial features and then at the intensity of her hazel eyes which mirrored all her unrealized dreams.

"Poor you," said Kannaki, when she could bring herself to speak, "and yet, maybe not so poor. A Third Undersecretary is surely not all that bad! Can't you sing and dance at the same time? Do you have to give up the joys of singing and dancing just because you're an Undersecretary?"

Sita didn't need to give this much thought, as she replied, "No. One can continue to dance and sing. But it's the song they insist you sing and the tune that they demand you dance to. When you're a government employee, you're a role model and the tune is always the same, the national anthem with an emphasis on the values they want to propagate. And the dance is always of the their victory over the opposition. I'm not saying that their values are false, but I'd be expected to sing and dance to them all the time. Can you imagine what would happen if one night they caught me dancing in one of the courtesan's rooms? A summary end to what could be a modestly brilliant career!"

A potential courtesan who cared for beauty and the arts, but whose spirit was now crushed by the prim of propriety. Echoes of the past in sculpture and bas-reliefs showed what she might have been, had she been allowed to be. How many other fantasies had been crushed by the same Victorian puritanisms?

"Enough of my hopes and dreams," Sita concluded. "Tell me about your project."

"Well, there's not all that much to tell," replied Kannaki. "I've always been intrigued by courtesans and the sixty-four arts and sciences. There seems to be so little written about them, so I thought it would be an interesting dissertation topic for my Ph.D."

"Do you have any specific plans for going about it?" asked Sita.

"Not really," replied Kannaki. "I thought I'd begin by locating some courtesans and interviewing them and see where that leads me."

"I take it this is your first fieldtrip," Sita responded, "so I'm not really surprised that you don't have a more precise plan of procedure." Then, downing the last dregs of her second cup of coffee, she said, "I suppose you might as well begin by seeing the local courtesans in action. My Uncle will be glad to escort us since he knows nearly all the musicians there. But we'll have to disguise ourselves as males — which I'm sure you won't mind, as fieldworkers have a reputation of intrepidness unparalleled in other scholarly types of endeavor. What do you say?"

If Sita had known that Kannaki had once found the courage to tear out her breast in the cause of what she had then felt was righteousness, you may be sure she would not have brought up the matter of courage. The only real problem was her long, lustrous hair, or rather how to hide it. But Sita knew of Favian, the hair and wig specialist, who could do anything to anyone and make actors and actresses come to life in any age or time. So they got done by Vivienne of Favian and with breasts strapped down, 'Masters' Sita and Kannaki met with Uncle who taxied them in the late evening to this place in an unsavory part of town, commonly referred to as the 'Red-light District.'

It consisted of a series of drab tenement houses, four floors high. At first there seemed to be nothing unusual about them, except that there was a slightly ominous air about the place. Uncle led the way up a rickety flight of wooden steps on the outside of one of the buildings and pointed to another structure across the way which he said was where the prostitutes plied their trade. The courtesans, whom he called *tawa'if,* performed in the building they were ascending and had little or no contact with them. As they approached the first floor they could hear the sounds of singing voices, harmoniums, *sarangi* fiddles, *tabla* drums, and *ghunghru* ankle bells spilling down the stairs in a multiplicity of songs. A long balcony stretched ahead of them as they reached the landing, with a succession of rooms opening into it. Some doors were closed and music was emanating from behind them; others were open and these rooms were silent. Seated on the floor of the open rooms was at least one relatively young woman, flashily dressed and made-up, looking hopefully at them as they walked by. On the other side of the rooms were the musical instruments, sometimes with musicians behind them ready to play. Occasionally there was also an elderly lady seated next to the girl, perhaps the mother of the courtesan. Uncle frequently paused to greet them — particularly the musicians, although he also had a respectful word for the courtesan or her mother. But he moved resolutely on until they reached one of the more distant rooms. Here he paused at the entrance, greeting the hosts, took off his slippers and ushered them in.

Sita and Kannaki tried to follow suit by taking off their slippers, but there were loud protestations from the courtesan, who insisted they keep them on — a sign of respect for the patrons — and directed them to sit on the pillows opposite the musicians. The doors were closed as Uncle introduced them as sons of visiting nobles and each of the performers by name. Renuka, the charming but over-dressed and over-perfumed courtesan, greeted them in Muslim Royal-Court style with *salaams* and deferential formulaic verbal expressions. Then, asking for permission to begin, she sang a plebeian romantic poem, *ghazal* — not one which had either intellectual or spiritual challenge — while remaining seated, but using extravagant and sensuous gestures to illustrate the verses. Her voice was raucous and her intonation insecure and she tended to shriek when she tackled the *antara* (higher register) sections of the poem. Yet they felt obliged to shake their heads periodically from side to side in appreciation and to top this off with exclamations of approval, '*wah wah,*' as Uncle was doing.

Then Uncle took them from this room to several others. Some of the courtesans danced, others sang, and still others did both. The musicians were competent, if not outstanding, but the courtesans always seemed to lack something: some were gross, others had poor voice quality or sang out of tune, and still others had no grace of movement or poor rhythmic sense. Yet they went through the rituals of appreciation, and Uncle handed them all monetary gifts as they departed, later submitting a detailed expense reimbursement report that would have done credit to any NEH grantee.

If there were any courtesans who were really good performers, they had evidently been 'captured,' so to speak, by affluent patrons and set up in their own apartments or houses; in any case, there were none that night in the tenement block.

For Kannaki this experience was a symbol of the way life had changed. Gone was the spontaneity and natural charm that had attracted her to Madhavi and the old world courtesans. Now the birds all sat, each in her own cage, waiting for customers, displaying faded and jaded feathers in a pathetic show no longer reminiscent of their days of glory when they had courted kings and ministers.

Later Kannaki met some of these courtesans in her earlier guise as a female, Earthly scholar and found them to be thoroughly disillusioned, without innocence and natural charm. She questioned them about their training and the sixty-four A's and S's, videotaping their responses, largely to put Shiva's Hi-Tech equipment to use. The footage was bland and predictable, and the interviews flat, revealing no exciting inner secrets. It was as though she were talking to parrots who kept reiterating that their patrons couldn't care less about the sixty-four A's and S's, only light music, dance, and a little bit of sexy poetry. What's more, they said, their clients were mostly rich businessmen who had no tradition of sophistication behind them, so they were obliged to eliminate most of the subtleties and focus on the grosser aspects of performance.

Kannaki also interviewed some of the musicians and videotaped several performances, at considerable expense, for courtesans still remembered the sixty-fifth art — how to clean out people's pockets. She discovered a few interesting things — nothing of Heaven- or even Earth-shaking proportions, but of casual import to those that care about such details. The teachers of the courtesans were not older courtesans who were too old to perform, as one might have expected, but were in fact the musicians. They trained the girls in song, dance, and poetry, while older courtesans were kept on by the 'house mother' to run errands, stitch and sew, and generally care for the welfare and health of the girls.

Sitting with Sita and Uncle a few days later and reviewing her research, it suddenly occurred to Kannaki that the courtesans in the tenements were the ones who had not made it, or they would have been set up in their own establishments by some wealthy lover of the arts. The next logical step would obviously be to interview one of the successful ones. Uncle suggested Chitra

Devi, a highly respected singer who was now Professor of Music at the University. He pointed out that not too many people remembered now that she had once been a courtesan. Since he had known her for many years he was sure he could persuade her to give Kannaki an interview.

The Professor was a remarkable woman who by her excellent musicianship and dint of perseverance, not to mention good luck, had surmounted the prejudice associated with her hereditary lifestyle.

It all began when she was nineteen, when a young man of considerable means became enamored of her and set her up in her own apartment. That was wonderful because she could sit and practice all day without distraction. A few years later he announced that he was going abroad for higher studies and insisted that she go with him as his wife. So she went, facing the usual problems of loneliness, homesickness, and boredom that trailing spouses do in a foreign land. To snap herself out of it, she decided to go to school. Not having had a formal education she had a difficult time at first, but eventually she was accepted in a major university, and since her husband had started his practice abroad she duly completed her Ph.D. in ethnomusicology.

Through all of this, she had continued to sing and had given numerous recitals in some of the most prestigious concert halls throughout the world. Finally, she had accepted a position as part-time lecturer, where she attracted a large number of dedicated students. In spite of this, she found the time to write several books which were reviewed favorably in the highest intellectual journals, as well as numerous research articles, until *Britannica* and *New Grove* were constantly peppering her with requests for her literary contributions. Then a tenure-track position in South Asian Studies opened up in that same institution, to which she applied. She was not even one of the finalists! No one questioned her qualifications, but just shelved her application. Why? Did the program really want to avoid having an Indian on their faculty?

Rumors hinted that a cultural insider could not possibly have the requisite objectivity for true scholarship. But was that really it?

Not long after she returned to her own country and become one of the then select group of foreign-returned musicians. Her successes abroad gave her an immediate entrée into the music scene, and her publications into the academic world in her homeland.

This summary, extracted from numerous interview sessions, cannot give the least insight into her effervescent character nor the extent of her vision. Thus I include the transcript of part of one interview:

Kannaki: "Did you truly suggest that universities should hire courtesans to teach the sixty-four arts and sciences?"

Chitra Devi: "Well why not? Students need to learn about life, not just their areas of specialization."

Kannaki: "But they all get their one or two 'breadth' courses exposing them to this and that. Isn't that enough?"

Chitra Devi: "You mean those courses usually referred to as 'Mickey Mouse' courses which they only take because they have to? They call them 'Mickey Mouse' courses because they are suitable only for cartoon characters, not humans. What humans need, and I mean all humans, whether they be scientists, engineers or even in the arts, is an understanding and appreciation of life, this extraordinary creation of the Gods that goes counter to their own laws of entropy. Who better to teach this than courtesans who have not only devoted their lives to this end, but also to communicating their knowledge in a salubrious and stimulating manner. Do you know that academic faculty are not required to have had a single course on methods of communication and have no knowledge of learning theories?"

A serious accusation, but true. To be a Professor means having a superior intellect (whatever that is) and the ability to publish the results of research in uncharted waters, whether right or wrong. The technique of passing on knowledge to future generations is, however, regarded as being purely incidental.

Chitra Devi: "Universities should prepare their students for the life outside and opening them up to those realities. Instead, they try to purge the very bowels of the educational environment. Once it was directed at communism, then drugs, cigarettes, sex and now verbal slander. Browns and nearly whites are called blacks if they have even a touch of negro blood! What happened to free expression? Why do we have to watch what we say? Why does the grapevine stretch its noose around one's throat and demand that yesterday's 'Afro-Americans' is out; from today it will be 'African-Americans.' Just by changing our verbal expressions can we change our personal predilections and prejudices? No, but the grapevine tells us that it will influence future generations to do away with the prejudices of our times which I would accept, except for the fact that history tells us that it won't be long before the grapevine starts to strangle us again with a new demand: 'African-Americans' is out; the new in: is '. . . .'"

Kannaki may perhaps have been overwhelmed by Chitra Devi's convictions in areas that she had never considered, so she waited silently.

Chitra Devi: "Courtesans on campus can change the university environment, which is now much too severe to promulgate the joys of discovery — unless one wants students and faculty jumping out of their baths and running through the streets naked proclaiming, 'Eureka, I have found it!' Put in courtesans and the scene would change; we could keep it all hush on campus because the discoverers would now run to them instead, and campus police would have a little better understanding of the things that go on in universities."

There was more in this vein and perhaps Kannaki was a bit precipitous in switching off her recording equipment, but she was zeroed in on courtesans and their sixty-four areas of learning. Chitra Devi had lived so much since her *ganika* days that she barely remembered the rigorous training she had undergone, so Kannaki moved on.

"Well, I don't really know," replied Sita, to what we are not absolutely certain. "I'm not sure that the big city world necessarily reflects the whole of the country. I was looking at the 1961 census reports the other day and saw that courtesans of one type or another are in every city, town and probably also in every one of the five hundred thousand plus villages in the land. The reports don't distinguish between courtesans and prostitutes — if indeed there is a difference — but there must be some somewhere who would fit your bill. At least it's worth investigation."

Kannaki couldn't deny the possibility, but feeling the strain of fieldwork she wouldn't have minded dropping the project right where it was. She was, in any case, feeling homesick and yearning for Kovalan, and now Sita seemed to be suggesting that her investigations be extended into five hundred thousand plus villages, not to mention the thousands of small towns and cities in the country! Suddenly she imagined herself aging into white hair and wild jabber-talk — notwithstanding her standing as an ageless Goddess — as she jeeped into her two hundred and thirty-two thousandth village, searching futilely for a sixty-four-arts-and-science courtesan! There was really no way she could do it, but, at the same time, she didn't want to admit to Sita that she was ready to quit. So she faked enthusiasm, but made up her mind that she would take just one shot in the dark, to see what another environment might have to offer.

Uncle recommended a small town, Jhajhuripur, which, he said, bards frequently described as having received a double quota of love — devotional as well as carnal. As Kannaki discovered, it was actually a large village, fairly prosperous in relation to others of its kind since it was a market center. Its greatest claim to fame was, however, the number and variety of temples and mosques that it housed. They were not pretentious, but every few days they drew pilgrims and celebrants from all around for one rite or another, so the place continually rocked between sleep and bustle.

Surprisingly, Kannaki felt quite at home here. At first she stayed in a hotel which was not exactly a prepossessing experience. But then she found a modest but clean room in a boarding house attached to a Junior College where she found an elderly lady who was dying to shower her with love and affection, not to mention breakfast, brunch, lunch, tea, snacks, and dinner. And so she was set, ready to face a protracted stay, should the worst come to the proverbial worst. As it turned out, the best was just around the corner, and the worst some distance away, but yet to come.

For a few days Kannaki just walked all around getting a feel of the dusty lanes and looking at the temples. Once or twice she saw women who might have been courtesans, but didn't feel like facing an embarrassing scene if they weren't. Then on one of her walks she heard a sweet singing voice and came upon a young girl in a garden moving elegantly from one flower bush to another, picking only the most choice ones. Kannaki stood outside the iron fence and watched, and as the girl came closer, she suddenly felt a tightening in her mid-section as the realization dawned on her that she had finally found Madhavi! There was no doubt about it, even though she was younger than her memory of Madhavi — only fifteen or sixteen, she guessed. But from the features, the tinkling voice and the grace with which she moved, there could have been no clone more perfect. The girl suddenly saw Kannaki and stopped in embarrassment while a delicate flush mounted her cheeks. And as the two confronted each other, silent messages darted back and forth, building a bond that had never been two thousand years ago, but now was and could never be torn asunder.

Kannaki finally broke the silence. "Forgive me, I didn't mean to invade your privacy. It's just that I was passing by and stopped to look and listen. I hope you don't mind."

The girl stared at her without replying, so Kannaki continued. "I'm just a visitor here in Jhajhuripur and I was just looking around the city. I hope you don't mind."

Later, Kannaki could never understand why she adopted such a distant approach, but just then the girl broke into twinkling, tinkling laughter. And when it had subsided she finally said: "My name is Madhukari and . . ." but stopped at seeing Kannaki's amazement, her sharp intake of breath, and the way her hand slapped involuntarily against her bosom. The listener will, I am sure, share with Kannaki the wonder of this extraordinary coincidence, for the words *madhavi* and *madhukari* are derived from the same root, *madhu*, which means, nectar, honey, spring flowers, love, and so many other nice things. Then after a moment, Madhukari completed her sentence, rather lamely at first: ". . . and I have no privacy. So there was nothing for you to invade. As to friendship, I have already given you my commitment; but as to love, it has already been given away and I take the deepest joy in it. Now that we're friends, won't you come in and help me collect some flowers for my beloved?"

Kannaki was entranced, but at the same time a little taken aback at Madhukari's openness and generosity. It usually takes a fieldworker great deal of time and patience to get into the confidence of an informant, but here it was being offered on the proverbial silver platter! Then Madhukari opened the gate and Kannaki entered speechlessly, not realizing that she was launching herself into one of the most vexing events to face the Godworld in recent memory.

Kannaki collected flowers with Madhukari, who led the way singing and dancing from flower bush to flower bush, until flushed, and with hands completely full, she led Kannaki to her own little flower bower covered over with the many colors of bougainvillaeas rampant with the joys of life. Laying the flowers down one by one in an artistic array with love and caring, she looked up at Kannaki and said,

"Now my lover is also yours, since you too have picked flowers for him."

Needless to say, Kannaki was horrified. Who was her lover and how did she get into this mess? What about Kovalan? What would he say about this?

Then Madhukari continued: "You should feel utterly honored. My lover is none other than our mighty Mahadeva, Shiva, Shankara, and this is his temple. I've been given to him since I was a child. I've taken joy in giving and receiving and my heart is full with him. Now I've drawn you by my side, as a true friend, to share that joy with me."

Little did Madhukari know that Kannaki was a Goddess living in Shiva's world, but with her own God husband. It was certainly a great honor for a human female to be chosen as one of Shiva's mates — and there was no shortage of them on earth, nor any shortage of those desiring to join the band — but for a married Goddess, to put it mildly, it posed some awkward problems. At the very thought of them, Kannaki's hands dropped her batch of flowers as though she was afraid of being venomized by a snake, and hurriedly took her leave of Madhukari without any form of explanation, leaving Madhukari amazed at this tantrum of her new friend.

All field researchers get into a pickle at one time or another. This was it for Kannaki. She had somehow been seduced into putting her foot in Shiva's door and was now feeling the cold, questing draft that blew in. Madhukari was disconsolate at having lost a new friend, and being a sentimental old fool, I shared in her distress. Then I saw Kannaki and she was in a state too, not only because of the voluntary parting from Madhukari and the lapse of her research, but also I think from the opportunity to be Shiva's lover, since she, like most of the Goddesses in the heavens, secretly had a crush on him. Thank whoever it is that serves as God in such expostulations, it didn't last long. Tears eventually dry up, no matter how intense the initial provocation.

The wisdom of the Gods had thought to include a degradation-of-memory chip to help mankind to cope with sad and especially desperately sad events.

Kannaki was going through a 'drop-back' phase that all field researchers seem to go through. I call it drop-back because, for one reason or another, they want to drop their research in order to get back to whatever it was that started them going in the first place. And some do — throwing up their hands in despair at the impossible directions their research impels them to take. But Kannaki, tempted as she was by drop-back, stayed with it.

Three long days later, Kannaki returned to the flower garden to find that even the birds had stopped singing. All was still except with her Goddess-powered hearing she could hear faint sobs coming from the depths of despair. She summoned up her courage, opened the gate, and ventured into Madhukari's flower bower, and the bougainvillaeas trumpeted the call of her coming and Madhukari became still as she looked up into Kannaki's face.

One might think that a being two thousand years old, and a Goddess to boot, might have little or nothing to share with a young girl, no matter how sensitive and graceful she may be. But obviously this was not the case. They spent many an hour in Madhukari's bower trading innocence for wisdom, and Kannaki got to know about Madhukari's world; but with regard to her own life, wisdom prompted her to preserve Madhukari's innocence. She maintained the guise of an Earthly scholar, and even that stretched the realms of her friend's imagination.

Looking at Kannaki's copious notes on Madhukari's life, now deposited in the Heavenly Archives (collection #3048), one sees the thoroughness with which our once diffident scholar had acquitted herself. Every ritual of the day, from the waking of the God, to putting him to bed, is fully explored and described — that is, except one. And that Madhukari called *gupta seva,* which translates to something like 'secret devotional service.' This secret service went on in the inner sanctum of the temple every day for about two hours but Kannaki could get no absolutely no information out of her on this, as she admits in her journal. Once she asked Madhukari if it had anything to do with sex, and Madhukari laughed, saying, "Sex isn't secret in our lives. It's our bread and butter and everyone knows about it. Do you want to see how beautiful it is? Shiva is so versatile, he comes down to my home after the day's services are over in a different guise nearly every night and makes love to me; sometimes it's beautiful and sometimes it's so sad, but then I love him even more."

For more lurid details of the *devadasi*'s sex life, the reader should consult Kannaki's journal, for she has not withheld too much in it. There's no doubt that she learned a few techniques to employ on Kovalan who desperately awaited her return, but there was no way she could go back without knowing more about *gupta seva,* which she felt could well be the clue to the sixty-four arts and sciences. Madhukari, however, refused to give her a single clue, saying with a determination far belying her sweet exterior that she had been bound to secrecy at her marriage to Shiva, and nothing would make her break her vow. If Kannaki really wanted to know, she should speak to Guru-Maharaj, the religious head of the temple.

For the sake of clarity, we should point out that this gentleman was not the same as the Maharajji we have encountered in other stories. In this context Maharaj is a form of respectful address to a Brahmin or other religious superior.

Why did Kannaki feel trepidation at this seemingly little step? Who knows? But with some anxiety she finally went and asked for an audience with him and was ushered in immediately. Guru-Maharaj sat on the floor with crossed legs and a beatific smile as she entered. Kannaki waited a few moments and just as she was about to interrupt his reverie, he spoke in a cultured tone with no appreciable accent.

"We have naturally been aware of your interest in our future number one *devadasi,* Madhukari. If you wish to make love to her, please remember that you will have to disguise yourself as a man, for all her lovers are to be seen as emanations of Shiva. Well, perhaps we could make an exception in your case on the grounds that Shiva has himself chosen, under provocation I suppose, the role of *ardhanarisvara,* in which half of him is a female. So you could go to Madhukari as that half. It will cost you a little bit, because it will be something new for her, but we can arrange it."

"Guru-Maharajji. You are very kind, but my interests are not inclined in that way. Well, that is not exactly true, but, let us say, not at the moment. I am carrying out research on the Sixty-four Arts and Sciences that, according to Vatsyayana and other sages, have been the preserve of courtesans. So far, my research has led nowhere and I am now at the point where I believe that courtesans have let the sages down by failing to preserve them — unless *gupta seva* is it."

"Let me first and foremost say that our temple and its traditions are unique in this country. We value tradition and we regard ourselves in the same light as the Smithsonian, preserving the world of the past, except that we are not interested in making flashy, incoherent television programs about our work as they feel obliged to do. As for us, we don't need money — our patrons do well by us and amply reward the services of our *devadasis.* The *gupta seva* is, shall we put it like this, our greatest claim to what one day will be recognized as the past's contribution to the future; more so even, than *Ramarajya,* the world of purity which is said to have existed two thousand and five hundred years ago, and is being touted by the hysteriographers of our population as the future of our salvation."

"How can I find about it?" said Kannaki. "Madhukari refuses to give me even the vaguest idea of what goes on."

Guru-Maharaj replied, "And rightly so. That information is reserved entirely for the *devadasis* and a very few of our most senior priests. It has been so since our temple was founded thousands of years ago."

"But you see," responded Kannaki, slightly exasperated, "it is essential to my research. I am not in a position to tell you just how important my project is, but believe me, it could have major implications for the future of mankind."

Guru-Maharaj was quite inflexible: "That may be; nevertheless, I may not reveal the secret of *gupta seva* since it was a condition of my appointment as head of this temple. That information is available only to *devadasis*, and there is no way you can have access to it, except by becoming one yourself. Now, please excuse me, as I must get on with preparations for the midday ritual."

This was a severe set-back for Kannaki's research, especially as she was now convinced that *gupta seva* was the secret to the preservation of the sixty-four arts. When she reported her conversation with Guru-Maharaj to Madhukari, she was delighted and said, "How wonderful. Now you can become a *devadasi* like me and enjoy my lover too."

Fieldworkers are faced, not infrequently, with situations when the only way they can have access to certain types of information is by accepting another faith. There are, for example, temples where only Hindus may enter. Since it is relatively easy to become a Hindu and Hinduism is not very demanding, numerous foreign scholars have taken this step to achieve their own ends. But this was quite a different matter, for becoming a *devadasi* meant a real commitment. Not knowing just what it entailed, Kannaki went to see Guru Maharaj again. After all, she was more or less a Hindu, even though that word was not in common use when she'd lived on Earth and there had been many changes in the belief system since then. So she thought that she might be able to get away with becoming a token *devadasi* for a short period.

But Guru-Maharaj made it quite plain that there were no short cuts. He said, "Becoming a *devadasi* is a serious matter and requires dedication. Firstly, you're not married, are you?" Kannaki replied, "Well, I was married long ago. But my husband's in Heaven."

"Oh! I'm sorry to hear that. You have our sympathies. In our tradition it is possible for a widow to become a *devadasi*."

Kannaki kept quiet. She hadn't actually told any lies, but not denying that she was a widow was tantamount to one and she hoped that Kovalan would forgive her.

"The other main requirement is that you must be able to dance and sing. Have you had any training?"

In Kannaki's time, all sophisticated young girls were required to learn these arts, but, of course, the repertoire was so very different now. Nevertheless, she could honestly say she had.

"Very well then," said Guru-Maharaj, "there is nothing to stop us from going ahead. I can make all the arrangements. Firstly, you must take some singing and dancing lessons to learn the special aspects of our tradition. When you're ready, we'll go ahead with your wedding to Lord Shiva so that you can be properly installed as a *devadasi*."

Kannaki again felt full of anxiety. She knew there was no way to keep this information from reaching the heavens. What would Kovalan say to such a marriage, even if it were being enacted in the name of scholarship? And what about Shiva? Would he want to take advantage of it when she returned to heaven, or would he understand and overlook it knowing that all fieldworkers had to put on a pretence of some kind to collect important data? Most of all, did she dare risk her happy two-thousand-year-old marriage for a mere research project? But even as she thought it, she knew that this was not a 'mere' dissertation topic that she was seeking to research, but the real reason for mankind's failure to live up to the high expectations that the Gods had once had for them. Surely Kovalan would forgive her when she came back with such important results.

So she acquiesced and began her lessons. Right from her first step and her first vocal '*aaaa*' everyone knew that she was exceptional, and in the space of just a few days her teacher was able to verify that she had mastered the whole repertoire, a testimony to the continuity of India's traditional arts.

Now the astrologers were consulted for an auspicious date, which unfortunately had to be postponed because Kannaki menstruated at the wrong time and had to wait for the impurity to leave her body. The next time she was in synch with the stars, and then the complicated wedding rituals began. One night she had to sleep with a dagger, and on another she had to have Shiva's trident branded on her arm. Their were numerous fasts, baths and anointings, burnings of incense, endless ringings of bells, and chantings of mantras. Days passed by. Then finally, there was the procession to the village tank, the final ritual bath, the tying of the black-beaded necklace to ward off evil, distribution of alms and wages to the ritual performers, and the sandal-paste mark placed on her forehead to certify that she was now a married woman. That evening she danced and sang in front of Shiva in the inner sanctum in the presence only of the *devadasis* and their musician family members. There was not a single person present who did not have tears in their eyes at witnessing that glorious performance. And Madhukari cried uncontrollably for days after.

Devadasi Kannaki received blessings from Guru-Maharajji, who was delighted with the way things had turned out. He could see Kannaki's grace and charm bringing not only prestige to his establishment, but could hear the clink of coins dropping in the donation boxes. Kannaki on the other hand, after all that she'd been through, was naturally impatient to find out about the secrets of the sixty-four arts and sciences, and so she spoke to him.

"Guru-Maharajji. Can I join the *gupta seva* session this evening? As you know, I've been working very hard for this moment and feel I've earned the right to it."

"My dear," he replied, "I know how hard you've worked and I'm indeed proud of your achievements. But the marriage has not yet been consummated and until then it is not over. I'll arrange for the consummation to take place tonight and then you can attend the session tomorrow."

"What do you mean, Guru-Maharajji? I have gone through the whole ritual, step by step. And still you say that it's not consummated!"

"Yes. The best part is still ahead. Tonight Shiva will come to your bed and you will join with him and spend a wonderful night in exultation of his body, and he of yours. Then you will truly be man and wife."

Kannaki was horrified. She was going to have to have sexual intercourse to consummate the marriage! Why didn't she think of that earlier? No one had thought to mention it and so it hadn't even occurred to her. Kovalan would never forgive that! And who would she be sleeping with? She knew that Gods didn't interfere with human rituals, so it wouldn't be Shiva, but probably some fat and pretentious big shot. Shudder the thought. What were the consequences of a Goddess sleeping with a mortal? Would she stop being a Goddess and become mortal again? Maybe she'd turn to dust, being two thousand years old! Had she been younger and single, she might've taken the chance and argued her case in the Heavenly Assembly later, but as it was, she just couldn't do it.

She only said good-bye to Madhukari, and it was such a sad moment! My profession loves to try to communicate these extremes of experience, but I find myself struck dumb in the face of such sadness. Then Kannaki flitted away to heaven, with a brief in-transit visit to the big city and another tearful good-bye to her friend Sita.

Kannaki never completed her dissertation and *gupta seva* still remains unexplored. If any young and pretty Goddess is looking for a fascinating and perhaps crucially important dissertation field project, I advise that she contact Kannaki, who is now back home delighting her husband with the arts of the courtesan. Hopefully she will spare a few minutes from her joys to give some homilies about fieldwork.

THE GODS FIGHT BACK

Since Shiva's initial forays into documenting Earth and its goings-ons, mankind had begun to explore realms which were properly those of the Gods. This was not so much the sending of probes into outer space — which the Gods found of little consequence in view of the immensity of it — but challenging the traditional areas of authority of the Gods.

Initially, the Gods had only two attributes: the powers of Making and Breaking, more elegantly expressed as Creation and Destruction. When Godkind was first imbued with these powers, they had a lot of fun making all kinds of crazy and wonderful things. Unfortunately, some of the Gods had just as much pleasure breaking them, sometimes even before the Makers could see what they'd made. So the game began to pall and would probably have died out except that by another miracle they acquired a third attribute: that of Preservation, or Saving, as on a computer disk. Now it was possible for a Maker to draw up a contract with a Saver to preserve the made, but that virtually put the Breakers out of business and the game once again began to stall. With no other miraculous attributes forthcoming, one of the Gods invented the concept of rules, which allowed both Makers and Breakers to negotiate deals with the Savers. Over millennia, the rules became more and more elaborate and complex, requiring experts to interpret and adjudicate. They were called umpires, but even they could not cope with it all and eventually had to resort to Instant Replays.

This got to be a bit much for the average God or Goddess, who actually preferred to loll about and do nothing. Many thought about the possibility of giving up the whole game, but then they would have to stop being Gods, and everyone kind of liked being divine. Finally they came up with the notion of relegating their responsibilities and giving proxy votes to elected officers, so that they could continue to play at being Gods without actually doing anything. Brahma was elected Officer of Making, Vishnu of Saving, and Shiva of Breaking. Fortunately, they liked having power and being officers, so it wasn't too bad for them.

Now they were being challenged in their areas of authority — not by demons, which would have been understandable, but by one of their own handmade creations: Man! Man had taken up Breaking as a vocation and was staging it on a Godscale. It started with petty wars in which mercenary soldiers destroyed each other voluntarily. Shiva first tolerated this as a party game, but it gradually began to get out of hand. Eventually there was no question that Man was well into indiscriminate destruction, not to mention spilling oil and the like, and if they were not stopped soon, Shiva would find himself in the bread line since there would be nothing left for him to destroy.

Not surprisingly, Shiva found this to be a matter of considerable concern. Under normal circumstances, the most powerful Lord of the Gods would have been enraged at anyone trying to steal his thunder, and might well have given them a heavy dose of destruction, since mankind seemed to be asking for it. But these were not the ordinary times one reads about as being characteristic of the celestial world, when Gods and Goddesses lolled about on the swards with their charming companions, only interrupting their reveries to bash in a demon head or two. No. There was a distinctly new look in the old place, a fresh air of questioning, and signs of unusual activity on Mount Kailash. The order of the day was research and scholarship, and with a bit of luck, finding out what went wrong with the divine plan for creation. Now man was threatening to cut off time summarily, which would mean that numerous divine theses and dissertations would forever remain incomplete since there would not be enough time for the mindless building blocks of scholarship — footnotes, references, bibliographies, indexes, and glossaries, not to mention new theories to explain the failure of the universe.

Shiva, while cogitating on this state of affairs, came up with some chilling thoughts. Destruction was bad enough, but what if the rumor now circulating, that mankind was on the threshold of a major breakthrough in the area of life-making — one of the deepest secrets of the Godworld — were true? What if they uncovered this secret before they had completed the destruction of the universe? And what if they designed an automatic start-up mechanism for the next universe to include life? He could see all the Gods joining him on the bread line! Something had to be done.

The simplest solution would have been to end it all right then, but he knew that the Gods needed time to complete their research. What worried him was that this might give mankind the extra time needed to complete their experiments with life and thus supersede the Gods as both Makers and Breakers! It was going to be touch and go, Shiva realized; research on Earth would have to be monitored closely, and at the first sign of man's success he would have to get into lightning action and go berserk. Everything had to be planned very carefully. Firstly, all preparations for the ritual of termination must be made in advance, so that the act could be implemented instantaneously. Secondly, he would have to enlist the assistance of Lord Vishnu, the Savings Officer, and the Preserver of the Universe, to keep the universe going until the danger indicator was just about to go into the red zone. Finally, a watchful eye would have to be kept on all life-related research activities on Earth and virtually everything else.

Easier thought than done, of course. Since Vishnu was the leader of the Opposition Party, he would have to be cajoled into cooperating. Like all good administrators, Shiva did not like the idea of asking the opposition for favors, which would, no doubt, put them in a position of strength; but Vishnu was critical to his plans, not only because Shiva needed him to thwart man's destructive designs on the universe but also because he already had a surveillance network on Earth. This he had been using to inform him of danger signs which might require his attention as Preserver. The network could already have apprised him of the dangers Shiva now saw; but since they were looking for demon-threats to the universe they might not have noticed man-threats to the Gods.

The meeting between the two Gods was, of course, held behind closed doors and on such delicate occasions, possibly affecting the security of the heavens, even storytellers are excluded. But from bits and pieces of information that leaked out of the chamber, we can reconstruct its main points, slightly embellished by the poetic license granted to writers and bards.

After the principal protagonists and their hench-Gods had been properly seated on cloud pillows placed on *kusha* grass, drinking the nectar poured by the diaphanously-clothed ones, Shiva opened his gambit with the expected platitudes:

"Dear friend and respected colleague, in the years we have known each other and worked amicably in the running of these heavens forever festooned with the breathtaking gifts of our forebears" — perhaps forgetting for the sake of rhetoric, that Gods don't have forebears, or do they? — "I have had so little opportunity to speak to you from the heart. My dear friend, many are the times that I have sat on this cloud admiring your wit and wisdom in carrying out your awkward responsibilities as Opposition leader, knowing that you have always placed the common good above all selfish ends and have therefore frequently seen fit to ignore, or at least minimize, my digressions and transgressions. I can say, without any hesitation, that I could not have hoped for a more congenial, should I say, antagonist? In any case, your many accomplishments have not passed unnoticed, and I would be most pleased to write a letter on your behalf for your next merit advancement."

Of course, Vishnu is no slouch as a God, and already suspected something was afoot, so his reciprocation of the compliments was cautious and a model of understatement. "Respected colleague, your dedication and forthrightness are well-known throughout the universe. It would have been unseemly to have questioned all your decisions, which I need hardly say we have not always seen in the same light. There have indeed been one or two moments when we have been tempted, shall I say, to be short-circuitous? I refer here, for example, to the episode of the deficit budget which we chose to overlook because we felt it inappropriate to raise questions about your credentials in the opening episode of the present series."

Vishnu had obviously been waiting a long time to get in this dig and one could see that he was rather pleased with the way he had put it. Shiva, however, ignored this marginal breach of etiquette and plowed right on. "I won't beat around the *kusha* grass. I really need your help and the support of your party once again. You see, something of a desperate nature has come up, and we can only tackle this with solidarity in our ranks."

Shiva paused for effect, hoping to keep Vishnu in suspense, and thus at a disadvantage. But Vishnu knew all about Shiva's devious tactics and he began to guess that the desperate nature of Shiva's problem was somehow connected with his pet project of documenting the Earth. As Vishnu bided his time, Shiva leaned forward, and in a quieter, more confidential tone, said: "This is a matter of utmost concern to me and I trust you will be as discreet as possible. I mean, it will do no one any good if our *Heavenly Sentinel* were to get hold of this information and have a lurid headline, 'Mankind Overpowers the Gods,' or something like that — and I am sure they could make it sound even more dramatic, being professional journalists and all. Well, to cut it short, the fact of the matter is that our power is under threat, and I mean serious threat. Mankind is turning out to be a real menace both to themselves and to us, inventing atom and hydrogen bombs, nuclear fission and chemical fusion and whatnot. What did we create? A bunch of homicidal maniacs, it seems. They deserve to destroy themselves. But I mean to say, they don't have the <u>right</u> to destroy on such a large scale. In the blueprints we drew of the universe, that right was ours, and specifically mine. How dare they try to take this away from me! Next they will try to take away your role and figure out a way of saving the world, and if they succeed in that, their next step — on which I have information from the usual reliable source — is to create life. What will it do to the Trinity and especially our father Brahma, who is eagerly looking forward to starting the whole process up again, being that creation is his only recreation?"

As Shiva wiped the brewing passion off his brow, Vishnu thought, 'The bit about destruction is no skin off my nose. About time Shiva was taken down a peg or two. In any case, destruction is not my business — what do I care? But what if they come after me next and take over preservation? How will I justify my existence?' His own brow knitted momentarily with concern, but playing the politician, he unravelled the knitting immediately and said in a cool voice:

"Surely you go too far. A few bombs can't destroy creation — maybe a country or two — but I can't see it going further than that. And I can't see their Greenpeace and Save the Environment campaigns as a real threat to my hegemony as Preserver of the Universe."

Shiva's response suggested that he was beginning to get impatient. "It's not just the principle of the thing, which is bad enough; but you underestimate its seriousness. All these fissions and fusions and combustions and ex- and im-plosions have just about ripped a hole in the protective screen around Earth. The place will become a hothouse and that means it will soon spin out of orbit, taking an erratic path which might even bring it dangerously close to our beloved Mount Kailash."

Vishnu was still not convinced. "You say might, but it also might not. Have you taken professional advice on the matter? Surely we should discuss this possibility with Vishvakarma, our architect for the universe, before taking any radical action."

"Naturally that was my first thought too," said Shiva, "and I must acknowledge that he dropped all the other work he was doing — including his design of the magnificent space terminal for the end of the rainbow — just to do these calculations." He then handed Vishnu a soiled and crumpled sheet covered with numerical hieroglyphics. "These are just his preliminary figures. Seeing their importance I didn't want to wait for his complete report."

Vishnu looked unseeingly at the sheet. "I see," he said. "Very impressive, er, I mean, conclusive. No doubt it is a very serious matter. You are right, we must take action. Gods are Gods; there is no escaping that reality. We must assert ourselves." Then, after a moment of thought, he suggested, "Why don't you just destroy them for being revolutionaries? That will solve the matter immediately. I am sure that this would be one destruction which my party would condone, once I give them all the facts. It will also be a relief not to have to continue to save and preserve this universe — after all, I've done it nine times already through my incarnations and each one has been thoroughly exhausting."

Shiva now sensed that he was getting through. "Exactly what I first thought. I said to myself, 'My colleague Vishnu has really been working hard to preserve this universe, in the process taking on the guise of so many creatures — boar, tortoise, fish, man-lion, dwarf, not to mention the highly revered souls, Krishna, Buddha, and Rama; surely he's done his bit and must be worn out. I should not impose on him further, especially since Kalki, the white horse, his final incarnation, is still to come.' But then I asked myself, 'What about the next universe? We just haven't collected enough data on this one to find out what went wrong. We have to keep the universe going long enough to complete our studies, or else we'll make a mess of the next one, too, and dear Vishnu will have to work overtime again.' And that's why I've come to ask for your help in continuing to protect the universe. It won't be long, I promise you. Already many Godscholars have joined the project and everyone realizes its importance and urgency, and we are making rapid progress. By the way, you must visit our archives one of these days. Admittedly, it's in a bit of a mess — but then, isn't that always the case when one is actively engaged in a project? In any case, the data is flowing in and the archive staff is working overtime entering information into the computers."

Shiva has always been a convincing speaker and Vishnu was clearly won over, but still being reluctant to concede, he stalled: "Yes, I've been meaning to visit, but you know how it is. Something always seems to come up at the wrong time. It's getting close to the granting period and a number of my students have approached me for letters of recommendation. It's something I hate having to do, especially as it always means one has to exaggerate the students' virtues and hide their faults. In the beginning, I tried to be honest, but I found everyone else was exaggerating and my students didn't have a chance. So what could I do?"

Shiva broke in, but in a conciliatory tone: "Don't I know!" he said, "I fully sympathize, since I'm going through the same thing. I know that you've been under considerable pressure, and I wouldn't have brought this matter up at this time but for its desperate urgency. Unfortunately, there's absolutely no way I can handle this without your help. There is an added problem that I must bring up, although your information network has probably given you all the facts already. Mankind is playing with a new kind of fire: the fire of life. If they discover its secret, we will be through as Gods. It is imperative that we monitor every research project on this subject, no matter where on Earth, and prevent them from completing their work."

As Shiva had already guessed, Vishnu's surveillance team had utterly overlooked the significance of this type of research. Vishnu had no recourse but to concede, but he was already planning to turn the situation to his advantage.

"At a moment like this, I agree we must show solidarity, and I think it is appropriate for the Opposition to make some upfront concessions, that is, provided the dominant party is equally responsive. I'll get my Celestial Intelligence Agency to look into the matter right away and to infiltrate the appropriate research centers, and I'll even hold off man's premature termination of the universe — on condition that you see fit to approve these," as he pulled out a list of concessions which he had been carrying in one of his inner pockets for Gods only know how long.

Shiva had expected no less, and with scarcely a glance at the list, affixed his signature to the paper.

When apprised of the details, the Heavenly Assembly greeted the news with applause: Vishnu had agreed to involve the CIA in monitoring life studies and to prolong the untimely end of the universe, in order to give more time for research! His stock went up at least twenty points and dipped only slightly when the concessions were mentioned; but he had agreed, and that was cause enough for celebration. Vishnu made it clear, however, that the CIA would be instructed to seek only a temporary, stop-gap solution — nothing like the assassination of a political leader or the takeover of a government — so that the Gods had better get on with their research in a hurry. The vibrancy with which Vishnu spoke can be attested to by the fact that there was a run on tape and video recorders right after the meeting.

Before the meeting concluded, Brahma, whose inherent modesty normally prevented him from asserting himself in meetings, found the temerity to speak:

"I think that my colleagues will support me when I say that I am neither hasty nor vindictive, but I regard man's playing about with the creation of life much more serious than their experiments with destruction — with all due respect to our King of Gods. Life controls death, in the sense that if there were no life, there could be no death, and it is life that is threatening us with destruction. I thus urge the CIA to look for ways to terminate man's experiments with life and to give this problem top priority."

The CIA team, headed by Vishnu's false avatar, 0007, went to work in its own nefarious way, with coercion and subterfuge, reaching its tentacles into both the sacred and the profane. Computers were made to cough up the most private secrets of individuals and institutions until credit reports and bank statements flew about like leaves in autumn, and people, like naked trees divested of their protection, stood about shivering in fear of the informer.

The CIA does not beat about the bush; it gets right to the heart of the problem, brushing aside all distractions and any opposition it encounters. Brahma's priority request had been granted, yet the CIA recognized that the most immediate problem was to slow mankind's headlong rush into destruction. This was not an easy problem to solve since violence is impregnated into mankind's being right from the nurseries, when Humpty Dumpty rhymes crack innocent craniums wide open by falling off walls or rolling down hills, and cartoon characters pummel each other into the most ludicrous shapes. It was no wonder that violence was taken for granted as a fact of life and that the media even exalted its most grotesque forms.

0007 saw right away that there was no way to turn mankind off from wrestling and horror movies. He even consulted the best psychiatrists who told him that watching violence did not necessarily mean practising violence, and that for most of the viewers the vicarious thrills of mayhem actually subjugated their own instincts in that direction. That was good enough for him. The answer was, if you can't change them, make the most of it. And so the CIA put their money into producing even more violent and horrific movies. Whether or not they succeeded in reducing the violent tendencies of man is open to debate; there is no question, however, that they had numerous box office hits, thus supplementing their inadequate budget to pursue their first priority: namely, to retard man from discovering the secret of life.

In his report to the Assembly, 0007 explained how they went about it.

"We gave the matter of life research a great deal of thought. Obviously, we couldn't just walk into labs and shoot the scientists. It was clear that we would have to be subtle. Use guile and deceit. Trickery — that was the way. Feed them red herrings, put up smokescreens, and trap them into the endless ways statistics can be manipulated to hide the truth. Get them to believe in the possibility of perpetual motion and cold fusion and the dangers of high and low cholesterol, smoking and non-smoking, aspirin and non-aspirin, sugar and sugar substitutes, caffeine and decaffeine, alcohol and non-alcohol, aerobics and lack of exercise, and everything else we could think of, so that they would carry out wasteful, time-consuming research into the dead ends of non-discovery. We are convinced that these double-pronged tactics will keep man from finding the real secret of life until Shiva's axe is ready to cut away their lifelines."

And so it came to be. The subversive, delaying tactics the CIA employed succeeded exactly as planned. They tampered with data, raising man's hopes which led to lengthy verification searches and finally to utter disappointment. The cold fusion episode was one of their masterpieces. Just a little tampering with data here and there and the scientists on Earth began throbbing with excitement at the possibility of a perpetual motion machine. Most of the laboratories suspended their own research projects to get in on the act and to verify the results found in a single lab in one of the lesser-known universities in the U.S. And it took them a whole year to discover the hoax! This kind of diversionary work, courtesy of the CIA, is still going on, buying time for Shiva's research.

Following 0007's report, Brahma expressed his enthusiasm for the CIA's endeavors and the Assembly voiced its approval in no uncertain terms. No deity questioned the ethics of hindering man's research to protect their own vested interests in Making and Breaking. Obviously, it was taken for granted that the Gods' ends were superior to those of man and thus justified any course of action, no matter how dastardly.

There was, however, a different concern expressed at the meeting by the brilliant Dravidian God, Ayappan.

"It has come to my attention that the CIA's covert activities have not passed entirely unnoticed. As a matter of fact, rumors are running so rife on Earth that everything underhanded is being ascribed to the CIA, and whenever a government is toppled or a celebrity murdered, the word goes out that the CIA is at it again. There can be no doubt that this is extremely bad for our image and I feel that we must make every effort to counter it."

Not too many Gods had given thought to the matter of their image on Earth, resting secure in the belief that, after all, man worshipped Gods and Goddesses and a little adverse publicity incurred by the CIA was not going to change that a whole lot. But Ayappan had different ideas.

"It is a problem of image," he said, "and images have become man's speciality — not three-dimensional ones, but those in one, two, and two-and-a-half dimensions: the storyteller operates only in the dimension of time, the film and video screen in two dimensions of space, and the surround hi-fi sound adds another half a dimension of conviction to the perception of space. All these create, in their own ways, a convincing impression of reality — but not the reality in which we live. Man, through assiduous practice, not to mention our help in experiments with drama, has learned the knack of illusion, where even a black-and-white photograph or a scratchy phonograph record of the 'thirties seems like the real thing. With this power of illusion, multiplied by two-and-a-half, he has recently been conveying a convincing, but utterly false image of what was and will be. And, believe me, the people believe it. Needless to say, I have solid documentation to support my statements, which I will present at the appropriate time. The fact of the matter is that they are distorting our world, our purposes and our very persons! Can you believe that they still depict us as being warriors fighting against demons? We have long since grown out of that and now accept our dear Demons as merely being the left of the right, not the wrong of the right."

Of course this drew applause from the Demon faction which spread slowly, and perhaps reluctantly, throughout the Assembly Hall.

"Ah! the art of illusion," Ayappan continued rhapsodically, "is what we built our world on. We called it *maya* and said that all our creations were illusory; but we only did this to make the unbelievable more acceptable. And here is *maya* once again — illusion, but this time presented by man on TV. It doesn't exist, and yet it is so convincing that millions or even billions of our creations believe in its reality. We set man on his way to become the master of magic, and with this magic he has created Superman and Batman who can accomplish extraordinary feats which even we would be hard-pressed to duplicate."

As usual, the Chair was impatient with Ayappan's lengthy exposition and wanted him to get on with it. Ayappan showed due respect, but nevertheless, rambled on:

"We live in a universe of illusions, most of which we ourselves have created. And that is right. We are the Gods and have the right to do so. Illusions are our stock in trade. But I think we made a profound mistake when we gave our illusions over to the simulatory world of drama. It has spread rapidly through the world of man and now they have become masters of that world. If I could show you the conviction expressed in just a five-minute animation film created by man or a typical TV commercial, even you would be tempted to believe in their make-believe reality."

Shiva hastily stepped in to let Ayappan know that it was not really necessary, but neglected to mention that there was no audio/visual equipment in the Assembly Hall, notwithstanding his own Hi-Tech proclivities. Ayappan continued:

"Now I come to the two recent TV series on the *Ramayana* and *Mahabharata*. They have enjoyed the most remarkable success as millions of our progeny have watched each episode gripping the edges of their seats. They are magnificent soap operas — there is no denying that; but they still depict us as we used to be, not as we now are. What little hint they have of our new scholarly goals are marred by rumors of our CIA and our foreign policy, not to mention our leading role as suppliers of arms to Third World countries. While there is, no doubt, some truth to these rumors, the important point is that we are much more than that. Our dedication to the goal of creating the perfect universe, and therefore perfect man, is not reflected in their epics. They must understand that, in the long run, we have their welfare at heart, and just because we are outsiders in their world does not mean that we do not know what is best for them.

"In view of this," Ayappan continued, "it is imperative that we solve our image problem at the earliest. There are basically two issues, as I see it. Firstly, we have to communicate to mankind our new world as it really is and our goal of producing the perfect universe; and secondly, we must quash the rumors that have been circulating about our nefarious activities. Both of these are tall orders. Our world is complex and it will be difficult to convince mankind of our superior motives, but I am convinced it can be done. We will have to hire professional writers like Mark Twain who understand our aims and purposes and have the ability to dress them up in an engaging style so that the work will be read and respected. Then I propose we produce a spinoff TV counter-series and market it through all the major networks. Of course there will be much initial opposition as people will not easily be prepared to give up their cherished, archaic notions about us, and no doubt there will be many who will call the work sacrilegious at first. But if we have an impeccable cast, we shall win them over. Therefore we must have the most famous writers whose words will be beyond question, and the most famous directors, actors, actresses, musicians and stagehands who are already so well-known and admired that their work cannot possibly be rejected."

And so after the Gods fought back in clandestine ways against the threat to their rights, Shakespeare and Kalidasa were hired to collaborate in writing the play showing the Gods in their best light, and are even now completing the last few scenes. They have called it *Goddyssey I* with the prospect of sequels to update their image as and when needed, and from every report it promises to be their greatest masterpiece. The huge cast is being lined up — Garbo and Gable, Liz and Blue-Eyes, Zeenat and Amitabh — you name it and they'll be there, not to mention Dizzy and Ravi and Michael and the Beatles. Directed by Bharata and Sellars, it will undoubtedly be the biggest extravaganza conceived, giving a glossy cover to camouflage their covert Godways.

VISHNU'S RIP ROARS

The seven Maruts were once important Gods who, armed with lightning and thunderbolts and riding on whirlwinds, were given the task of regulating the storm patterns on Earth. But in the course of time and numerous misadventures, they finally found themselves in an abject state of misery and physical discombobulation. As they sat about as lumps of frightened flesh, Shiva happened upon them and, out of compassion, rescued them and fashioned from the lumps seven identical little boys who he gave to his wife Parvati to mother. It perhaps does not say much for Parvati's motherly abilities, though she was otherwise perfect in all respects, that the seven never really grew up, and as storm Gods were utterly erratic, giving monstrous headaches to meteorologists, not to mention travellers, prize fight organizers, opening nighters, and the like. Since they all looked alike, were the same age and wore the same outfits, I have chosen to give them arbitrary numerical designations. But as will be seen, they were not all quite the same.

One day, Number One, completely out of the blue, spoke thusly: "Brethren, do you not see what is going on around about you? Is it of so little concern to you that the purpose of our birth has been diverted by the stream of intellectual scholarship that has hit the heavens? When are we going to do it?"

This may seem enigmatic to you listeners, but to the Maruts it was straight talk. They had been created initially to destroy Indra, once King of the Gods, though the records are now somewhat murky as to who concocted them. Unfortunately for them, Indra had gotten wind of this preordained scheme and postordained it by chopping the one Marut embryo into seven while it was still lying in its mother's womb, and then after birth chastising the seven into the fleshy lumps Shiva had found. Growing up in Parvati's opulent home, they learned to be carefree and careless, except periodically, when their prenatal memory surged back, as in this instance.

Number Two — or was it Three? — who had been for several days impatiently sitting in a kind of lull, saw this moment as a signal to snap out of it and began to bluster, "Yes. Yes. Let's get to it pronto and leave no quarter unchurned."

This started the others revolving like a slowly mushrooming maelstrom and soon I could only catch the comments here and there. I think it was Number Four who came next, trying to get a grip on his bearings. "Hold on. Hold on!" he warned. "Rushing about like hot air without a hot plot is not going to get us anywhere. We need sage advice, or at least a *How To Do It* book."

"Yes! Yes! Yes!" said Number Five, who loved the sound of sibilants, "Yes! Yes! Let's seek some savvy seeress sage and see what her crystal foresees for we."

Whereupon Number Six, who always liked to blow in the opposite direction, responded: "Get with it. You don't have to have a savvy sage to give seasoned advice. Any herb can do it." To which, of course, Number Five hissed, "Shush up and show me, sibling show-off."

"Look who's talking, you . . . lispian. There, I said it. And you deserve it," retorted Six.

Since we haven't yet heard from Seven, I guess it was he who came next. "You guys are always looking for a tea cup to storm about in. Let's cut the wisecracking and get cracking! I say we go to Papa Shiva for his input."

And so the storm Gods, knowing full well that an unruly entrance would trigger sudden just retribution from Shiva's third eye, drifted gently into his presence. When the dust had settled and Shiva had acknowledged their presence by twitching said eye, Number One, who had appointed himself as spokesGod, ventured forth. "Illustrious Papa," he began. "We have been growing exceedingly concerned that we are not approaching the fulfillment of our destiny. In fact, I would say that we have made little or no progress for thousands of years. It is surely high time that we hatched a plot to ensnare Uncle Indra and, at least, harass him a little, even if we can't knock him off right away. But we need a scheme — and it is for this that we are here."

Shiva was quite taken aback at this obsolete request. Gods didn't do that sort of thing any more — how could his own children be so far out of it in this day and age that they still lived for petty vengeance and this 'fulfillment of destiny' garbage? It would be just his luck to have a bunch of thrill-seeking wards, without a serious puff of intellect. Maybe it wouldn't have been so bad if all the younger generation of Gods had been like that, but there were now so many bright young things who specialized in hot-shot scholarship and were out to take him down an academic peg or two. If even one of his stormy kids had the wherewithal to take up an intellectual cudgel or two in his defense! But they all seemed to be oafs and goof-offs.

"Sons," said Shiva. "If you wouldn't spend all your time frittering and farting away your lives, you'd notice a thing or two. We don't go around killing any more, or hadn't you noticed? We don't even kill demons now, let alone other Gods. This is the period of enlightenment, as you jolly well ought to know, if for no other reason than you are the sons of the King of Gods. Do affairs of state mean so little? What do you spend your time doing — chatting up a breeze? Rumors have reached me that you're even being negligent in your storm duties and that my favorite Southern California has been going through years of drought. You'd better go down and remedy this right away and make March the wettest in history, or next year will bring complete disaster.

"And as for your plans to mortify brother Indra, you'd better stuff them for another time and place. I can't believe that anyone could have so little sense about what's going on. I suppose you'll tell me that you know nothing about the problems I'm now facing, as the hot-shot Gods are beginning to question my fieldwork methodology. I face the distinct possibility that they'll do their damndest to discredit me and my work — and you bring up your archaic perversions at this very time! Get lost and don't come back until you know what's what, when, and how."

Suitably chastised, but now more 'couldn't-care-less' than ever, they drifted off, that is, all except Number Two (or was it Three?) who was not without gumption, not to mention a modicum of interest in this and that. He stayed on and timidly asked his father to explain who was out to discredit him and why. Shiva was naturally pleased to find one of his sons taking an interest in his world and prefaced his explanation with, "Actually, it's quite complicated and there's a lot of subterfuge involved. I have to back up a little for you to understand what it's all about, so I hope you won't get bored."

Number Two may have felt some concern at this, since Shiva was sometimes known to be long-winded, but filial considerations, at this moment at least, overruled all others and he very properly said, "No, no, not at all. I'm very interested," which wasn't a complete falsehood, since 'very' is a relative term.

Shiva then began his recap, saying, "Very well then. Make yourself comfortable. I'll try to make it as short as possible," and settling himself into a meditative pose, he proceeded. "As the handwriting on the wall of time predicting the doom of all things began to come sharper into focus, we Gods realized the end was near and it was high time for us to find out what we did wrong, before it was too late. So we began carrying out fieldwork on Earth as a model case.

"All would have been well, except that mankind began to challenge our prerogatives by threatening to destroy the universe before we could complete our research. Then, at an historic meeting of the Heavenly Assembly, we decided to fight back and established a policy of feeding red herrings to humans and tampering with the data they uncovered to throw them off the true scent, thus involving them in wild and endless searches into nowhere. This we thought would slow them down in their research into Making and Breaking the universe.

"This diversionary policy was first established by brother Vishnu's Celestial Intelligence Agency under the direction of his false incarnation, Triple Oh Seven. I say false because no true incarnation of Vishnu could ever have done the things he did. He seemed to go power-mad, and even the Black Hole of Calcutta seemed like a tea party next to his Machiavellian machinations.

"Since then, a Senate Committee, DRIP (Diversion of Real Intellectual Pursuits), was formed to oversee the activities of the CIA. This committee has now become one of the most powerful and best funded committees in the Senate. I can't say that they're not doing a good job, but it sure is taking a lot of funding away from other projects. One of their best efforts was to persuade the Mahatma to start a non-violent, passive resistance movement, a marvellous idea which really caught on in a big way. DRIP master-minded that project magnificently, convincing the populous that a skinny, half-dressed shrimp of a man had found a real alternative to war and destruction. But, mind you, elsewhere they were also promoting war and destruction at the same time! It seemed crazy to me, but few of the Gods were inclined to listen to my words. I said, 'Why put so much money into keeping the Mahatma looking poverty-stricken and living a simple life, when he wasn't? Why carry around his huge entourage and a bunch of goats everywhere he went just so he could have goat's milk at every stop?' But no one listened and they approved one budget request after another.

"Now I admit that if they'd succeeded, we could have carried on our research without undue haste, but any student of history would have guessed that the Mahatma Plan was doomed to disaster from the very beginning. There is just not enough passion in non-violence, vegetarianism, meditation, and the like to leave a lasting impression on man. After all, man was created through the sacrifice of Purusha, and I'll tell you there was blood everywhere, even though it was for us a systematic, dispassionate dismemberment and we don't like to talk about the blood. Born from blood to live in blood — that is the way we set man's course. How could a Mahatma, no matter how great, reverse this directive of the Gods?"

Shiva was moved by the intensity of his own oratory skills. Wiping his brow, and with a deep breath, he continued, but in a different vein. "Even though it didn't work, I must admit it was still a good diversionary tactic. It kept man confused for quite a while. I can see that now, but, in the end, it had no more lasting effect than their earlier plans to fund Don Quixote to fight windmills. No doubt, the Mahatma was a better scene, but it was still doomed to failure before it began. At one moment, I was afraid that it might succeed, and I tried to warn the DRIP Chair that we didn't want to get man completely turned off the idea of destruction, because destruction was inevitable. It was bad enough for man to play God by destroying the universe, but if man were to try to take over Vishnu's role of preserver, I would have SCUDs and Stealth Bombers trying to deter me from carrying out my duty when the time came. How then would we get on with our ultimate purpose of composing a perfect universe?

"I've tried time and again to convince the DRIP committee to be careful, but I don't know if I'm getting through to them. They keep coming up with hare-brained ideas and trying to slip them by me without going through the normal protocol of Assembly approval. For some reason, they think that I'm against them. But I'm not. Not at all. I may not approve all their ideas, but, sure, I realize that they're trying to buy time for our research. I keep having a sneaking feeling that they might be true believers in the principal of diversion and may be trying to divert all aims and purposes, including ours. Yes, I mean our heavenly purposes! If that's true, we're in for a lot of trouble, and I mean, big trouble!"

Shiva in full flow is beyond any restraint. But fortunately this was a relatively small run-off, as he continued. "I don't know why they have it in for me. I may have my doubts, now and again, when their budget exceeds that for research, but there should be no real question about my being supportive of their efforts. No question, whatever — at least, in my mind. But they don't seem to understand. They evidently think that I want to use the whole heavenly budget to further my research and I guess they've never really forgiven me for the fast one I pulled on them over High Definition TV. OK, now I can admit that I wasn't utterly scrupulous on that occasion, but it was for a good cause and I thought it was important at that time. So I was wrong on HD TV being the ultimate. Big deal. Everyone knows that Gods aren't always omniscient, especially when it comes to this weird creation of ours that we call humanity.

"Anyway, I am now convinced that they want to get me. I don't know who's behind it, but somebody is after my hide, so to speak. I've been tempted to bug their headquarters — and now we have really good recording equipment for it; tiny, almost invisible, and excellent recording quality! But after Watergate I haven't dared to take a chance."

Number Two had drifted off from time to time through this exposé but woke up, and I mean right up, when he heard about bugs and recorders. This was his kind of thing — Perry Mason and all that. Before he knew it, he'd volunteered his services, saying, "Papa, I can really give you a hand here. It wouldn't take me any time to disguise myself as a gentle breeze and waft through their offices with a minicorder, and no one would be any the wiser."

Shiva gave this some thought before responding, "Son, I greatly appreciate your offer, but you must understand that Gods have never stooped so low as to use bugs or spies. Times are, of course, changing and there's a strong feeling that one should live with the times. Since my reputation might be at stake, there is no way I can give you approval to go ahead with your scheme. But on the other hand, there is nothing to stop me from teaching you how to use a minicorder effectively — and by the way, I have a tiny digital beauty, just in case, you, uh . . . want to play around with it.

"Actually, I already have a few sources in the DRIP camp who let me know what they're cooking up in a general sort of way. It's a pretty good network, but mind you, it wouldn't hurt to have a few more details — if you get my meaning. It would certainly enhance my supposed omnipresence, don't you think? But whatever you decide to do, I want to make it absolutely clear that you are not working for me, and in the event that any unpleasant situation were to arise, I would have no hesitation in disowning you."

Having said that Shiva put his arm around Number Two's shoulder and gave him a little affectionate squeeze to endorse the opposite. Needless to say, Number Two was thrilled by this and the prospect of some real action instead of the usual huffing and puffing which was his normal lot. He set to work on mastering the recorder under Shiva's expert guidance and made a number of practice recordings in difficult conditions. Then he worked hard at being a gentle breeze, which was not quite as easy as he'd thought. As Storm God he was accustomed to forthright expression and gentleness was just not in his repertoire. Now he told himself, 'Think balmy, tropical islands, frangipani fragrances, and leisurely strolls along moonlight beaches, preferably with a charming companion.' He worked hard at it — even though his siblings regarded him as a sissy and a deserter. Little by little his technique began to improve until finally he could pass for the real thing. But then he had to figure out how to conceal the minicorder, and that was not an easy task. He tried this and that and finally developed a remarkable technique of keeping it hidden behind butterflies and gently floating will-o'-the-wisps. Then with Shiva's approval and secret blessings, he went off on his mission.

All went according to plan and in no time at all he returned as an exuberant gentle breeze with a report and an intriguing digital tape.

In the meanwhile, word was going around that DRIP was organizing a fundraiser. Actually, they were calling it Seminars On Diversion (SOD), which meant that it was going to be a DRIP-dry event as seminars tend to be as a general rule. But they were giving it much more than the usual publicity and the media blurbs were hinting that these seminars were going to reveal something of major import. Naturally, everyone who was anyone planned to turn out.

Number Two's report was not conclusive, by any means, but Shiva found it ominous in its implications. There was, indeed, something going on behind the seminar exterior. Everyone was being very secretive, and the audio tape only revealed hidden references and hastily cut off sentences. One fragment seemed to refer to someone being ripped, followed by general laughter, and another to the importance of timing the attack at exactly the right moment. Not much to build on, but it seemed clear to Shiva that these comments had been directed at him, since he'd been excluded from their confidences. He sensed that things could get tough at the DRIP seminars and that he would need all the support he could muster. Since he was more than pleased with Number Two's initial efforts, which had at least given him an insight into what lay ahead — not to mention that he was delighted that one of his storm sons had shown more than the customary dust and bluster — he became more expansive than usual.

"Son, my only caring storm son," he said, "I really need a right-hand God to help me through this vexing time, for my spies — I mean my omni-presences — tell me that there are mumblings and rumblings among the Godly hoi polloi against me and my projects and that they are going to surface at this fund-raiser. How it's going to happen, I still have no idea. Your — may I call it investigation? — conclusively verifies their reports. There is no question in my mind that it is going to be a rough session and I'll need all the support I can get. By your selfless act of courage in breezily storming the citadels of our foes at the risk of failure, which would be undefended and unlamented — yes, you have earned the right to be my right hand. How would you like to be my Field Marshal in this campaign to help me defend my honor and my documentation project? What do you feel about that?"

Poor Number Two, delighted as he was to be offered such an honored position, had no idea what it meant, nor did he know much about Shiva's projects. But with the enthusiasm and bravado of youth he accepted without a second thought — or, for that matter, even a first — and speaking in a voice a fifth lower, he intoned: "Honored Sire and Pater. Thou doest me great . . . honor. It shall be my devoted duty to lead wherever thou commandest, and fail you I shall not, nor transgress the bounds of your dictums. Thou, sire, may count on me as a master counts on a devoted slave, and thus shall I be. I pledge my troth."

Having said this the Storm God subsided. Shiva was a little taken aback at this sudden uprising of archaic speech and figured that he might have been underestimating his stormy sons just a little. But being a master of composure, he shifted from expansive to matter-of-fact, deal-is-done attitude, and said, "Right then. There's a lot of work to be done. First I've got to give you a crash course on everything, from my life and works to protocol at heavenly meetings. Now to start with, you do not call me Papa, or Pater, or Sire. You call me . . ."

We needn't go through the details of the crash course that followed, since much of it will become evident in due time. Suffice it to say that Field Marshal Number Two was pretty well informed by the time the seminars began.

The expectant crowd arrived in formal attire, but since it was a mixed bag of Gods and Goddesses, they wore togas and *dhotis* and sarees and Nehru jackets mingled with jeans and the 'sky-clad' Digambara Jains. With flash bulbs popping and camera crews working overtime, the Gods paraded into the seminar hall, graciously granting interviews and signing autographs as they went. It was truly a memorable moment in the heavens, and there was no obvious hint of any unpleasantness ahead. Nevertheless, a discerning eye could have seen that the portends were already there in the foyer, even before the privileged deities entered the seminar room.

The wigs entered, seating themselves from big to little in hierarchical order, composed themselves, and then waited for the moment of revelation, which was not immediately forthcoming. Yet they waited patiently, remarkable for such a motley lot. DRIP operated on Indian Standard time, which is flexible and suits performers perfectly, but is usually less than heaven — one does not dare say the word in the context of the Gods — for the audience. They remained orderly through the long wait; perhaps they were feeling out their neighbors, but whatever, ruliness ruled the wait. Finally an MC emerged and picked up the microphone.

"Gods, Goddesses and others — I should have said gee-gees and others — ha! ha! We are here assembled here to witness a momentous moment in our history — and DRIP is IT."

The band then struck up their victory song: "tra la . . . tra la . . . tra la . . . ."

The Storyteller now begs the listener's indulgence for breaking into the following monologue, but he is bursting with anxiety —

DRIP is IT? Diversion from Real Intellectual Pursuits is IT? That was their goal and no one in the Assembly gave a single thought to the moral implications of diverting humans from finding the truth. All they cared about was that it would give them time to finish their research — but what about mankind's research? What if earthly fieldworkers were to use similar types of deception to retard the progress of their subjects? Maybe some had been doing it, but surely not at such an overt level.

The Gods chose to give souls to humans and animals, and maybe even to plants and all living matter. They put them all into their karmatic design, where they, and only they themselves, were responsible for their futures. And now the Gods seemed to feel no qualms whatever about interfering with their own design of the universe. DRIP was utterly immoral, as I saw it. What right did the Gods have to divert humans in any manner whatever from the free choice they had granted in their original Bill of Rights which was imbedded in their Doctrine of *karma* and transmigration of the soul? And yet they were doing just that, depriving mankind of the right to find their own destiny!

Shiva, my dearest God of this age, I have no desire to be critical and I think I understand that morality is context-relative. In your context, it is imperative to find answers before it is too late, in the process individuals may have to be sacrificed, and the promises of the Gods violated for the common good of the future. But from my vantage point I say, 'Why give them souls in the first place? Pain and anxiety, joy and fulfillment, I can understand. Take them away or invert them. Do what you will. But when you give a soul to any creature, you have given a commitment that that little bit of soul is, as I understand it, an integral part of the universal soul and that is beyond the construct or destruct of the Gods.' —

The Storyteller apologizes to the listener for this digression; however, we have missed nothing of substance.

Continuing the report of the meeting, the MC is introducing the first speaker, Varuna, an old and once highly respected Aryan God who had fallen out of favor over the years. He was now Chair of DRIP.

"Distinguished guests. Our meeting today will be in three parts. Firstly, we'll be hearing reports on DRIP projects that are continuing. Then we'll be hearing about some exciting new diversionary proposals from our very best scholars, followed by a short business meeting, if need be, dealing with bylaw matters, new elections and budgets. Then, if any time remains, we'll open the discussion to the floor for new business. Since we have a lengthy agenda to cover, I'll introduce our Secretary, Yama, who will now report on existing projects."

Yama, God of Death, experienced in the judgement of good and evil, had been unanimously elected as Secretary, not so much because of his experience but because he was the only God with office facilities and a diligent accounting and recording staff. His report is much too long to be given here in detail and may be consulted in the Heavenly Archives. Here follows a summary of some of the more interesting projects on which he reported.

A large part of his presentation was concerned with DRIP's support of wars on Earth — World Wars I, II, and III, Korea, Vietnam, Cambodia, Iraq, not to mention the 6-Day War in the Middle East, and others in Nicaragua, etc., etc. The idea of diverting man from real intellectual pursuits by getting them involved in wars must have seemed like a good idea to many of the Gods because they approved the immense funding that was needed. Like Shiva, some of the Gods were opposed to this so-called Defense spending, not for ethical reasons, but because it was taking funding away from their own projects. Yet it is easy to understand why the Gods went for it. They knew all about rampages against enemies, having had a great deal of experience of this in their early years and having not yet really grown out of this earlier conditioning. Besides, Secretary Yama was particularly

partial to death in all forms, shapes, and sizes, not to mention that
he was fully cognizant of all the other parameters of life, which
with his eagle eyes he diligently patrolled for flagrant and even
minor violations — when it suited his purpose.

In all fairness, it must be mentioned, however, that there
had been another form of opposition to the 'killing fields'
approach sponsored by DRIP. A few — a scant few — Gods
including Shiva, had pointed out that wars meant killing and
destruction and therefore the development of sophisticated
mechanisms for destruction which could only hasten the end of
the universe. This was what DRIP was supposed to divert. But in
their response to this, DRIP drew attention to the Mahatma
campaign and the passive resistance movement, and argued that
by playing both games, and backing both sides of the coin they
could not fail to confuse humanity and distract them from real
intellectual pursuits. Ultimately DRIP won hands down because
Gods understand death and violence better than life and peace.

Yama then drew attention to several other projects in hand
which were also working splendidly. One of them was the
misguided application of statistics which could be used to
confound the relationship between cause and effect. For instance,
he stated that DRIP was making man carry out ridiculous
experiments, like giving huge doses of This or That to helpless
small animals and discovering that they had a higher incidence of
death due to x disease than those who had not been subjected to
these doses. The cause was then said to be This or That. It never
seemed to enter anyone's mind that if This or That is the cause of
x, why don't all the subjects get x disease? The beauty of this
scheme was that the same experiment could later also be made to
show that these huge doses of the same substance reduced the
probability of catching disease y. And DRIP, Yama pointed out,
was seeing to it that all these so-called discoveries got maximum
media exposure so that humans were getting into a state of
complete confusion. No one knew when the Medical Board would

choose to ban any substance and laud its substitute, then switch around a few weeks or months later and go into reverse, canning the substitute instead. By these tactics, DRIP had put mankind on a sickening swing — This up today, That down; now That up and This down, until even the most rational Earth minds were spinning in perplexity. Yama gave numerous specifics which had the Gods congratulating themselves that they didn't have to make the same kind of decisions.

There was a great deal more in the same vein, and when Yama had concluded his lengthy presentation, there was no doubt in the Gods' minds that DRIP had justified the budget expense and had been extremely productive in spreading misinformation which confounded mankind on many different levels, and they reacted with a healthy round of applause.

Although he joined in with a show of clapping, Shiva was not all that happy. Every time a DRIP project succeeded, it meant a larger budget for them and less for documentation and research. Both he and Number Two were, however, beginning to hope that if the reports went on long enough, the personal attack on Shiva might not materialize.

Chair Varuna then announced a short recess before the second part of the agenda would be taken up, and the Gods and Goddesses filed into the foyer. The first session had not been uninteresting, but I feel sure many would have left long since except for the fact that the advertising had promised an important revelation, and indeed there was a continuing and even growing sense of anticipation in the air.

When the second session began, the Chair introduced Ayappan who was unquestionably one of the most brilliant Godscholars of the time. Ayappan had come up with another project for DRIP on which high hopes were pinned. Fortunately, we have access to the transcript of his presentation and will use his own words:

"Gentle Gods and Goddesses," he began, "in my researches on Earth I have noticed that mankind is fascinated by puzzles, and individuals spend hours and hours tinkering with them. It's interesting to note that statistics show that it is the intellectuals who are most fascinated by them. The range of these puzzles is surprising: from contests of mind like chess, Chinese checkers and even word and board games like Scrabble, Monopoly, Careers and Trivial Pursuit, to manipulative puzzles like jigsaws and wire contraptions, to the more literary ones dealing with detective stories and the like. Some of these puzzles have been propagated by DRIP, as you no doubt know. They are already distracting man from real intellectual pursuits, but from time to time new ones have to be invented to keep man's interest alive in these diversions. Since we target intellectuals rather than the common man, we need to build them around challenging intellectual ideas. One such is the concept of holism, in which a whole entity is said to be larger than the sum of its parts. A perfect example of this, with which we are familiar, was Purusha, whom we systematically dismembered to create this universe. Although we used all his parts, the one thing his whole being had which the parts didn't, was a particular kind of spatial orientation which made him perfect; that is, the way the parts were aligned in space. This orientation was not one of his parts but was yet a part of him. By dismembering him, we relocated his parts and thus lost an essential aspect of him. In this sense all entities are more than the sum of their parts.

"I'm proposing that we introduce a new game on Earth, which we hope will rival Monopoly, and one that will take away thousands of effective research hours from intellectuals. I propose we call it 'Orientation,' but I remain open to other suggestions. In this game we provide copious amounts of data and facts of all sorts; the player is then left to provide the orientation which will prove that the whole is larger than the sum of the parts. Just the summing up of the parts will keep them occupied for quite a while, and it is up to us, the designers, to build in numerous attractive and elegant solutions which don't work, and only one which does. I think we have the know-how to do it. If not, perhaps we can get a genius from Japan or one of the Third World countries to assist us. We could gear this game to different levels of intellectual skills, like crosswords. Once this catches on, which with proper marketing I am sure it will, I anticipate tens of thousands, if not hundreds of thousands of hours of release time from real research to be generated by this game."

When Ayappan sat down, the audience burst into applause. Here was a true genius in the world of the Gods, and yet, believe it or not, he had not been granted tenure! And there would be a long and painful fight ahead before he could relax in a privileged seat on the Senate.

Ayappan was not the only brilliant star in the firmament. In fact, there were many others, each one shining as bright as funds permitted, basking not only in the glow of their own brilliance, but also the artificial enhancement engendered by the munificence of the grant-giving agencies. The father of many of these suns and the proud recipient of numerous legends was Surya, the principal Sun God. In recent times he'd been going through a period of eclipse, especially when it came to matters of state, which in this age meant that he hadn't taken scholarship into orbit, figuring that it was not likely to last longer than a solar wind. But he was certainly bright and his light could reveal many things that others could not see. Now he was making a comeback into his old prominence as he stood up to submit his report:

"Respected Gods and Goddesses. Mr. Ayappan has made, I hope, a convincing case for holism. I want to follow this up with another scheme we have for DRIP which also concerns holes but of a different kind — I mean the kind that motivate golfers and gophers. Well, that's not exactly it either, only metaphorically speaking. I'm talking about those empty spaces which occur in the middles of things which one feels an irresistible urge to fill up. No. I can see that I'm not doing a good job of this, because what I'm really referring to is the non-existence of something — and yet what I'm talking about isn't really in the world of things, it's in the world of the mind — something like a gap in a string of ideas. That kind of a hole, I mean a hole in one's knowledge, a missing link in a chain.

"Holes have been a special problem of mine, especially the black holes in space, where matter seems to have gone into a 'within itself, crushed into nothing' mode which no one really understands. I've tried to examine these in some depth more than once, without too much success I'm afraid. If any of you are interested in my research in this area, I have a few of my publications on this table in front of me. But the important point is that I keep being drawn to this subject, not only black holes but all kinds of holes. Every time I see a hole I want to know where it leads to and what's at the bottom of it; not that I'm foolhardy enough to put my hand down it without taking proper precautions, but I'm really dying to find out."

Surya then took a long break to towel off, after which he seemed to collect enough impetus to continue.

"One day at a DRIP Planning Committee meeting while we were rummaging through our bags of ideas, it suddenly occurred to me that maybe holes are IT. I mean we might have to dig a few more, maybe even come up with a few black ones for added interest, but we'd have a winner, I am convinced. And so there it is in a nutshell."

With that, Surya wound his tortuous way back to his seat, through a sea of blank faces. From his bare bones exposition, no God or Goddess could possibly have understood what he was getting at and for a moment or two, no one seemed to know how to proceed. It was evident that Surya had touched on something meaningful and important, but what was he trying to say? Finally Varuna rose from his seat on the podium, and using all the diplomacy of which he was capable — for Surya was a highly revered deity — addressed the gathering.

"A most interesting presentation, most interesting, as I am sure you will all agree. There are perhaps one or two small points that may need further clarification, if the honored speaker would consider returning to the podium," as he beckoned to Surya, who grudgingly retraced his tortuous return, knocking over a bottle or two of true vintage in the process. Obviously, he thought he'd said it all quite clearly. Varuna then continued:

"I think we'll conduct this as a question-and-answer session. I'll kick off with a small question myself," and turning to Surya, who was mopping his brow, he continued. "You said, 'Holes are it,' and, mind you, I'm inclined to agree with you. I think you have a very strong case and you should stick by it, as I would if I were you. We could go further and say that the majority feeling here would be thoroughly supportive. But, uh, there may be a few who may not have the requisite background to follow all the implications of your proposal, and I wonder if you would be kind enough to express in your own, shall we say inimitable style, more exactly what you meant by It."

Surya seemed surprised by the question: "IT? IT? Why, that should be obvious. It's what we were looking for. I mean, why were we having a meeting of DRIP in the first place? And why were we rummaging through grab bags? An idea — that's what IT is."

No doubt Surya expected to see enlightenment around him, but words were clearly not the source of his effulgence. After another moment or two of uncertainty had slipped by, Shiva, who knows how to handle all kinds of difficult situations, stood up and spoke:

"Dear friend." What a master stroke! With just two words and the warmth with which he said them, he evoked a friendly, intimate scene of an after-dinner cigar by the fireside. The comforting smell of leather and dust. The good old days, before smoke-free environments became the in thing. The kind of comfort and well-being that inspires confidences. Having let it sink in for just the right length of time, he continued: "We've been friends for how many years? Perhaps more than we care to recall. After all these years of friendship and close communication, I hope you will not take offense if I seem boorish in pointing out that your brilliant idea needs to be savored, pondered and ruminated over in the environment I have evoked. Therefore, let us look at IT in this flickering firelight rather than the overpowering brilliance of your very own self."

There's no doubt that Surya now felt much more at home, as he took a deep drag on his Havana. Now there seemed to be no one else in the room, just two old friends in familiar surroundings. After watching the dancing flames in the hearth for a moment, he replied:

"My dear Shiva. You certainly know how to put one at ease. I suppose I've been a little hesitant in talking about It, because it's the first real idea I've had in a long time, and a lot is riding on it for me. You see, I've already done some market research and the figures are pretty conclusive. Man is equally as fascinated as I am by holes, and I think DRIP can use this to really good advantage. Say we judiciously plant a fossil of an imaginary creature, or a ruin of a temple that never existed under mounds of Earth, and let them be discovered, so to speak, naturally. Next thing, newspapers get hold of it, they interview all the leading experts and, if we hit the jackpot, scholars might even put on a conference or two over it. It might lead to disputes and debates and what-not. The beauty of it is that they will try to use this fake data to fill in the holes in their understanding of the universe. And, of course, it'll completely divert them from reality, which is what DRIP is all about. That's why I've being saying, holes are IT."

Now finally everyone understood. The possibilities were staggering. The Gods could tamper with the past in endless ways and lead man into a never-ending maze of intellectual convolutions. The gathering rose as one, not only in response to the beautiful simplicity of Surya's new form of hole-ism but also to acknowledge Shiva's brilliant stratagem.

Afterwards, Shiva was surrounded by his followers as though he'd won a difficult court case, and Number Two was pirouetting about like a joyous whirlwind. Surely now the ominous note that has been sounding throughout this story had been laid to rest!

The meeting should have concluded at this high point since the new proposals for DRIP had met with much acclaim. But now, as the seminar was winding to a close — or so all thought and hoped — the troubles began. It was during Varuna's perfunctory call for New Business that the Lord Vishnu chose to stand up.

"In all of these seminars we've heard a great deal about the diversionary aspect of DRIP and there have been some very highly commendable proposals. But what about RIP, I mean, Real Intellectual Pursuits. What are they? Is anyone ever going to define the terms? To whose reality do we refer? Sometimes we've talked about *maya,* the world of illusion, which we are supposedly masters at creating. But is illusion real? Or is all reality an illusion? And equally, we need to question what we mean by intellectual or even what we mean by pursuits. We get carried away by catchy acronyms and stop thinking. DRIP. I don't even know why it's catchy but it's clearly clouded our vision and from now on we'd better start using fog lights in the face of acronyms. I can't believe that we've given so little consideration to these vitally important matters. In intellectual circles such as this, you cannot take your terminology for granted. We ought to know that. RIP must come before DRIP. We must know what RIP means, in all its implications, before proceeding with any DRIP projects."

There was shocked silence. All the brilliant ideas and all the planning gone for a loop in just a few words. Vishnu continued. "The first order of the day must be to appoint a RIP committee which must sit until it has fully clarified the terms and delineated our purpose. DRIP projects must cease until then — even if it should mean that man destroys the universe in the meanwhile. That is the only ethical and intellectual approach we can adopt."

This was an impossible ultimatum and murmurs of dissent rippled through the hall. In fact, it was surprising that they were not more emphatic. It was evident that not even Shiva wanted to give up on DRIP. So much had already been invested in it that no one was ready to write it off just on ethical or intellectual grounds. Yet Vishnu was not one to be trifled with. As leader of the Opposition Party, he wielded considerable power, and even Shiva thought twice before crossing him. Although no direct confrontation was made explicit, it was obvious even to Vishnu that his proposal had no support.

"Very well," Vishnu continued, "I am going to have to give you some concrete proof in support of my contention. I am sorry to say that it will cause discomfort in some circles, but I see no alternative."

You have guessed right: This is the moment, and Shiva knew it too. Inexorably, Vishnu went on.

"We think we know what is real and what isn't. Right? And we have been attending regular soirées at the King of Gods' residence for some time and seeing videotapes of his documentation of human events. Were they real? Were they even representations of reality? I suggest that they are illusions. And I'm going to prove that they are not only unreal, but that they distort reality and even convey a false impression of reality.

"I know many of you witnessed Shiva's videotape of Maharajji and his Temple of SHIT. It's an excellent story which has been honed and refined through many tellings. But I was suspicious right from the start. It sounded too glib to me. Then my attention was drawn to a magazine in which the same story was printed. It wasn't quite as detailed and there were one or two

episodes that had been omitted. But there is no question that it was
the same story, including Mother's appearance and even some of
her own words. So I decided to investigate. I went down to Earth
to interview Maharajji myself. It so happened that he was not at
the temple, and on enquiring, I found out that he lived a block or
two away. It wasn't a mansion by any means — but on the other
hand, it was considerably more elegant than the broken-down
room that we were led to believe he lived in. Maharajji still had his
magnificent flowing white beard — but that was the only
similarity. Gone was his yellowed robe; instead he wore pants and
a shirt, and on his wrist, a smart digital watch."

Vishnu paused to see the impact of his words. Shiva, of
course, gave no sign of anything, but Number Two was clearly
beside himself. He would one day learn how to hide his
mortifications like a true God. Vishnu resumed his exposé.

"I don't think I need to go into all the details, which are
described in my report. The whole thing was a scam, a first class
swindle. Maharajji is not a real swami, from what I could
discover. It's true that the temple was dedicated to a little-known
Goddess by the name of Banodokri, but no one seems to know
anything about her or why her temple fell into disuse. People
confirmed that the self-styled Maharajji sits there sometimes. But
he doesn't seem to have any rights in the temple and it's clear that
he's been selling the story of SHIT to newspapers, tourists, and
all kinds of gullible people, and that's how he makes his living.

"The question that bothers me most is, just how much of
what we've seen at the soirées is illusion and a distortion of
reality? Can we depend on any of it in our preparation for the next
cycle of events? Pointing a video camera at a subject — does that
ever produce reality or even a semblance of it? Surely, one has to
carry out contextual research, and study phenomena in terms of
both space and time, in order to discover reality. We need to know
what's going on beyond the frame of performance and the video
camera. Then only can we say that we truly understand anything,

and if we're going to base our next creation on research carried out on this one, we must be sure that the research is valid and thoroughly documented in terms of text and context. It is my contention that point-and-shoot research should be completely disregarded in our design for the next universe."

This was certainly a turn up for the books, as the expression goes. No one recalled such a direct confrontation of Gods except on a battlefield. Here Vishnu, who is truly a dear affectionate God, is seen in a most unusual light, as exposer of magical illusions of reality. The listener should, however, be advised that Vishnu is most widely known, not as critic of Godly practices but as the ultimate illusionist which he makes manifest in his many incarnations. Was this whole experience an illusion that he had created?

The revelation had finally appeared. Shiva stood condemned, for he was the prime exponent of the point-and-shoot philosophy. He stood there phlegmatically while Number Two looked as though an unforeseen typhoon had split his bearings. But he never lost faith in his dad and said in a tearful tone,

"Papa. I have faith in Papa. He would never let anyone come between me and my faith. You'll see that he'll prove Lord Vishnu wrong. No, that would hurt Vishnu and he would never do that. He would never hurt anyone. But he'll do something to vindicate himself, and also Vishnu, whom he loves dearly . . . I know . . . I know . . . I know . . ."

ABDICATION?

Shiva had seen his share of awkward moments in his days, but probably none could match Vishnu confronting him at the DRIP seminars. That was something else! Even though Shiva had his feelers out and Marut Number Two had buzzed around a bit in the enemy camp, Shiva did not have the slightest inkling of the seriousness of Vishnu's purpose. And then for it to happen right at the end of the seminars, when everyone was tired and there would be no possible opportunity for him to defend himself, was what he found most frustrating. For the next few days the discerning eye could see a listlessness in Shiva's step and a one- or two-degree Kelvin drop in the light of his eyes. All he could think of was the viciousness of Vishnu, for surely it was downright wicked to have tackled him from behind, utterly without warning. And instead of receiving at least a fifteen yard penalty, he was now being feted by his admirers! Yet underneath Shiva knew that Vishnu was far from vicious, and as upholder of the universe he was impeccable in his meting out of justice.

Shiva relived every moment of the seminar and regretted not having the sessions covered by a flock of cameras, a la BBC, CBC, NBC, CNN, and whoever else. Still, he began to understand some of the elaborate details of the plot, like the conversational snippet that Number Two had captured on digital audio, regarding the importance of timing, and he could see that the whole thing had been orchestrated with cold-blooded precision — the kind of precision one associates with the robbing of a bank; or even better, the demonetization of currency which has to be carried out with the utmost secrecy so that when it is announced, everyone — except for the tiny circle of those in the know — is floored. Not just floored, but out for the count.

So it seemed that Shiva had been done in, good and proper. But one must never count Shiva out. Was there ever a more resourceful King of the Gods?

After the listless days and the light lux drop comes the firmness of resolve, bringing with it spring in the step and ozone in the air. Soon Shiva began to get a glimmering of the way to go. But first, in the true spirit of science: research and more research. Leave no stone unturned, no avenue unexplored. And who better to do the legwork than our devoted and dedicated Marut Number Two? There followed numerous meetings between the pair as gradually plans of actions were hatched and buried. And the young storm God, armed with his DAT recorder, mysteriously disappeared from time to time in guises ranging from calm to gale and brought back ever new data to be sifted through by Shiva. Gradually, the glimmerings began to glow into penetrating lasers of strategical design.

It was inevitable that sooner or later stray beams would emanate into Vishnu's camp, bringing with them an eclipse of the revelry that had been continuing since Vishnu's denouncement of Shiva's methodology. Shiva was up to something, but what? Vishnu agonized over this for days and finally knew that he had to find out. He just couldn't stand the thought of losing the decisive advantage he'd gained when his RIP had roared. In a hush-hush party meeting he hinted that he had to know and his volunteers came forward ready to go for glory (and possibly tenure) or inglorious grief (and possibly banishment). Unfortunately, Vishnu's camp was not hi-tech, and his crew had access to only bulky, clumsy, analog portables. Not being able to conceal them easily, they were obliged to spy from a distance and returned from their missions with exemplary recordings of just tape and environment noise.

In the meanwhile, Shiva had broken down his problem into two major issues. Firstly, how to respond to Vishnu's accusations — that was obviously the most important, and he was making good headway in solving it. Secondly, how to communicate his response to the kind of large gathering that DRIP had mustered for their meeting when everyone who was anyone had been present. If he were to announce that he was organizing a function in order to respond to the accusations, he knew for sure that attendance would be low and probably limited to his own followers. After all, who wants to listen to the kinds of circumventions and prevarications that are characteristic of defenses against accusations? No, he had to think of a stratagem to pack them in and a straightforward approach was not it.

As usual, the Storyteller was not privy to the numerous meetings Shiva had with Number Two and his other dependable devotees. I presume they plotted and planned and tried out this and that, and eventually I could tell from the increasing frequency of their self-satisfied smirks that they were just about there.

Then, quite out of the blue, Vishnu's camp suddenly had success. One of their old, clumsy recorders had picked up a few isolated words above the hiss and noise of the machine — just occasional words in the stream of Shiva camp conversations:

" . . . resignation . . . abdication . . . in good grace . . . save face . . . no alternative . . ."

Of course there was jubilation in the Vishnu camp as even Vishnu, cautious though he always was, felt obliged to admit that it meant that Shiva had decided to concede and to step down.

When I heard of the recording, it seemed pretty conclusive — on the surface — but I couldn't help having a doubt nagging somewhere in the back of my mind. It was just not like Shiva to up and quit, no matter how hopeless the situation seemed. And why had I noticed smirks in the Shiva camp just before this discovery? Vishnu's roar had seemed so non-vincible that the general feeling was that the only decent thing for Shiva to do was to step down. So when the rumor that Shiva was abdicating, riding on the wings of credulity, spread throughout the Godworld, it was accepted as the inevitable. The only question was how and when.

The answer was not long in coming, for the next issue of the *Sentinel* carried the following story:

SHIVA DISCLOSURE

SOIRÉE SET

King Shiva announced today that his next Saturday soirée would be of seminal importance to future Godaffairs and was thus opening his residence to all and sundry in the Godworld. When questioned by our reporter, he revealed that he had given much thought to the rumors that had been circulating since the DRIP SOD and had come to the painful conclusion that there was only one decent course of action for him to follow. When questioned further as to the nature of this course of action, his only comment was, "Surely you will allow me to do it in my own way." Does he plan a twenty-one gun salute as a good-bye? Come and see for yourselves.

Of course, they all came to see the fall of the high and mighty — that is, all who could stand the valet parking service which Shiva was obliged to arrange, since his residence was mounted precariously at the end of a dead end narrow winding road on Mount Kailash. This was utterly unlike the DRIP event. For one thing, all the Gods and Goddesses were informally clothed, knowing full well that they would have to sit on the hillside around the open air amphitheater where the soirées were held. For another, Shiva was known for his hospitality, not to mention his choice of gracious serving nymphs who would be sure to keep the vintage libations liberally flowing from beginning to end — and beyond, if need be. Thus there was a festive air around the place, not at all suggestive of the demise of a King; rather more that of a coronation.

Shiva was in his most resplendent 'ashes and sackcloth' outfit with all his usual appurtenances, greeting his guests and seeing them comfortably ensconced on the least protuberant gneisses and granites that dotted the hills around. The nymphs charmingly flitted about in diaphanous wraps, vying engagingly and not a little erogenously with each other in the performance of their calling. The nectar and *amrita* flowed, the weather cooperated, and the Marut storm Gods, for once, put on a reasonable light show in the skies. What a setting for another dramatic moment in Godworld history!

Normally at these soirées, Shiva would have begun with one of his field videotapes, but in view of the suspicion with which they were regarded since the attack on their integrity, he had planned a different tack using live actors, musicians, and dancers. They had worked up a little musical sketch, a parody on recent Godworld events. Vishnu was given a long pointed nose on the edge of which perched a pair of opticals and, with his flowing black gown, looked every inch the prosecutor as he whirled and pirouetted, periodically pointing his index finger at the stage Shiva in accusation. This Shiva was seen as a pompous old country squire, cringing and blustering, and looking every bit the guilty party. When the sketch ended with Shiva being chased offstage by an executioner brandishing an ax, the audience responded with thundering applause that set up standing waves echoing in the hills around. And Shiva, too, clapped as loudly as the others.

So the stage was set for his entrance, and as he stepped on the boards, the Gods and Goddesses once again broke into applause, no doubt thinking what a good sport he was to allow the players to mock him at his own soirée.

Now I was beginning to put things together. Shiva was a master of psychology and he'd set the whole thing up. What intricate planning! He must have been responsible for the tape recorder picking up those stray incriminating words that started the rumors of his abdication. Who knows how he did it, but it had worked because it had drawn all these Gods and Goddesses to witness the rare sight of a GodKing abdicating. Now, by allowing that sketch, which he himself had probably written to be presented at his soirée, he'd drawn the sympathy of the audience in his favour! I still couldn't see just what his purpose was, but I was beginning to appreciate some of the subtleties of his game plan. Even if there had been enough time to think, I am sure I would never have guessed what was to follow. As the applause died down, Shiva began to speak:

"Friends, I thank you for visiting my humble abode." This, of course, drew the expected disbelieving exclamations. "This is the time for me to acknowledge all the help, support, and votes of confidence I've received from you in the past. But now I stand accused of distorting reality and thus endangering our research for the next epoch of creation. My first inclination after the Seminars On Diversion was to resign as King of the Gods, and I would have done so long since. Although I still feel inclined that way, my friends dissuaded me from acting over-hastily. Therefore I thought we should do it — should you give me leave to do so — in pomp and splendor in the company of your august presences. However, since we accord a last wish to the condemned before the hangGod tightens his knot I too have my last wish which I plead with you to grant. That wish is merely an opportunity to respond to the accusations. Then I shall call on you to begin the countdown for my abdication."

Needless, to say, no one would dream of denying such a last wish, although I think a few were disappointed that they would have to wait for the denouement. But what circumstances (apart from the pointy gneisses testing one's hemorrhoids) could be more pleasant in which to wait? Would that dentists' waiting rooms were people-coddled by libationry nymphs!

Then Shiva continued: "Since I have not been drowned out by objections from the opposition, I presume that my last wish has been granted. I trust it will not deficit our wish-budget.

"I'd like to begin by pointing out that I hold my accuser, Lord Vishnu, in the highest regard as both guardian of the universe and a significant scholar in his own right. Yet his churlish attack on the integrity of my methodology demands response. Had we been living in another age, I might have been tempted to throw down my gauntlet at such an accusation, and by exercising the function of my third eye, bring the attack to summary retraction. But the fact of the matter is that I utterly agree with my accuser that we need a committee to define what we mean by Real Intellectual Pursuits. I would go even further, however, and argue that we need a committee even more urgently to determine what we *really* mean by reality.

"Before expanding my argument, I feel obliged to draw your attention to a small anomaly in our accuser's accusation. Perhaps it is of little consequence as I don't wish to seem moribundly pedantic, but the accusation charges me with the distortion of reality — before we have defined what we mean by the term! I expect most of us know in a general sort of way what we mean by reality, but do we? I mean, in all its many implications? If we do, then perhaps both my accuser and I are wrong in calling for a new committee. If not, I plead that the accuser is wrong in questioning my version of reality, without a heavenly Oxford/Random House type of standard definition to support his claim."

At this point Shiva paused, perhaps to let himself observe the reactions of the audience. It was clear that a few eyes had opened wider and there was an inordinate rustling of program notes, snifflings, throat-clearings, and the like, as Shiva continued: "It would be unseemly for me to harp on such abstract issues." Somehow the musicians heard this as a cue and began to harp on abstract themes and only tailed off when they heard Shiva was still in mid-speech:

"I would rather focus my case on the specifics of the accusation, namely, the issue of the Temple of SHIT. My accuser went to great pains to show that what we had seen on my video tape of Maharajji did not represent reality, but was in fact a distortion of reality. I think that any thinking God or even Goddess would agree that a videotape is not reality. What then is it? My accuser says that it is a distortion of reality, whereas I say, it is deeper than reality. Consider an abbreviated replica of reality for a moment:

"A man wakes up in the morning, stretches, yawns, looks at the time, decides to steal a few more winks, falls off, wakes up with a start, decides it's getting really late but can't resist a final few moments of shut-eye, falls off again, wakes with 'Oh God, I've done it again,' totters up and into the bathroom, uses the toilet, stumbles over to the wash basin, looks at himself in the mirror rubbing his hand over his chin, wishing that the stubble would go away, hunts for his toothbrush and paste, puts too much paste on brush, spills some in sink, curses, wipes bowl, drops his brush, redeems it with another curse, brushes his teeth, up and down and sideways, rinses mouth, gargles, washes face, hunts for his razor, brushes face with shaving cream, begins to shave, cuts himself, curses, continues cursing and shaving, washes soap residue off, finally looks into mirror and says, 'Ugh,' steps into shower, begins humming to himself, emerges, dries himself, combs hair, now feeling more 'human' looks at himself in the mirror again with a 'perhaps all is not lost' expression, dresses — shirt, pants, tie, breakfast, office, lunch, dinner — and each event is buried in endless details. The whole series of events is reality! And it would take as much time for us to capture it as it does for a person to live it. Reality has no shortcuts, and there is no way to abbreviate it. Perhaps we might want to document some events in this degree of detail, but there are billions of humans on earth and their realities are even beyond our resources of time and energy, not to mention how boring it would be to look at them going through their mundane day-to-day activities day to day.

"In short," Shiva continued, after a sip of his nectar, "reality is beyond documentation. It can only be lived, never relived nor reviewed. Thus one can argue that all research is phony — not the act of research itself, but its methodology, since its principles are based on data drawn not of reality, but from abbreviations and abstractions of reality as perceived by the researcher. And who determines which abbreviations and abstractions are most representative of reality? The individual scholar? Yes, that is the way it goes currently, but should there not be a broader consensus view? That's why I share with my colleague the opinion that we do need a committee to examine what we mean by *real* but propose that it be ROR, to look at Representations Of Reality and not the roar of Vishnu's RIP."

Intellectual issues are not known to be among the favorite subjects of Gods or Goddesses, but they were hanging in as Shiva continued. "Now why do I say that a videotape is deeper than reality? It's because people who know they are going to be on videotape want the most consequential parts of their lives to be recorded. That is not reality. No. It transcends reality. It incorporates their hopes, ambitions, dreams, and frustrations, which emerge only in such a context.

"And what about the other kind of field documentation which involves the fieldworker spending a great deal of time living in a limbo state of participant observation? Is that closer to reality? Perhaps, but I would certainly say that it is still far less than reality and may possibly distort reality more than does a video camera, because it not only involves the researcher's subjective decisions in the interpretation of events, but also leaves him to decide which of the millions of events taking place is meaningful to the comprehension of their reality — whatever that may be. On the one hand, it is the camera with its dimensional and framing limitations that dispassionately records events; and on the other it is the fieldworker, with the limitations of his conditioning, who interprets the meaning of these events. It is obvious that videotapes are not reality, yet they capture some aspects of reality. The fundamental question that ROR would have to determine is whether or not contextual research, involving observation and interviews, brings one closer to reality, since both the researcher and the subject introduce unknown quantities, namely their prejudices and inclinations which color both their perceptions and conceptions of events. With regard to cameras, we know their capabilities by their technical specifications, but with researchers no specifications are provided. "

Knowing that this was a vitally important moment in his career, Shiva persisted with his defense, even though he sees that many of the Gods are now taking a greater interest in the libationers than his exposition.

"Fieldworkers believe that they can avoid their subjective outsider views from interfering with their interpretations by availing themselves of the opinions of local informants. What they seem not to realize is that informants are also misinformants, unavoidably influenced by their own backgrounds and conditioning which also filters their perception of events around them. They usually choose the most erudite informant, for they need, in addition to interpretations of the events, song texts and translations written out clearly in longhand which they can later computerize for their dissertations. Their research often concerns non-literate peoples, and yet they attempt to pass off this longhand literacy of long-winded oral texts as reality!

"And what about the researchers themselves? Are they not slaves of their times which dictate the fashions of their research methodology? Today this is in; that is out. Today they protect the identity of the source of their information; yesterday, they cared not a jot. Villages and towns are now anonymous, but tomorrow they may decide that anonymity is like giving references without specific source and page number, and may therefore have to expose personal details of their sources in order to gain respectability in that new scholarly climate."

Shiva actually went on without interruption, but I, out of consideration for the listener, provide a break in his narrative. This is the moment, like a commercial, when you may go to get a cup of coffee, or do the needful, as the case may be. I have nothing to add of any great consequence at this moment, except to say that the pot was beginning to boil after a long watching period. Shiva, the immaculate speaker, knows that it is time to get down to brass tacks, and when you return from wherever it is, he will continue with the fulfillment of his last wish. Ready now? You're on, Shiva:

"I can't deny the evidence Mr. Vishnu has put forward that Maharajji is not a full-time swami, and that some of the details seen and heard on the video may have been contrived for the occasion. Isn't that the case with all performance, whether or not there is a camera present — that some embellishments are added just for dramatic effect? But can one concoct a completely alien representation just for a camera? I don't believe such a thing is possible, but even if it were, why would one do it? To deceive the researcher? I'll admit that we've known that to happen with occasional facts and characterizations, but distortions intentionally or unintentionally introduced by the researcher to deceive the reader are a far more serious problem — and we have evidence of that from the work of many scholars.

"Maharajji has a good story to tell and occasionally sell, if a buyer happens to be around. Does that make him a swindler? In any case, shouldn't we be looking at the content of the story to see whether or not it has any validity rather than criticizing the motives of the performer? In brief, the crucial matter, I believe, is whether or not SHIT is a real problem on Earth, a problem that should be taken into consideration for our next universe design. I happen to think so, but I would welcome a final resolution of this issue by a ROR committee.

"Some of you will know that I am fascinated by swamis, and Maharajji is certainly one of them. Whether or not he is a real swami, there can be no denying that he spends many hours at that forsaken temple and was there when I arrived unexpectedly. Why, and what does he do there all alone? It seems highly improbable that he sits there hour after hour waiting for the occasional tourist or news reporter. He uses no publicity to draw them to the site which, as you have seen, is hidden away by underbrush. At first I presumed that he had been sitting there and meditating, but couldn't sense any powerful vibrations emanating from him. When I returned to Mount Kailash, it occurred to me that Banodokri, the Goddess of the temple, would know, and so I looked for her address in the record book of Minor Goddesses. But there was no entry under her name. And I checked Social Security, Unemployment, IRS, TRW, and credit card records and still found nothing. Was there really no Banodokri and was the whole of Maharajji's story a complete fabrication? Was she only the symbol of SHIT in Maharajji's mind?"

I couldn't believe what I was hearing. Since the Temple of SHIT episode, Banodokri had become my favorite Goddess and I had often dreamed of her wafting into my presence in the purity of her white robe. I loved her gentility and the firm conviction hidden behind her unassuming manner and laid-back profile. And now to be told that maybe she didn't and hadn't ever existed was as bitter a pill as I've ever had to take. Even as clouds of darkness were descending over me, Shiva continued:

"I must confess that I didn't want to believe that she was not a Goddess and so I didn't give up searching for her. One day it occurred to me that minor Goddesses have a tendency to come and go, and when they come on big, their files are transferred to the 'Major Goddesses' section and when they are in the go routine they wind up in the 'Dusty and Obsolete Files' section. I knew that she had not come on big so I looked in the dusty files, sneezing fitfully in the process — and finally, there it was:

> *Banodokri: 1107-? Goddess of insignificant matters. Last known as residing on Bhuvar Loka, between Heaven and Earth. Address:*
>
> > *1, Lost Place,*
> > *Shunya Circle,*
> > *Planet Nine,*
> > *Bhuvar Loka*
> > *ZIP 22441683264128256357911000000002222222224444444*

"I could hardly believe that my not wanting to believe in her non-existence had paid off. Nevertheless there it was, dusty but incontrovertible. The only question was, was she still there or had she gone off with a new boyfriend, as minor Goddesses sometimes tended to do? There was only one way to find out, and so I went. Believe me, we must do something about our transport system to the Bhuvar Loka planets — only once a month, and that providing our sunGod Surya doesn't happen to be playing roller derby with his sunspots at that time! But I made it there, and the planet reminded me of a ghost town of lost causes and nearly-forgotten hopes and dreams. In its own way it was truly beautiful and sad. Everything moved in slow motion but with a dignity that I found unmatched elsewhere. Of course I had my camcorder going the moment we landed and the scenes of the stately grace of that place can be seen in our archives.

"And then I looked for 1, Lost Place and as I was looking I realized that there was certainly a play of words intended: 'one lost place,' 'one last place,' 'won lost place,' 'won and lost place,' 'won last place?' And Shunya Circle meant an empty circle; 'one/won lost/last place in an empty circle?' Then, there it unmistakably was — a modest little undistinguished dwelling in the middle of a circular void. And I thought to myself, 'Why? Why would a Goddess leave Mount Kailash for this void? Surely our real estate prices hadn't escalated so much that Goddesses — even though they be minor — couldn't afford to purchase at least a small bungalow on some nondescript Kailash street?

"I had a most remarkable interview with her which of course I videotaped, a copy of which has been deposited in the archives. But just as I was completing the interview a most wonderful thing happened. Blessed Sister, who by now knew the story of DRIP and RIP, said to me: 'They are already suspicious of your video interviews. Why do you think that they will accept this?' Strangely enough, I hadn't thought of that. I suppose it's because I believe in the efficacy of videotapes and take for granted that sooner or later others will, too. But Sister was right, of course. It was a video interview that had started all this ruckus and I couldn't present more video evidence until video had been vindicated. Then Sister spoke again. 'There is only one course of action to follow. I must come with you to Kailash and speak to them in person.' Naturally, I couldn't believe my ears. I would never have imposed it on her, but she was determined to come. And after a long and painfully difficult journey, Sister is here and it is my very great pleasure to introduce her to you all."

And with that, Shiva gestured and Banodokri came on stage still in her simple, white gown and stood quietly next to him. Everyone was stunned, not only at this remarkable turn of events but also her transcendent presence. Some began to clap and others to fidget, not knowing how to respond. I know that my eyes filled with tears as I saw her standing there in her purity and beauty. I now understood why Maharajji had stayed faithful to her over the years.

When the desultory clapping had subsided, Shiva spoke to her. "Sister, I know everyone is anxious to hear your story. Could you first tell us about Maharajji?"

She spoke in a soft voice, but with not the slightest trace of nervousness at being confronted by the august presences around her. "He's a dear boy and completely dedicated to me. I seldom visit him any more — I don't need to. He never has any doubts now and he has infinite patience. Perhaps I should go to him more often, as I used to in the olden days. He so enjoys my company. But I'm so enmeshed in contemplating my void that I find it difficult to leave."

Shiva prompted her to continue, saying, "Sister, I'm so sorry to have imposed on you to leave your void and come here. I'm sure we are all most grateful to you for helping us to clear up some of these thorny issues that have been causing friction among friends and colleagues. Could you please tell us a little more about Maharajji? He claims to have lived for thousands of years in your temple and is confident that he will continue to do so until the end of time. Is that really true?"

"Yes, my dear brother," responded Banodokri. "It is true. I never used my Goddess powers in the usual way, granting boons to all and sundry, as other Goddesses sometimes do. I've just used my powers to keep him alive, for I know that he will keep me and my dreams alive on Earth. And as long as my powers are not taken away from me, I intend to keep him alive."

Shiva was tempted to reassure her, but not having his attorney nearby to counsel him on the prudence of doing so, resisted the temptation and said, "You must have great faith in him and I am beginning to understand why. Can you tell us about the origin of SHIT?"

At that, Mother Banodokri seemed to show a slight sign of embarrassment, but continued anyway. "It happened a long time ago, when I used to visit him more frequently and we used to spend hours talking about values. I happened to be talking about truth and by sheer chance used the sequence, sincerity, honesty, integrity and truth. When he heard that, he became excited and interrupted me saying, 'Mother, that's it, don't you see — SHIT.

That's what those values have become — shit. And as long as I can hold on to that catchy term, I promise never to be unfaithful to you.' At first, I was taken aback by the crassness of the acronym, but then I thought, 'He's right. I don't use the term because I don't need any props. But humans need something more concrete to hang onto than just abstract ethical values, and if this is important to him then I should not interfere.' And now I know I was right. When things have not gone well with him and his spirit has tended to flag, I have heard him chanting 'SHIT. . . SHIT. . . SHIT . . .' all through the night, over and over again. And soon his resolve would return."

Shiva now sounded slightly apologetic. "Sister, as you know, Maharajji's veracity has come to be questioned by some of our colleagues. It is now known that he has an apartment near the temple and that he no longer wears his robe all the time. How and when did this happen?"

Banodokri replied, "It's really quite simple. When I realized that the universe would be coming to an end soon, I urged Maharajji to leave the temple occasionally and to experience the world as it really is before it ends. At first Maharajji resisted my suggestion, saying that he was happy just sitting in the temple alone and thinking about me. But I pointed out that it was a necessary part of his education and finally he consented, but he didn't go very far — just a block away. And although he now wears jeans sometimes, I know that he is happiest in his old robe sitting in his usual place."

At this point there was a slight commotion on one of the hill slopes as Vishnu stood up and requested permission to speak, which of course Shiva granted. As Vishnu walked down the slope to the stage area, everyone wondered what was coming next. I hoped against hope that he hadn't found a weakness in Mother's testimony that would lead to her embarrassment. But there was nothing I could have done, in any case. And then Vishnu began:

"Sister, we all thank you greatly for having come all the

way from Planet Nine to help illuminate this thorny matter which has been disturbing our peaceful existence in Heaven. Brother Shiva has spoken eloquently in support of his methodology, and I for one am prepared to concede that there is something to be said for straight video documentation — not that I feel that that is the ultimate. Your presence here and your testimony prove, in my opinion, that video documentation does need to be supplemented by contextual data before its validity can be established conclusively. Still I feel I must commend my brother for having raised this whole issue which otherwise may never have seen the light of heaven. There is, however, one little point on which I would like to have clarification. I now understand why I found Maharajji living in his modest apartment instead of his temple room but what I don't understand is why he's been selling his story to magazines and tourists. Surely he wasn't doing this under your advisement, or was he? I can't believe it was for the money, which must have been on the level of peanuts — even for a minor, inactive Goddess."

Mother then looked at Vishnu with an odd little smile. "Poor Maharajji. Everyone is always suspicious of him. He's thousands of years old, but in some ways he's still a child with childish dreams and hopes. But there's no soul purer or more dedicated on Earth and I have the good fortune to have him as my one and only devotee. I wouldn't exchange him for all that you Gods could offer. And he knows it. Still he dreams of a world where my temple would be as resplendent as any and thousands would flock to offer homage to the values we stand for. I gave up those dreams a long time ago and as the ages pass, I know that it was never in the cards. But he — he still has his visions and periodically embarks on his publicity campaigns. Before this, he tried to influence bards and storytellers like Jogis and Bauls to travel all over and tell our story, but people just shunned them and called them mad jongleurs and went about their usual ways. Now people read about our remote temple and of Jaisinghji and our obscure values and say, at most, 'Cute story,' and continue to go about their ways. In fact, our story gives them a few moments of diversion from their humdrum lives — like seeing a comedy turn — which actually makes their existing lifestyles more acceptable. Of course, I can't tell this to Maharajji without destroying his innocence which I prize so dearly. So I leave him alone, and each time he tells our story I see within him a flash of hope that maybe this time he's hit the jackpot and my temple will shine and resound with lights and bells and music, drawing crowds from every direction and corner of the Earth."

Everyone sat charmed by Mother's words and even more by her demeanor. I knew I was totally in love with her and I think the feeling was shared, at least in part, by many others present.

"Sister," Shiva said, "we all owe you a great deal for clarifying some of our concerns about Maharajji and SHIT. But I think many of us would like to know why you left Kailash to go and live in seclusion on Planet Nine."

Mother hesitated before replying, "Brother, don't ask me that. I have no wish to cause hurt or criticize others. There are some things that are better left unsaid."

Had I been conducting the interview, I would no doubt have left the subject and moved to something else. But Shiva, in his infinite wisdom, chose to pursue it.

"I am sure that you're right about this, but there is something about being on Kailash which makes it impossible to leave sleeping Gods lie. Please tell us why. We all want to know, and if we've transgressed in some way we all want the opportunity to reform. Perhaps your words will strike home and maybe they will cause embarrassment to some. But it will only be temporary, I assure you. In the end, we'll all be grateful to you."

It was obvious that Mother was still reluctant to speak, as she stood there with her head lowered. Surely Shiva would show some consideration after all the testimony she had already provided. But, no. Shiva could be pigheaded beyond belief! And he persisted.

"Sister, we must know — no matter the consequences." Then, turning to the audience, he asked, "Do we not all agree on this?" The response was sporadic at best. Most Gods felt oppressed by the thought that Mother's words might not let Gods lie sleeping, notwithstanding Shiva's assessment of conditions on Mount Kailash.

But Mother refused to yield. It was just not in her nature to criticize others' actions. Once again begging to be excused, she stepped off the stage. Shiva was nonplussed, and for a moment couldn't think of what to do next. Then he remembered his erstwhile intent and spoke.

"We have no option but to respect Sister's resolve and proceed with our purpose. The time is now ripe for you to summon the hangGod and instruct me to abdicate."

Everyone looked at Vishnu seated on his gneiss on the slope. After a few moments, he stood up and descended again to the stage. Then, composing himself, he made his final statement.

"As a result of the proceedings of this session it is my opinion that the time for the hangGod is not yet. There is much work still to be done and little time left. A change of Kingship at this stage will undoubtedly slow down our research and disrupt numerous projects. Besides, I look forward to debating with my brother on the nature of reality in the committee which, I am sure we all agree, is utterly essential. Whether its focus should be that of RIP or ROR is a matter that we can thrash out in our first meeting. In the meanwhile, I want to thank our host for his gracious hospitality and introducing us to the illuminating presence of our long-forgotten sister, Banodokri."

As he walked offstage to the accompaniment of rousing applause, I realized that Shiva had done it again. It was a night to remember and the celebration continued into the wee hours, but Mother was already on her way back to Planet Nine.

THE IMMACULATE DECEPTION

Shiva and Vishnu were now righteously meeting in debates over reality and all seemed at ease in the heavens. But if one looks closely, the ointment is always laced with flies and one or another is bound to raise its head and rotate its eyes for more trouble to get into. And so it was now.

It began rather quietly when an underGodling casually questioned, "Are we sure that we've failed and that the universe is going to end? How do we know for certain? Maybe this is part of a larger design and when things are into a completely hopeless, impossible entanglement, then, presto! *Deus ex machina*! And the ever-thickening plot suddenly thins to nil viscosity and the universe spins on into infinity."

For a moment, Gods in earshot were taken aback by this possibility, until one of the seerGods pointed out that it was not really practical for Gods to put their trust in Father Deus who had been banished from the Hindu Godworld quite a while ago. Nevertheless, an interesting issue had been raised.

The next development was not long in coming — once the think-bug is invoked, there is no telling where it will lead. Another underGodling saw fit to speak up:

"Admittedly, it is improbable that we can expect a machina from Deus, in which case the universe is doomed to failure. But where exactly does the fault lie? Everyone presumes that the program was faulty and the superGods are right now putting in a great deal of energy in trying to find out just what went wrong and how to right wrong for the next creation. But what if the design were right and the execution wrong? What then? Is anyone looking at that possibility?"

And that, indeed, had not been considered by anyone. All the Gods entrusted with the responsibilities of creation were highly revered and respected and it somehow seemed a kind of blasphemy to question their performance in the line of duty. Yet the question-air that prevailed then in the Godworld was amenable to the entertainment of even such challenges. The Gods thought and thought about this issue while Shiva and Vishnu were away facing problems with reality. Finally the seerGods conceded that in order to clear up these underGodling concerns, it might be desirable to organize a hearing. Not being quite clear what a hearing heard or what it entailed, they left it in the hands of the non-tenured Gods, who found an eager Chair to head a new committee to get the ball rolling. He was the elephant-God, Ganesha, who is known everywhere as the Remover of Obstacles and Lord of Auspicious Beginnings.

So, many of the Gods and Goddesses found themselves respectfully summoned by a courier to attend an Earth Hearing organized by this self-styled Heavenly Ethics Committee under the chairmanship of Ganesha. There being no established protocol on such matters in the heavens, the message went on to say that attire was optional. Possibly it was this — the thought that some Gods and Goddesses would choose to come in the buff — that drew a reasonable number to the proceedings.

The venue was surprisingly unprepossessing, considering heavenly resources, just a cave that might have been used by plotting old-world pirates; but the pudgy, one-tusked Ganesha, donned in a fancy white wig and black judicial robes, riding astride a snarling rat, with his brief on the back of an accompanying tortoise (to preclude the possibility of it running away with the case), obviously planned it that way so that his image would evoke the undertones of Long John Silver at Halloween and thus add, in his conception, to the gravity of the scene. As the Gods and Goddesses filed in some of them felt inclined to snicker at the sight of the rat-sitter, but one glance at his baleful red eyes chilled all proclivity towards banter or josh.

With an inordinate rustling of official papers, the Lord of Auspicious Beginnings rapped on the table with his one tusk and brought the hearing to order:

"As this is the first celestial hearing, I ought to explain what is meant by a hearing. It is an opportunity to hear what others have to say. But everyone can't be hearing all the time, or there would be nothing to hear. So a hearing also implies talking — but not everyone talking at the same time so that no one is hearing. A hearing is actually an exchange between designated discoursers with the majority of you hearing the evidence placed before you, but keeping your minds open and your traps shut. Since I am the chosen one to designate the discoursers at this hearing, I shall do so with my unerringly-aimed trunk, and I will not tolerate any deviation from this protocol."

Ganesha tends to be rather heavy-handed at times, but one must understand that he has little choice.

"There is another aspect to hearings," Ganesha continued, "which some of you may consider an invasion of privacy, which, of course, it is. Hearings lie somewhere between idle gossip and open accusation. So there are, in effect, two parties; one whose purpose is to question and the other who is obliged to respond. It is in fact a game of attack and defense, and in the process mud is often raked and slung. Yet hearings are not indictments and there are no formal accusations and no judgements. If the circumstances should so warrant, the proceedings may, however, lead to a formal charge to be considered by the Celestial Grand Jury which, as you know, has the power to banish the accused to remote places beyond the galaxies, but only in extreme circumstances. I say this to let you know that the game could turn into deadly earnest. But the beauty of the game is thrust and parry, with neither side exceeding the limits of propriety, yet challenging them and taxing their elasticity."

I couldn't believe my ears! By referring to it as a game, Ganesha was making light of this Hearing of the Heavenly Ethics Committee; but surely any discerning observer could detect in this an element of petty behavior quite unworthy of Gods. Instead of focusing on issues, they were now going to become vindictive and attack each other in an attempt to find one or more scapegoats on whom to pin the failure of the universe! The whole exercise seemed like an excuse for criminations and recriminations, with charges and countercharges flying about like lances on battlefields. How could they call this a hearing on ethical issues?

"It is a necessary part of this game," Ganesha continued, "that I, as Chair of the Committee, designate the defendant on the basis of the committee's report which lies before me. I thus request the illustrious God of fire, Agni, to take the stand."

Few announcements could have been more heaven-shaking and the cave was filled with babbles of amazement and protest above which one could hear cries of "No," "Unfair'" "How dare they," and the like. And indeed, I could see their justification. Agni was one of the most senior of the Gods in heaven and had been the recipient of more acclamatory versification than any other God. And here he was being put unceremoniously on the rack! But at the same time, I could see why Agni was the obvious choice as he was here, there and everywhere, in Heaven, Earth, and in between. His flamboyant character made it impossible for him to stay out of the limelight.

In the beginning, he was the God to whom the powers of ignition had been endowed by the Creator, and had had a distinguished record throughout his career. He had developed an impressive strategy of controlled burning which enabled the majority of the stars to deplete their fiery energies at a steady and predictable pace. This was a remarkable accomplishment, as all those who have studied astro-dynamics will, no doubt, appreciate. Of course, there was the occasional supernova as a star went berserk, spewing vast gobs of energy all over the place, like

semen from an elephant in rut. This did cause a few raised
eyebrows, especially as Agni always seemed to get flustered,
rushing about hither and thither trying to find his calculator to see
if he could pinpoint his error. But these instances were few and
far between galaxies, so his record continued to be regarded as
virtually unblemished.

On Earth, too, Agni was greatly revered not only for
himself, but because he was thought to be the link between the
world of man and the world of God — did he not appear on Earth
as fire, in mid-air as lightning, and in the heavens as the sun?
Thus oblations in the form of liquid clarified butter were offered
not only to him but also through him to the other Gods. Little did
man know that Agni's lightning was only a down elevator and that
there was no corresponding up for man to reach the Gods. They
saw Agni's smoke rising and thought that that was it, but their
offerings which went up in smoke dispersed in mid-air and never
reached the heavens. Whenever an offering failed to produce its
desired result, mankind, instead of questioning the validity of his
procedure, always ascribed it either to operator failure or
inadequacy of the offering, with the result that Brahmin priests
became ever more meticulous in the performance of their rites and
poor Agni found himself periodically being thoroughly doused in
liquid butter. When man got carried away either by excessive
religious zeal or by excessive greed, Agni would be drenched and
his spirits thoroughly damped, so that it seemed that his only
recourse was to burn down a forest or two to replenish his
energy, not to mention his enthusiasm for his vocation. Of course,
this was to come up later in the hearings, but at the time, who
would have thought that a burnt-down forest or two could have
such massive repercussions?

Skanda, the God of war and son of Shiva, was entrusted
with the task of leading the prosecution. Actually, it is said that he
was not born of woman — that Shiva cast his seed into the fire
and Skanda was the result. Thus some hold, much to the distress

of Skanda, that he was really the son of Agni, God of Fire, not of Shiva. Now he was evidently out to prove that Agni was not his father — and what better way to do it than to put Agni on the HEC Hearing rack?

After Ganesha had auspicious-ised the Hearing and the protagonists had taken their stands, Skanda began his interrogation.

"Mr. Agni," he said, "am I correct in saying that the Supreme creator gave to you the responsibility of controlling conflagration in the universe?"

"That is correct," replied Agni.

"Do you feel that you have carried out your responsibilities conscientiously and effectively?"

"I believe so," Agni answered.

Then with exaggerated calm, Skanda spoke: "Do you know about the 'greenhouse effect'?"

Agni was a bit taken aback by this, for he hadn't a clue. "Not exactly," adding "Sir" as an afterthought, and then feeling foolish to be addressing his own son as Sir.

"Well, let me explain," said Skanda. "The Earth is now faced with a depletion of the ozone layer which means that cosmic rays will increasingly penetrate through the atmosphere, causing the temperature of the Earth to increase, the Arctic and Antarctic ice to melt and the level of the oceans to rise, sweeping man off many parts of sunny California and causing impossibly more destruction in Bangladesh and many other places, with ultimate consequences that are too gruesome to mention here. It is our opinion that all this is a consequence of your giving man the power to control fire, without first exploring the full ramifications of your act. And we believe that you did this solely so that you could be relieved of carrying out the conflagratory responsibility entrusted to you in order to pursue your own personal satisfactions. Therefore we ask you to defend yourself in terms of potential charges of mal-nonpractice, excessive permissiveness, self-glorification, and sheer irresponsibility in the discharge of your duties, not to mention destruction of earthly resources."

The seriousness of the allegations took Agni by surprise. At a certain stage, he recalled that he'd been bored with having to light so many fires for mankind, and had decided that he could save himself a great deal of effort if he gave them the right to light their own fires — and indeed it had worked pretty well for quite some time.

"Wait a minute," said Agni. "You can't seriously blame me for being responsible for the greenhouse effect. Besides, it still hasn't been proved. All I did was to give mankind some rubbing sticks — how much damage can one do with that? Well, I admit I also taught them about flint. But still, that kind of limited fire power can't lead to the kind of holocaust that would have to take place to cause your greenhouse thing. Anyway, you don't understand what it was like for me to have to go down to Earth every evening, rushing from one house to another lighting cooking fires and hearth fires. Finally it got so bad that I had no time for more serious astrophysical affairs. What was I to do? The budget didn't permit me to hire a single assistant, so I was being run off my feet. And when I did give them rubbing sticks and hearth fires began to spring up here and there of their own accord, it was really heart-warming to imagine fur-clad families huddling around it, sending me their blessings for the gift. OK, I admit that once in a while a hearth fire or two did get a bit out of control but surely you're not going to throw the book at me for that. Besides, my instructions call for me to start fires periodically as part of a 'controlled burn' strategy to keep the underbrush from getting out of hand — why else was I given lightning?"

Skanda remained expressionless as he pressed on. "Let us take the potential charges one by one. To begin with, mal-nonpractice. Do you deny that on occasion you failed to render improper services to mankind when such would have been in the best interest of the Gods?"

"Now, just wait a dab-blamed minute," Agni sparked. "There is nothing in my Manual which says I have to go around giving improper services to anyone."

"But notice under clause IV of article II of your Manual," Skanda rejoined. "It says here, and I quote: 'To render proper conflagratory services as needed, in the best interest of our aims and purposes.' I emphasize the 'our aims and purposes' bit. Now don't you think it would have been appropriate for you to have rendered an improper service when it was in our best interest, say in the case of the hydrogen bomb which you could easily have made into a damp squib? If you had thought about it you would surely have realized that the bomb would jeopardize our creation."

While Agni was thinking of a suitable retort, Skanda went right on. "And what about excessive permissiveness? Can you deny that you let even young Boy Scouts into the secret of rubbing sticks? If that is not excessive permissiveness, I don't know what is!"

One could see Agni's temperature rising, but Skanda continued unabated. "Now we come to self-glorification. Can you deny that on occasion you have revelled in making your displays ever more spectacular to the extreme distress of firefighters and unfortunate homeowners, just to see yourself being exalted in television newscasts? Would you also deny that these exhibitions demonstrate sheer irresponsibility in the discharge of your duties? And what about the forest here and there that you demolished now and then just to satisfy your flamboyant ego? Would you not regard that as unnecessary destruction of Earthly resources?"

Everyone knows that Gods sometimes indulge in self-glorification and usually we look the other way when it happens. Who doesn't know the story of Shiva admiring his own mirrored reflection so intensely that he gave himself the evil eye? So what if occasionally Agni did the same? Was this sufficient cause to trigger a hearing?

With all eyes on him, Agni began his defense.

"I see that my overall track record has not been taken into account by my prosecutor. If I may say so, it is nearly unexceptionable — even if I do say so myself. I can't deny that there may be a few little blemishes here and there, as would be found in all our records. But focusing on these occasional blemishes doesn't give an accurate picture of my dedicated service to my heavenly responsibilities which go back to the ignition of the first star in this creation.

"Now considering the accusations, I am most struck by the greenhouse thing. Frankly, I can't see the connection between my giving rubbing sticks to early man and the depletion of the ozone layer. I mean, for thousands of years after the rubbing sticks, man just played with fire, and life continued virtually unchanged. It's all very well to accuse me of being irresponsible in giving mankind the secret of fire, but I did consult the oracles before acting, and they looked quite far into the future and could see no perceptible impact from it. And so I went ahead.

"Then after a long time the Chinese invented gunpowder, and before I realized what was going on, people were shooting each other dead all over the world. How to interfere at that stage? Negate the laws of nature that our designers had worked so hard over? And who knows what else might have been unleashed, had I done so? So I didn't. But if you really want to know my opinion, I think you ought to question Vishvakarma, the architect of the universe. He's the only one who can tell us why mankind lay dormant for such long ages and then suddenly became activated, and in a few short centuries went from the Industrial Revolution to artificial intelligence."

At this point, Ganesha raised his portly self off the rat — much to the rat's relief — and spoke.

"We have heard the case and the defense. It so happens that the prosecution had already targeted respected Vishvakarma next for the hot seat. Obviously, any determination on the Agni case must await the testimony of our next hearing. I now call upon Mr. Vishvakarma to take the stand."

Is nothing sacred? Vishvakarma, the father, the generator of all things, the supreme architect who knows all worlds and the spaces in between, and is even said to have given the Gods — Goddesses are, as usual, not mentioned — their names! He who is beyond our comprehension! And yet this self-appointed Heavenly Ethics Committee has the temerity to call him to task!

As Vishvakarma came to the stand to be duly sworn in, Skanda rubbed his hands in anticipation of the havoc he was hoping to wreak.

"Mr. Vishvakarma," began Skanda, "I have not had the pleasure of your revered acquaintance, but I welcome you to our Hearing. The fact of the matter is that, as you know, the general opinion seems to be that this universe is doomed to failure and preparations are being made for the design of the next one. Do you share this opinion?"

Caves are notorious for magnifying sounds which echo on and on. But now there was an exaggerated stillness and nothing to echo until after a lengthy pause, Vishvakarma spoke in what, I must say, was a surprisingly thin and reedy voice for such an august personage:

"I must confess that I have recently not been listening to newscasts as diligently as I should. It may be something to do with my hypertension. But yes, I think that appears to be the handwriting on the wall."

"With all due respect," Skanda continued, "I would have thought that you would have had your eyes and ears glued to the daily reports of the state of the universe, since you were the one who created it all."

Vishvakarma replied, "You're right, in a sense. But news reports and papers hardly give you that kind of news — they always talk about killings and accidents and floods and earthquakes which involve a few people here and there. They never give any news of things that are going well, except in the Obituary columns. There you get to read about all the good things a person did in his life, and none of the bad. So I end up by getting hyper.

"In any case, it's not that simple. You see, I was working from a template when I created the universe."

"What, a template? And who supplied this template?" demanded Skanda.

"I'm not at liberty to say," Vishvakarma responded.

"How strange," said Skanda. "We have always been under the impression that you are the designer, and now we hear for the first time that you worked from a template provided by some unknown character whose name you refuse to divulge."

Vishvakarma replied, "I haven't given 'him' a name yet because she hasn't needed a name until this moment. If you really want one, let's call her Mother Epicure, for she has a refined taste and loves good things."

"Very well then," said Skanda, "Mother Epicure, whose vita we will no doubt find in our archives, gave you a template, and with that template as your guide you created the universe. Is that correct?"

"Yes," replied Vishvakarma, "in its basic essentials. But, of course, I also had the Designer's Manual."

"Well then, would you say that your design of the universe is coherent and logical?" asked Skanda, trying to make it seem like a casual question, but everyone could sense that it was anything but — except perhaps Vishvakarma, who replied:

"I suppose so. I did the best I could, but it was a pretty complex problem and one always has to make some compromise or the other, especially when builders tell you that your abstract vision can't be realized in just the way you want it."

"Are you then trying to say that your universe is not utterly perfect?" asked Skanda.

"I suppose so," replied Vishvakarma.

"Hmm. I'm sure you'll understand that this comes as a bit of a surprise." After a ruminatory pause, Skanda continued: "Very well then, what aspect of the universe is, in your opinion, the most perfect of your creations?"

"I would say that it's mankind," replied Vishvakarma.

I knew that he wasn't going to say something idiotic like *nouvelle cuisine* or anything like that, but mankind! That was what all the trouble was about! Skanda was taken aback, too, as I could see. But he composed himself rather quickly and went on with his questioning:

"I see, and yet I don't. Do you really believe that mankind is truly perfect? That is to say, entirely as you envisaged it on, so to speak, the drawing board?"

Vishvakarma seemed to hesitate for just a moment before he replied. "Yes. Not initially perhaps, but yes. I regard mankind as my most perfect creation. Whether that constitutes perfection in the abstract sense or not is for others to decide."

At this point, Skanda requested and was granted a short recess to consider his next plan of attack.

In the meanwhile my mind raced on. What did Vishvakarma mean? Man was threatening the Gods by challenging their sole right to create and destroy. Was he saying that his creations were so perfect that they were, in fact, the new Gods of the future? Was that it? And what would happen to all the old Gods and, I suppose, Goddesses? Would they some day become like fossilized dinosaurs for archaeologists to dig up and weave grand theories around? Surely not. Not our powerful and now vital Gods fighting back with scholarship and DRIP and RIP. No, I couldn't believe that mankind could really out-God our beloved Gods — notwithstanding their foibles which only Gods know are not utterly insignificant. I folded my arms across my chest in disbelief as I waited for the next round to begin.

Skanda soon returned to his former stance, seeming more belligerent than before, and with "The prosecution is ready to continue," began:

"Mr. V. — I trust you will forgive the abbreviation since the frequent recurrence of your lengthy name might tax the forbearance of our potential publisher — you have stated that mankind is the most perfect of your creations. And I think we can go along with that, up to a point. But when we go beyond that, we find some anomalies. When mankind — and I don't mean to exclude womankind — is seen, we see perfect symmetry in their figures, with features aligned along a vertical reference frame. Eyes and ears, two; equidistant and identical. Arms and legs, in similar disposition; hands, feet, fingers, and toes all well thought out and arranged symmetrically. And we even appreciate the design of the lips, the nose, and the generative organs, all centrally located in terms of this vertical frame. But we would like to ask, why did you feel the necessity to resort to this centralization when it came to noses, lips, and generative organs? Why not have two mouths and two pairs of lips, or for that matter, two penises and two vaginas, which might have served your purposes twice as well?"

Vishvakarma had, of course, considered all possibilities when he was designing mankind and was not at all fazed by the question. He'd considered the possibility of two penises and two vaginas, but he'd felt that it was too much of a good thing. Besides, he realized that double impregnation was utterly unnecessary, since he'd already visualized that Earth would soon be overcrowded. But he chose not to bring up this issue, focusing instead on the practical, as he responded:

"Eyes, we needed two of, so that mankind could have depth perception. And we needed two ears to determine the direction of the sounds of danger — not to mention opening up all kinds of stereo possibilities for hi-fi sales. But why did we need two mouths? To support dentists? They already charge enough with one set of teeth to make up for two. Besides it would only have encouraged more double-talk. I thought about it in great depth — and I couldn't see any reason to give two sets of generative organs either — so instead I doubled the pleasure of one. Wasn't that a neat solution?"

"Yes, I must admit that you've found some excellent solutions," said Skanda. "Very neat, I must concede. But, of course, it's only skin deep. When we get under the skin, things seem to get really messy. And what happens to symmetry? Why, for instance, is the human heart not in the center of the body, but shifted over to the left?"

"Well, I admit I had some problems there," replied V. "I tried it like that at first, putting the heart between the ribs. But it kept getting punctured at the littlest excuse. Then I tried to expand the rib cage to cover it, but then the body just didn't look right — it seemed to protrude in the wrong place. Finally I decided to tuck it under the ribs on the left — it could as well have been on the right, but I flipped a coin and left won. It works just as well there as it would have in the center, but it's protected by the ribs. This way the ribs look much more sleek, and one can join the ancient Greeks and Rodin in really appreciating a good torso, not to mention what it does for breasts, which poets have raved over throughout history, as I'm sure you will agree!"

"Now I think I'm beginning to understand," said Skanda. "I wondered about the liver being on the right and the funny way the stomach and the duodenum curl to the left, but most of all, the way the intestines seem to be stuffed into the body as though it were a bag. And that's the way you did it, isn't it? You designed the outside first, making it perfectly symmetrical, in accord with your concept of beauty. Then you fitted in the inner parts as best you could, without any consideration for aesthetics whatever. Obviously, you were concerned more with the external look of things than with following through on larger principles such as symmetry of the universe. And I guess you don't have any regard for the theory that form should follow function, for no one could possibly guess what goes on where from just looking at the external body."

"There are lots of nasty little things going on in the body that aren't particularly pleasant to look at," V. replied. "One doesn't want to show evidence of human sewer systems and the like on the surface. That's as bad as designing a building with all the drainpipes and wires running on surface walls. I was trying to create exalted beings and try as I did to exalt human sewer systems, I must confess it was without success. The only alternative I could find was to hide them so that one could concentrate, without distraction, on the lofty and sublime design of my creations, who needed neither to urinate nor defecate. And that has inspired artists to claim that the human body was the most perfect shape in all creation!

"And surely, I have succeeded in that. You may belittle my handling of the innards, but let me tell you it's a great deal more difficult to create beauty that functions well than it is to design a 'form follows function' monstrosity."

I must say that I was impressed by V.'s point and felt like applauding. Beauty creates desire, and desire breeds stories, and as a storyteller, I knew that if the human body had been pudgy and shapeless my repertoire would probably have been cut in half.

But Skanda was obviously not of like bent and tenaciously pursued his role as prosecutor.

"Is it not true that if one pursues form for its own sake, function will necessarily suffer? I mean that there must be occasions when a functional element just cannot be accommodated within the aesthetic form — then a compromise becomes necessary. Since there can be no compromise when it comes to beauty, it must be function which suffers. I thus confront you with this question: In your design of mankind, were there or were there not occasions when you compromised function in order to satisfy your penchant for beauty?"

V. hesitated before replying. "The answer to your question depends on one's viewpoint. If I look at it the way you evidently do, the answer is unequivocally: Yes, there were. But, you see, I don't look at it in your light. For me, beauty is itself functional. It is not an extraneous element overlaying a set of functions as you see it. Therefore, my answer would be: No."

"Let me put it like this," Skanda continued. "Would mankind not have been served better if you had chosen to provide two hearts instead of one? But, of course, that would have spoiled your exterior design which you hold in such high regard."

V. now had a hint of a smile on his face as he replied, "I see that you're not familiar with the constitution of the Designer's Manual. Conservation of energy is one of its first principles and duplication of resources is expressly discouraged. A second heart would provide no other service than to serve as a back-up for the first, and if one were to provide back-ups for every organ there would be a tremendous waste of both energy and resources, especially if you consider how many individuals with perfectly healthy organs get run over by automobiles or bumped off in gang wars every day."

"Alright then," Skanda said, perhaps sensing some kind of victory, "Why did you provide a lung back-up? After all, many people are known to live with just one functioning lung."

"I can see that you may have difficulty understanding or accepting this, in view of the way you regard beauty as being incidental to function," replied V. "Nevertheless, I'll try to explain, although if you've never experienced the disdain that a woman can put into a so-called 'heaving breast,' you may never understand it. Chests and breasts are erogenous zones precisely because the lungs which lie beneath them constantly dilate and contract, setting them into continual in-and-out motion. Not only is this movement enough to attract attention to them, but changes in the rate and depth of this motion register emotion; that is, e-motion or erg-motion, the energy-state of experience which is communicated directly through the senses to the perceiver, without the need for verbal coding and decoding.

"Now imagine, one lung and one heaving breast — too ludicrous to communicate anything but humor — like flaring one nostril, or raising one eyebrow. Mankind is so used to seeing symmetry that any non-symmetrical movement causes amusement. I admit I couldn't work out a scheme in which one lung could cause two heaving breasts — so I used two lungs."

One would have thought that by now Skanda would have thrown his hands up in despair at trying to pin V. down into an indiscretion. But he still had a few cards to play.

"There is one more little point which I'd like to bring up. You've been talking a lot about beauty and erogenous zones, and some of it makes sense even to a non-beautician, like myself. But what about the brain? You made it in two halves, more or less symmetrical, though each one processes different types of information. Why did you feel the need to divide it into two halves instead of leaving it as a whole?"

V. gave this one a great deal of thought before he replied. He knew that this was the big one.

"I had a lot of trouble with brains," he admitted. "The problem was, at first, how to incorporate all the processing power into such a tiny package. But then I came up with the idea of neurosistors — like transistors with neurological ends. And I could do it. Next I was faced with the question, what areas needed neurosistance? And there I must admit I was bogged down for quite a while. I tried out numerous possibilities with the animal kingdom — so-called 'animal,' only because I failed to come up with a good solution. Then I thought I finally had it, and I implanted it into humans — though why I chose humans for the implant I'll never know, unless it's because I felt that they were the ultimate guinea pigs.

"But to respond directly to your question. At first I had a single brain which processed all kinds of information. It caused a lot of problems. You see, I couldn't figure out how to insulate one neurosistor from another so that the different types of inputs wouldn't interfere with each other. One minute a person might be listening to music, then suddenly the music would stop and the speech mode would switch on and one would be hearing verbal clichés about the music. And just as one was getting into that, the music would start again in mid-sentence! That worried me a lot. How were we going to sell music disks and cassettes and CDs if they were interrupted every few moments by internal commercials? And what company would sponsor our programs with the possibility that their commercials could be cut out internally, without so much as an individual having to finger a remote control?

"So after much deliberation, I decided to partition the brain and to shift the music CPU — Central Processing Unit — to the right brain channel, and that solved it. But, of course, one always loses something — notice how hard it is to talk about music now? That's why musicologists have such a hard time convincing anyone that they're not just musicians who couldn't make it."

I could see that the Chair had had enough of this rambling examination that didn't seem to be going anywhere. It was obvious that V. was too sharp for Skanda and I hoped that he'd call an end to the session. But instead, Ganesha said,

"We've listened, rather interminably, to the prosecution's case and the defendant's response, and so far I see no reason for this matter to go up before a higher tribunal. In case the prosecutor has an ace up his sleeve, I will allow him just one more opportunity to pin his adversary to the mat."

The way he said this, one could visualize the massive Lord Ganesha, rising off his rat and wrestling his foe into submission. But Skanda, who was not known for massivity, would have to resort to guile in place of brute force, notwithstanding his martial background. And so Skanda stood up, knowing that this might be his last stint at prosecution if he couldn't come up with a big inning.

"Mr. V.," he said. "Believe it or not, I've done a bit of homework. In the Designer's Manual it says that your goal shall be to produce a 'universe of near certainty.' What exactly does that mean?"

V. replied, "It's plain and simple. In every segment of my design I had to include an equivocal element which would leave open at least a distant possibility that everything was not a completely foregone conclusion; otherwise, gamblers would never have started in business and horse racing would have been no fun whatever, not to mention what it would do to baseball games, Dow Jones, and the stock market!"

"And how does this relate to mankind?" asked Skanda.

"Well, I had to do the same with them," replied V. "I began by setting the human synapses to zero gain, but had to leave a small window open for random configuration."

"So you left a way open for mankind to break into the industrial age and beyond. Is that correct?"

V. was flustered for the first time in the interrogation and responded, "But yes, I had to do it. I had to follow the dictates of the Manual."

Skanda now turned to the chair in obvious triumph and said, "Your Honor. It is our contention that that uncertainty clause was inserted into the Creator's Manual to incite mankind to dream, but not to leave any real opening for their dreams to come true. It always has to be someone else who wins the jackpot, like one's neighbor's, brother-in-law's, friend's, girlfriend's aunt who wins, not the party of the first part. I thus contend that the defendant is guilty of leaving the wrong window open which enabled mankind, the party of the first part, to break through into the uncharted waters that now threaten our Godhead."

There was nothing that V. could say in his defense. The odds against mankind finding that window had been astronomical

— and yet, by a series of absurd coincidences, they had found it. And there could be no denying that V. was ultimately responsible for it. So it was a real victory for Skanda.

But in his summary of the hearing, the wise Ganesha tempered its importance:

"Now that we've heard the parties thrust and parry, I find the result inconclusive. While it is clear, as our earnest prosecutor has maintained, that V. was responsible for deciding which window to leave open, it is the Designer's Manual which must take the ultimate responsibility, since it required V. to leave a window open, not only in this context but in every element of creation. In my opinion, leaving windows open all over the place is an irresistible invitation to come and go and is certain to invoke the laws of uncertainty.

"I am even prepared to concede that the prosecution may have succeeded in establishing that the window left open by V. was indeed the window through which mankind entered the world of accelerated progress; nevertheless, to make a conclusive case, they would also need to prove to my satisfaction that leaving a different window open would not have achieved the same result."

"I thus find both defendants, Agni and V. largely, if not wholly, guiltless in this matter. The investigation has, however, served to direct me to point my trunk in accusation at the author of the Designer's Manual. Mr. V., would you please read the author's name."

V. opened the Manual to the appropriate page and read the colophon with a twinkle in his eyes:

"This work has been written by Anonymous under the direction of the committee on Public Works, in the third regeneration of the universe."

"Since it was written ten regenerations ago," V. commented, "it may need some slight revision here and there, but I must say in its defense that I have found it to be a most useful and enlightening work."

So in the end, the Hearing came to nought. Skanda had proved that he had potential as a prosecutor, but there were few opportunities for prosecutors in Heaven and so he spent most of his years collecting unemployment, which was a pretty good deal up there. Agni and V. gained a bit of notoriety, but so what? Gods need that to enhance their visibility anyway. A revision committee was eventually formed, but to the best of my knowledge, they are still opening and shutting windows.

When Shiva was told about the episode, he said flatly, "There's no Goddess by the name of Epicure." Then he thought about it for a few moments and said, "Wait a minute. Epicure, hmm. EPIcure ... epiCURE ... epicURE. Something rings a bell." Then he broke into laughter. "It couldn't be! That Vishvakarma! He's always making up stories and posing riddles. I bet this is another of them. Goddess Epicure!" he said, and broke into another peal then mumbled, tentatively: "Hmm. It could be a reference to that kookie cult devoted to the unfettered reaffirmation of enchantment — see, Cult-Unfettered-Reaffirmation-Enchantment! CURE. Seems a bit far-fetched, but one never knows with V. Hmm. I wonder what the EPI could have been? Now I come to think of it, there was a pretty young girl-Goddess who was at the epicenter of the cult. Hmm. I'll have to work on it some more; it's really a puzzler, just the kind of thing that V. loved to pull on us."

It's good to end a story on a humorous note, and Shiva certainly helped me out here. But somehow I have a slightly perverse nature. I can't help thinking about what Shiva was really saying beneath the banter. The listener will know by now that I'm really partial to Goddesses, and Epicure had sneaked her way into my top ten. But now to be informed by Shiva that no such Goddess exists will demand a major reformatting of my mento-emotional program. If this is indeed the case, and I have never had reason to doubt Shiva when he is speaking straight, then who had given V. the template? Was it part of the Designer's Manual, or was there no template? V. was always making up stories, Shiva said. Could his whole explanation of creation, or perhaps part of it, be a complete fabrication? If so, I would say it was a brilliant, extempore concoction. It had me fooled completely, and even now I can't think of a better explanation to account for the fact that humans and animals are symmetrical on the outside, but have organs stuffed any which way on the inside. The symmetry is obviously window dressing, presumably to cover up reality which is neither coherent nor symmetrical, and sometimes downright ugly. But who was the dressing for, the Gods? Mankind? Vishvakarma himself? An Epicure somewhere that Vishvakarma was trying to please?

Or was he just hiding his poor design skills behind a pleasant exterior?

INVERSIONS

Whew! Finally a moment to breathe and to take stock of what's been going on. This Godworld sure has its extremes. Firstly Gods and Goddesses are busy, busy, busy, creating the universe, and, believe me, that takes a lot of work. Then when it's created, everyone sits around basking in the sun, frolicking and sporting about and indulging in all kinds of excesses — you know, the kind of things that Gods and Goddesses are famous for. Then, slowly the handwriting begins to appear on the metaphorical wall, that the universe is a failure and that Shiva will soon have to apply the finisher. For a while, no one wants to admit it. Gods are pretty much like humans in some ways, and so they pretend not to see these ominous billboards signalling the end as they begin to appear by the super high- and low-ways, until they begin to blot out the celestial scape. Even then, it takes the conscience of a Shiva to get back to work and start researching the causes of failure. Once that process starts, everyone wants to get onto the rollercoaster, and there's hardly an instant for a storyteller to breathe, for this is the moment that gives birth to the most fascinating stories.

Even in such times there are lulls, and this was one of them. I might have enjoyed a pleasure cruise, had I been younger — but they're all fully booked years in advance and one can never tell when a lull's coming in this busy season. So I'm kind of reconciled to lying about and daydreaming, using my favorite means of transport, flight of fancy, to take me around. Besides, it's cheaper, quieter, and there are no schedules to worry about.

I suppose it was inevitable that my thoughts would wander through the maze of happenings in this active pre-destruction season. In spite of all the research that had been done,

I couldn't help feeling that the Gods and Goddesses had not yet found the real reason why the universe was failing. It seemed to be so cleverly thought out and, as I lay there and gazed at the sky with its galaxies, stars, planets and moons, I found its beauty overwhelming. There was no doubt in my mind that the designer, Vishvakarma, had merged function with beauty in an extraordinary way. One would have thought that the scheme for mankind was just about perfect too, with the doctrine of *karma* which was designed to lead mankind gradually higher, from one life to another, until finally each soul reached emancipation. I thought it was a pretty neat idea to give individuals more than one shot at getting there so that everyone had the same opportunities in the long run. There had to be a flaw in the reasoning somewhere.

At difficult moments like this, I tend to seek counsel from my wiser half.

I: If the scheme had worked, souls would continually be rising towards emancipation. Are they, and if not, why not?

MYSELF: If they were going up, the world would be a better place to live in every day. But the concept of moral law, *dharma*, doesn't go along with that. In fact, it has a distinctly pessimistic turn to it. In the first period of creation, the *krita* age, truth reigns supreme and *dharma* is identified with truth. Then in the next age, *treta*, 1,728,000 years later, one quarter of truth is said to be replaced by falsehood and deception. Then, 1,296,000 years later, in the *dvapara* age, comes the next thump, when truth and falsehood become equally balanced. And so we move on to our present *kali* age, 864,000 years later, when truth and morality are down another quarter point and three-quarters of everything is dominated by lies, not to mention such pleasantries as murder, rape, etc. Then, and here's the clincher: 432,000 human years later the world ends, when presumably lies and bad guys take over completely.

I: Wait a minute. Who could have made up that story? Not the Gods, for sure. They wanted the universe to be perfect and to go on forever.

MYSELF: That's true. It couldn't have been the Gods. At the same time, they needed some kind of a morality code to make *karma* work. I mean one would need to know how to behave in the present life if one wanted to be advanced to a higher evolutionary soul-scale in the next life.

I: So why didn't the Gods come up with some scheme consistent with their creation?

MYSELF: Well, I suppose it's because it's not that easy to do.

I: What's so difficult about it?

MYSELF: It seems pretty evident that what's moral for one isn't necessarily moral for another. Take a woodcutter, for instance. It's right and moral for him to cut down trees, provided he doesn't go hog wild and chop them all down, in which case he'd be a bad woodcutter since he'd put himself out of business. That would definitely send his stock plummeting next time around, but on the whole chopping is good for him. And chopping's also good for a warrior, if what he's chopping down are his enemies. In fact, if a woodcutter happened to be his enemy, it would be perfectly appropriate and *dharmic* for him to chop the woodcutter down and thereby up his stock for the next life. So far so good. But it would be absolutely inappropriate behaviour for the woodcutter to chop down the warrior — even to save his own life. That would be against his *dharma* and if he succeeded, he'd be born as something even more miserable in the next round. So it just wouldn't be worth it. If I were the woodcutter confronted by a warrior, I'd just lie down and go to sleep and dream of becoming a warrior so that I could eventually get my revenge and someday go on a chopping spree myself.

I: Sounds pretty complicated, I'll admit. I can't even imagine trying to work out everyone's *dharma* seeing the variety of life styles on Earth.

MYSELF: I imagine that the Gods must have struggled over it for quite a while, but couldn't come up with anything like a coherent answer. That's why the word has so many meanings and the whole matter's so utterly complicated. I think the Gods found it too complicated to work out the details of *dharma* and left it up to man to cook something up. And I would have to say that they cooked up a mean pot of stew!

I: Well then, whoever invented the rules of *dharma* must have known that it was bound to fail, for they predicated the end of the universe. Why didn't the Gods interfere when the rules were first dreamed up?

MYSELF: I guess the Gods didn't really care about mankind's morality problems, just so long as souls were moving up and down in keeping with their concept of *karma*.

I: Are you suggesting that the Gods were not really interested in the purification and emancipation of human souls, but just wanted them to keep moving up or down? What would be the point of that?

MYSELF: At first I thought that the Gods had planned for *karma* to be a positive thing. Do good, and up you go. One would think that enough people would want to go up, and therefore, there should be more good entering the human world all the time. But the *dharma* doctrine says, no. More bad is entering. It's already bad enough, but soon bad is going to take over completely. What does that mean, if it were true? That the Gods had failed to provide enough incentive to go up! Maharajji's complaint regarding SHIT was perfectly valid. But was it because they were incapable of providing incentives, or did they really not want emancipated souls cluttering up their secret plans?

I: Well, what do you think?

MYSELF: Let me ask you the same question. The Gods created the four broad classes of people, from the bottom up: the Shudra serfs, the agriculturalist or commercial Vaishyas, the warrior Kshatriyas, and the priestly Brahmins. Well obviously the top two, priesthood and warfare are not everyone's cup of tea. Where's the incentive for a Vaishya to move up from making pots of money, to getting his head chopped off, or sitting still all day mumbling magical mantras? I'd rather buy a fleet of Cadillacs or an Infinity of Lexuses.

I: I see your point. They intended to give mixed signals right from the start. So they really don't want souls to be emancipated. Then why go through this facade of *karma* dragging mankind up and down from one life to another, like a yo-yo? Why not leave them to sort out their own *karma*, or let them be in the same state from one life to another?

Even as I asked myself the question, the shocking answer began to dawn on me. It had to be. There could be no other explanation. *Karma* was the ultimate example of the Peter Principle! As soon as people began to cope with their particular lifestyles, the idea was to bump them up to something else, like kicking them upstairs into administration, so they'd have to start all the way from the bottom again, learning the ropes. The Gods didn't want mankind to become really expert at anything by giving them an opportunity to re-examine the same problems in the next life! Of course! That was the reason man was making such a botch of everything!

Now I got really excited. Vishvakarma must have known that his design of mankind was potentially capable of challenging the Gods, but instead of modifying it so that man would be made safe, he'd introduced *karma* to reduce mankind's effectiveness. If only there was some way to bypass *karma*, mankind would become infinitely wiser and maybe even head off this impending doom. I could see each person being offered a choice: *karma* and move up, or stasis and get with it — and I'd bet my socks that a bunch of people would opt for the latter. The question was how to suspend *karma*, and I had a feeling that man could figure out something, if only they knew what I now knew.

The storyteller's guild will be horrified to find out that I now felt obliged to enter into my story and attempt to influence its outcome. We have our code, you know. It says that we can color our facts in whatever way we like, but have to do so impersonally, making it seem as though they have been doctored by one of the characters, not the storyteller. Our own eyes are only permitted to see reflections of heros and heroines and our own tongues to wag only the tails of their dogs. And all along, I've been playing the game. Well, sort of. Every now and again I've thrown in my two bits for what it's worth. But now the time has come for me to enter openly into the fray and challenge the code of the guild.

It's not so easy, unfortunately. How does a storyteller go about marketing an idea? Surprisingly, though we have the gift of the gab, we're not much good at selling. It's the 'foot in the door' aspect of salesmanship that sticks in our throats and stifles the gab. I knew that *karma* had to be stopped. But how? My wiser half came, once again, to the rescue.

MYSELF: It shouldn't be that difficult. *Karma* is, after all, just a computer program and programs are constantly being updated. All you have to do is to find a brilliant programmer to poke into it and produce a new version, and bingo! Why don't you try the fabled Silicon Valley?

So off I went, hoping that some whiz would jump at the chance to save mankind; but they'd all encountered mankind-saving opportunities before and, I suppose, my long white hair was a bit freaky so one brush-off followed another. I did finally get in to see an executive from a small firm called Breakers Anonymous. The conversation went like this:

ME: It's good of you to take the time to see me.

JOE: Well, I admit I'm playing a hunch — but what the hell! I've got to take some chances or I'll be stuck as a junior exec. for ever. Now give it to me Fax fast, I'm loosing break-time.

Joe was probably sixteen or seventeen. No doubt a genius in his home town, but here, just another precocious kid surrounded by High Q.'s.

ME: I'll get right down to it. You see, I think I've found the answer. There's this program called *Karma*, invented by the Gods to prevent mankind from achieving excellence in any field.

JOE: Interrupt. Are you trying to suggest that we're not excellent at what we do? Give me any write-protected program and stand by and watch the dust fly! I wouldn't go around talking about that non-excellence crap in this place.

ME: No, no. I didn't mean to say that . . . eh, . . . you're not excellent. No. No. I have the highest regard for you all in this valley, and that's why I'm here.

JOE: O.K. I'll live with it one more time. Give it your best shot.

It's amazing how a potentially venerable Storyteller can be flustered by a seventeen-year old hotshot. I wanted to say, 'Of course, I believe you. Now here's this program — do you're dust-flying bit with it.' But then I suddenly realized that I didn't actually have the program, I mean, not on disk; and the thought of trying to explain what it was all about — and Fax fast — to this supercilious snippet, was enough to make jello out of my resolve.

So that was, of course, that.

What next? There aren't too many places where one can get people to listen to the truth, unless one can find a remorseful financier to sponsor another independent church. Unfortunately, most of them are already taken — I mean the financiers. I even thought about going to Hyde Park Corner and taking my turn with the other 'sages', until I remembered that I'd gone there with my girlfriend, ages ago, but with nothing like the saving of the universe in mind. I toyed with other notions, sane and wild, but all came to nought. In the end I decided that I was trying too hard to make things happen and so went back to my original state of repose, lying about and dreaming of what might have been. But even that was not to be, for thoughts of how to make it be, made my repose into a pose of repose.

I kept thinking that there had to be some way to interfere with *karma*, and in my half dreams I visualized myself rushing to the rescue of mankind — indeed the whole universe — with white hair flying and riding a red Yamaha with flaring nostrils, triumphantly waving the document that declared *karma* null and void. After numerous aggrandisements, I finally decided to get serious and asked myself: 'Now what would Sherlock Holmes do in a situation like this?' It's pretty certain that he wouldn't consult Watson. No. He'd take out his violin and play in his usual execrable manner and look out into some remote place. There, he'd see the flaw in his previous reasoning and return with the solution. Just like that! Well, I didn't have a violin handy, but I was as good as any one at looking out into remote places. So I settled myself comfortably and began looking. I looked and looked and looked — and got nowhere. Then I suddenly realized the obvious. It didn't work without a violin, or else Holmes wouldn't have used one. The only instrument around was a single-stringed *tambura*, the kind of instrument that ascetics twang away at when they sing or meditate. Seemed like just the right thing, so I dusted it off and twanged along with them.

Let me say right off, that it's not automatic; I mean, it's not twang and you're away. Actually, it was pretty distracting at first and awfully boring. Then, after a while, my mind sort of went limp and I suppose I went somewhere and did some things, but what and where, I haven't a clue. Then, like one of television's special effects, I finally found myself swirling round and round, head over heels. And when I came out of the spin, I found myself taking my place at the end of a long line of ascetics seated in an open courtyard — *sadhus, sanyasis, fakirs, yogis, jogis,* and *babas* — each one playing a magical instrument. I still don't know what it all meant, but at the head of the line was the 'Frizzy-Haired *Baba*,' and suddenly I knew I'd found my answer!

Now, as I think about it, it seems rather obvious. Even the word *baba* should have given me a clue, for it's a word with many meanings. It not only means an ascetic or the head of a spiritual order, but also grandfather, father, and child. Three generations and all *babas* — spiritual guides. If the grandfather had been good at his game, in accordance with *karma* he would have been bumped up, probably to *nirvana*, salvation. If he'd been a failure, he'd have been knocked down a notch or two. But grandfather remained a *baba*, as did father, as well as the child.

This was surely clear proof that *babas* had figured out a way to out-karma *karma*! Then I remembered the story of the Frizzy-Haired *Baba*. From childhood he'd claimed to be the reincarnation of another famous *baba* and so he'd absorbed all the knowledge of the first one. As a result, he now had tremendous magical powers, the full extent of which no one knew. I had to go and see him.

Not surprisingly, he'd expected me and I found myself ushered in past the long line of envious devotees. I never know how to act in front of *babas* and hesitated momentarily before greeting him. He was smiling and knew exactly what I was going through. "No need for formalities," he said, waving me to a seat beside him (but slightly lower). "When you came to our ascetics' meeting the other day, I was able to read your mind and know that you have something very important to communicate. I already have a fair idea of what it is, but you must clarify a number of details for me."

"Baba," I replied. "I'll be happy to do so. But first can you tell me whether or not I'm right in my interpretation that both your teacher and you have learned how to bypass *karma*?"

"Not only my teacher and myself," said Baba, "but we have been doing it for six generations in my tradition, so that what you see in me is the result of six lives of meditation and concentration. I don't usually talk about this very much, but your case is certainly an exception. I'll tell you how it all started."

"The first *baba* in our line was self-made. One day he just decided to drop out of school and decided he wanted to become a hobo. His parents never saw him again. He bummed around doing this and that, meeting fascinating drop-outs, some who had been brilliant scholars, others wealthy businessmen, and a few, like himself, who'd never been anything. Over the years, he gradually developed a tremendous appetite for information, and through enormous effort and concentration became a walking encyclopedia. When people discovered this, they wouldn't leave him alone. They came from far and wide for answers to the most obscure questions, and he was seldom without the answer. At first, he revelled in being the center of attention, but as he grew older he began to think about death and what would happen to all the information he'd stored in his memory banks. Perhaps if he'd found a student as brilliant and as dedicated as he himself had been, he might have tried giving crash courses. But, as it happened, there was no one around who was prepared to undergo the rigorous intensive and extensive training that it would take. So, instead, he applied his mind to solving the problem in another way, how to package all this information he'd acquired into the sheath of his soul. After a great deal of trial and error, he succeeded. Now, he figured, if he could only swap souls with someone else, at the precise moment of his death, then it would be this other soul facing the vicissitudes of *karma,* while his own soul with packaged memory banks, rested securely in the bosom of his chosen heir, Baba II. And so it came to be. Obviously, I can't divulge the secret techniques involved in these processes, but they're all there in our communal memory banks, and as long as each one in the line continues to pass them on before they die, our line will continue forever, each generation getting more powerful than the last."

"It's exactly this 'forever' notion that I wanted to talk with you about," I said. "I happen to know that the Gods believe they've failed in producing a perfect universe and are intending to end it very soon so that they can start planning a new one. They don't care how many people have to die in the process. It's as though they're obsessed with the necessity of creating perfection."

Baba thought about this for a few moments, then responded: "Hmm. I'm beginning to see many things. But tell me why you're here to see me."

"I had this notion that Vishvakarma forgot himself when he was creating mankind and created beings that could challenge the Gods. When he realized this he could easily have pulled out a circuit or two; but I guess he liked the elegance of his design so much that he decided to put in an external control by inventing the doctrine of *karma* to ensure that mankind's soul would have to keep jumping from one lifestyle to another, so that in each new life they'd be starting from scratch. Then I thought about you and how you'd managed to keep going as *baba* from one incarnation to the next. So I knew that you'd broken the spirit of *karma*. Now, I thought to myself, if only you'd help me to pass on your secret to others, in a few generations, mankind would be able to achieve its true potential and challenge the Gods' right to destroy them and the universe. No matter how low our moral standards are said to be, we would never on Earth agree that parents have the right to destroy their children; but the Gods don't even think about the issue, as though we're not their children, just their playthings — Godtoys."

Baba again thought about this for a moment before he responded. "No. I'm sorry to have to tell you that I can't divulge our secret of soul perpetuation. But don't worry. I have an idea that will give the Gods something to think about. Now you may go home, at peace, and observe the forthcoming events for your next story."

I didn't have long to wait for the next chapter to begin for *baba* soon broke free of Earth's gravity and arrived quietly on Mount Kailash. There he sat down at a busy intersection, set out his begging bowl and his bedding roll and began meditating. Probably he would have been arrested for some trumped up charge, like delay of game, except that the police system was, like the fire brigade, virtually non-existent. Instead, many Gods and Goddesses found his presence there quite arresting. Soon crowds collected — and everywhere there are crowds, a new behavior pattern sets in. If one wishes to use an unambiguous word for it, I can suggest hooliganism. The irresponsible Maruts started blowing at Baba, adding gobs of spit to their breath when no one was looking, but Baba remained quite unperturbed and lost in his reverie. Playful Monkey-God Hanuman zinged banana peels and peanut shells at him, but still he remained immobile. Then the sensual Goddesses, the *Mohinis* of the Godworld, did their best to entice him — but nothing worked. Baba was above and beyond. And soon a cult sprang up as Gods and Goddesses took to sitting next to Baba on the sidewalk and into the street, just to be near him, perhaps wondering what he was all about.

You see, such phenomena just didn't happen on Kailash. It was a sedate world — unless perhaps one penetrated beyond the spiky iron gates and snarly guard dogs of such elite establishments as the Hills and Airs of Beverly and Bel. And we all wondered, because they never returned. Now again all were wondering when finally Baba spoke:

"Oh Gods and Goddesses! Many from my world would give their right arms to be sitting in your presence. But I . . . I give not a jot. Not even a tiny finger — for you are less than it. And yet I care for you. I have looked at your aimless ways and purposeless lives, driven like sheep by a disembodied shepherd's flute sounding in the wilderness. So I have come. I have come to sit in your busiest intersection, and I dare you to move me."

After a suitable lapse of time, during which Gods and Goddesses exchanged glances and raised eyebrows, but did nothing else, Baba continued. "This is where I want my *ashram*, my hermitage. Right here at this intersection and nowhere else."

All the traffic suddenly pulled over, as though a siren had sounded, and a resplendent *ashram* glowing with gloom newly reprieved, serenely descended right plumb square in the middle of the intersection. It was not just the miracle which impressed, but the elegance and grace of it all, as the *ashram* shimmered in the foul stench induced by the hithering and thithering of vehicles still unrestricted by smog laws. And the hithering and thithering was stopped perforce as the intersection that was, was now not. Miraculously the air began to clear and divine sinusitisses fell away like jacaranda flowers — and the *ashram* shimmered no more, and yet no less, for the smell of incense and tropical flowers permeated the air around. Baba then led the Gods and Goddesses in with a 'come my children' type of gesture and they all filed in.

So began the Baba cult on Mount Kailash. And the Gods and Goddesses continued to come day after day finding solace, not only in the newness of the experience but also in Baba's words which reflected the accumulated wisdom of six generations of *baba*hood. And they learned about the inner peace that meditation can bring and the secret joy of participating in devotional group singing. The songs were like the *nirgun bhajans* sung on Earth, not in adoration of the Gods and Goddesses, but of abstract concepts set in the form of precepts which Baba composed for the occasion, putting them to glorious soaring melodies and subtle rhythms which sink into the marrow of one's being and set the molecules of the body dancing in ecstasy.

I often went to the ashram myself. Baba, interestingly enough, gave me no sign of recognition, although he permitted me full access to all that went on. I think it was his way of telling me that a storyteller is only an observer and may not interfere in the course of events. I would have liked to have pointed out to him that, in my opinion, the mere presence of an observer was a form of interference and that he should have prohibited me from entering the ashram if he wanted me to keep my hands off. So I observed, in plain sight, and when I was moved by his songs, I sang, justifying it to myself in terms of participant observation which was by then a commonly accepted practice among fieldworkers. Baba let it go, so I continued singing and meditating, sharing in the peace and joy which was being spread in the Godworld.

Baba's sermons were equally captivating. On one occasion he talked about entropy. This is the way he explained it:

"The Gods created the universe from *purusha* who existed in perfect equilibrium and therefore in a state of maximum entropy, which means that all the tremendous energy residing in the perfectly ordered *purusha* lay in a completely unusable state. However, the energy invested by the Godly designers of the universe in dismembering *purusha* released his energy, and suddenly their creation's entropy flip-flopped into the reverse mode. From that very moment the Universe was doomed, at least according to human understanding of the Laws of Thermo-dynamics, for they have not discovered any evidence that the process of increasing entropy can be stopped or reversed, which means that all the energy released by the dismemberment of *purusha* will eventually end up in an unusable state and the universe will die out.

"When I found out," Baba continued, "that you were carrying out research to find out the reasons for the failure at such a late date, I knew there had to be something else. And, of course, it's there, right under our noses! I asked myself, 'Since the universe began with *purusha* who was in a state of perfect order and will eventually end with perfect disorder when all the available energy has run out, why should life have been created, since life has the capacity to create order out of disorder?' Entropists might say, 'Ah! but it takes them more energy to create order than they gain by the order they have created, and in the long run, they're only increasing the entropy rate.' Nevertheless, looking at it from my perspective, I asked, 'Why would the Gods want to create a reversal mechanism at all, even though it is merely a small eddy in the overwhelming flow of entropy? Were they doing this merely for entertainment, or did they really believe that life could in some way halt and even reverse the flow?'

"Then I knew that mankind was destined to replace you Gods and Goddesses as creators, preservers and destroyers of the universe. It was no game on your part; you had created life, and ultimately mankind, to reverse the flow of entropy and to create order out of the fast disappearing order which you couldn't handle on your own — like the matter of creating drama and giving it to mankind to produce, because you knew, even then, that they

could do things that you couldn't. But you didn't think about the
consequences, that if mankind succeeded, they would oust you
from Kailash and establish their dynasties here.

"Obviously, Vishvakarma had an inkling from the start
and so he built in the *karma* clause which he thought would slow
mankind down. And so it did. In spite of that, man went ahead
and achieved things which you had thought were impossible.
Then, when your Heavenly Assembly realized that man was
beginning to threaten the basic rights of the Godworld as creators,
preservers and destroyers of the universe, they decided to become
selfish and started putting impediments in the way, creating
DRIPs and drabs of distractions which prevent man from getting
to grips with the real enemy — Entropy.

"Now I say to you, 'Let go. No one wants to give up an
ages-old lifestyle, but there comes a time when you must move
on, and this is it. Take off the shackles of *karma* and withdraw
your DRIP guerilla forces from Earth and let mankind find their
own salvation. Then I will show you the truth about yourselves."

The essence of this sermon (if one can call it such) spread
throughout Kailash and soon younger Gods and Goddesses were
congregating at street corners singing the 'Let Go' theme:

Let go, let go,
The open road
Is where we wish to be.

Move on, move on,
The open road
Will lead us to be free.

The senior Gods ignored them at first, but when they
started shaving their heads and snarling up the traffic 'something
orful,' Shiva scheduled a general meeting of the Heavenly

Assembly to discuss the issue. Knowing it was to be a momentous meeting, everyone came, the younger ones singing 'Let Go' as the elders entered. When Shiva called the meeting to order, all became quiet.

"Friends, I apologise for scheduling this emergency meeting at such short notice, but I think you will agree with me that the circumstances warrant some sort of action on our parts. As you all know, Kailash has been host to an intruder from Earth for the first time in its recent history, and I should say that we've been most hospitable; well, at least we haven't required visas and health certificates, nor have we subjected him to security checks and customs examinations. I should also mention that he has appropriated Municipal property for his *ashram* and we have not lifted a finger to discourage him. In view of this, I think it's a bit presumptuous of our guest to be critical of our deeds and doings. Where else could he get away with this? My first thought was to evict him summarily, but I see that a number of our gathering feel otherwise, and not wishing to act hastily, I've called this meeting.

"Since there's no real precedent for this kind of meeting, I will lay down the formalities for procedure. Firstly, I call upon Vishvakarma to comment on Baba's assessment of entropy and the universe."

Vishvakarma took the stand and began his response. "There isn't too much to say. It didn't happen quite the way Baba sees it, but I suppose he has all the essentials right. I'm disappointed that he focussed on only the negative aspects of creation, never once talking about the beauty of the universal design or giving any credit to me for creating the perfection of humanity. Very discouraging, after all the time and energy I invested, not to give credit to the moments of inspiration that went into it."

Shiva, being not only his close friend, but a consummate diplomat to boot, spoke in support.

"No one can belittle the magnificence of your creation. In fact, I'm going to ask our members to give you a rousing recognition of your endeavors."

Shiva began the applause himself. The response was warm, if not rousing, but some of the younger Gods and Goddesses made themselves conspicuous by not participating. Then Shiva continued.

"So Vishvakarma, almost from the beginning of creation the designers knew that something had gone wrong and entropy had taken over. Why didn't they ask me to end the universe right then? Why did we have to go on for such a long time believing that there was a chance for it to succeed?"

Vishvakarma replied, "When we were absolutely sure that it had gone wrong — and it wasn't right away — we had a meeting and discussed various possibilities, one of them being of course, to start all over again. But I felt that there was a solution and I still believe that it exists. The Laws of Entropy demand that everything moves from order to disorder. The obvious way to undo entropy was to create a force which would counter this and create order out of disorder, and I said that I could design such a force. That force is life, and especially, mankind, and I created it, and even today I believe that it can do the job."

Vishnu then asked to be recognized and spoke. "It's all very well for you to throw around orders and disorders, but is it not my responsibility to preserve the universe? If you built in the secret of preservation into your design, what have I been doing all this time? Why was I not consulted when all this was going on?"

"Well of course we considered bringing you into the picture," Vishvakarma hastily answered. "We also thought about bringing in Shiva. But you see, your duty was to preserve the universe until such time as it was to be dissolved by Shiva. You have done that admirably and at great sacrifice of creative energy. It's not you for whom I feel concern, since your duties were always terminal, but rather for my dear friend Shiva. If my design were to work, as I believe it still can, the universe would be self-perpetuating and Shiva would be out of a job. Many a time, lying in bed, I've considered the possibility of man being extinguished so that Shiva can fulfill, and be fulfilled by, his mission of destruction — but I'm afraid that it may now be too late."

A hum of incredulity spread through the chamber as the Gods and Goddesses tried to comprehend Vishvakarma's statement, which clearly indicated that there was now no way to stop mankind! That meant, *ipso facto*, that they had already become the new Gods!

Shiva, with his customary self-control, not revealing anything of the turmoil that must have been racking his being, spoke: "Thank you, Vishvakarma, for your forthright and sincere testimony. I will now summarize our options, as I see them. Firstly, we could ignore all the evidence that has been presented, expel our uninvited visitor and continue as before."

This was greeted with loud boos and cries of 'shame', as Shiva held up his hand to still the responses and continued: "Secondly, we could form a committee to look into the matter."

This was greeted with even louder boos, but Shiva persevered: "Thirdly, we could change our diversionary tactics and withdraw our DRIP contingent, leaving mankind to find the answers without interference."

This was received more favorably, but still every one was waiting for the fourthly which had to come:

"And fourthly," Shiva said, "we could also revoke the *karma* clause. This would give mankind a real opportunity to counterbalance entropy, but at the same time, it would positively set the seal on our future."

I could not believe that the Gods would ever have considered such a step, although I knew they were well protected by retirement funds, social security, medicare and what not. Baba had done it, and although there were numerous abstentions, the majority vote went solidly in favor of the fourth option.

I went to see Baba the very next day, walking past the innumerable 'For Sale' signs that had appeared overnight. This time, Baba deigned to recognize me, just long enough to tell me, 'I told you so.' Then, once again, I became anonymous, while Baba was deluged by his new followers desperate to hang on to his every word. Then we sang, and we meditated, and finally, Baba spoke.

"You have done the right thing and I commend you for your courage. Yet, believe me, it was the only course for you to take. Now you must shake off your own *karma* and make yourselves free to find true happiness. You see, you've been afflicted by the same curse as you had inflicted on mankind: *karma*. While they've had to go from one life to another and another, virtually endlessly, seeking to perfect their souls, you've had to go from one creation to another and another, also virtually endlessly, to create a perfect universe. Just as their future lives were influenced by their good deeds and their mistakes, so have yours, only you've had to carry out your own research to find your successes and your failures.

"Who is driving you to create the perfect universe? Why must you go on and on striving for perfection? What force is greater than Gods and Goddesses? Why can you not just sit in peace? I want to help you find the answers to these and many more questions.

"So let us begin by looking within ourselves . . . ."

GLOSSARY

adbhuta — the sentiment *(rasa)* of wonderment as experienced by writers who make it to the glossary

Agni — the God of Fire and one of the chief deities of the Vedas who with his seven tongues laps up all the butter offerings consigned to him, and occasionally suffers from bouts of biliousness

Amitabh — First name of a famous Indian actor (any Indian will gladly supply the last name)

amrita — nectar of immortality? water of life? Soma juice? or just a lost dream?

antara — the second musical theme like the second floor, higher than the first one, *sthayi*

Ardhanarisvara — lit. 'God with half woman (characteristic)', i.e., Shiva with one bosom

Aryan — a group of tribes armed with Vedas and Gods that invaded India from the Northwest in the 2nd millennium B.C., leaving one wondering where India would now be if they hadn't

ashram — hermitage, famous for one-course meals and the absence of golf courses, swimming pools, and saunas

Asura — originally a term for Gods which turned out to be inauspicious so they forced it on the Demons

avatar — incarnation which Deities adopt to visit the Earth in order to fulfill a particular purpose, not to mention doing the things they can not do in heaven

Ayappan — a Dravidian God not generally mentioned in Aryan literature, but of great importance in South India; is regarded as the son of the two male Gods Shiva and Vishnu (in his female aspect), and created expressly to destroy the Demoness Mahishi who had carelessly been granted immunity to anyone born of woman or Goddess; the plot thickens here as Ayappan, a brilliant minority person, nevertheless faces big problems achieving tenure in the Heavenly Senate

baba — a spiritual guide; one who turns out to be the guide of Gods

Bali — a monkey king said to be son of Indra who made the mistake of challenging Rama, not knowing that Rama was an incarnation of

Vishnu and that he had no hope of winning; moral: do your research before jumping into the soup

Banodokri — one of many local Goddesses in India worshipped by particular castes and tribes; the modesty and gentility of this old lady-Goddess explains her non-persona status in the Godworld

Bhairava — the terrible manifestation of Shiva which can be provoked at the wink of an eye

bhajan — a devotional song to work people into a frenzy

Bharata — lit. 'actor'; name of the author of the famous work on drama, *Natyashastra*, a tradition which he claims was passed on to him by the God Brahma as the fifth Veda — Ha!

bhayanaka — the terrible sentiment *(rasa)* which in these stories only the Goddess has the courage to dramatize

Bhuvar Loka — the land that lies, and lies between all that matters, the worlds of the Gods and the one world of mankind

bibhatsa — the odious sentiment *(rasa)* — horripilating thought

Brahma — first member of the Hindu Trinity; THE CREATOR; but in these stories, a modest, gentle, caring old guy who has seen it all, time and time again

Brahmin — The upper echelon and priestly caste of Hindu society, which isn't necessarily a good fun place to be

Buddha — the father of Buddhism, a human prince who was adopted as the ninth incarnation of Vishnu, no doubt confounding his followers

CIA — Celestial Intelligence Agency

CHP — Committee on Heavenly Personnel

dasa, dasyu — indigenous inhabitants of India conquered by Indra but not yet vanquished, thank God (Gods?)

Deus — Roman God (cf., the Greek God Zeus) whose Indian counterpart, Dyaus, was known as 'Heavenly Father' in the Vedas; but his name is seldom mentioned in later literature, suggesting that the heavenly father myth is now running a bit thin

devadasi — girl given over by parents to the service of a God which involves a multitude of activities, the full extent of which should never be disclosed; knowing, however, that Gods are particular about those around them, they have developed India's artistic traditions to the highest levels in their pursuit of God-joy

Devi — a general term for Goddess whose character ranges from gentle, beautiful, and motherly, as in Goddesses Uma, Gauri and Jagat-mata, to violent and bloody, e.g., Kali and Durga. All in all, a fairly good general description of American women

dharma — an unavoidable problem, consequential to the doctrine of *karma*: if one is going on the *karma* UP elevator one needs to know which button to press; *dharma* is the instruction manual; unfortunately mankind has not yet cracked the code in which it is written

Digambara Jain — The only group that is really allowed to practise what they believe, and the sky is the limit and the only clothing they will accept

Dravidian — probably the largest of the original groups that inhabited India before the Aryan conquests; they were driven to the Southern peninsula of India, where they are still dominant, no thanks to the Aryans who still try to impose their 'lingua franca' on them

DRIP — Diversion of Real Intellectual Pursuits

Durga — Goddess, wife of Shiva, extolled in India's East in neon lights, biscuits, and matchstick designs of her form; nemesis of Mahishasura; see Devi

dvapara — the third of the four ages (*yuga*) of this disaster called creation in a magnanimous moment

Ganesha — elephant-headed deity, Lord of Wisdom and Auspicious Beginnings — how did he get into such a prestigious position? Of course, he is the son of Shiva — is anyone suggesting nepotism? Whether or not, he is a great character and your Storyteller, would be poorer without him

ganevali — lit., singing girl or woman — why should this be a derogatory term?

ganika — a courtesan of old, versed in the sixty-four arts and sciences, and possibly a few others that are not mentioned in the records

ghazal — verse form in the Urdu language, a hybrid of Persian and Hindi, said to have been invented in army camps as a means of communication; if so, all their time seems to have been spent on love matters, not war, for ghazals are devoted to love poetry — I could go for a war like that!

ghunghru — tinkling ankle bells that evoke endless memories of the gone, the here, and the hereafter

gupta seva — the storyteller does not believe in hiding the truth, but confronted with the Secret Service, under Vishnu's CIA profligate corps he has second thoughts; the secret *seva* of the *Devadasi* must remain secret — what is already happening to them is bad enough!

hasya — the sentiment *(rasa)* of laughter not too popular in the Godworld — maybe we should send Jerry, Woody, or Robin up there, just for laughs

HEC — Heavenly Ethics Committee

Ilango Adigal — actually a prince, not a storyteller by trade — still, I'd say he did a pretty good job of *Silappadikaram*, almost as though he were a professional

Indra — Vedic God of War and Thunder, armed with his bolts and several belts of Soma juice, he above all is responsible for extending the Aryan domain into India; but once that is over with, along with his 'King of the Gods' stint, he becomes involved in petty affairs, falls into the second rank of Gods, and faces an uncertain future

jogi — a mendicant musician who makes the music he likes like he knows what he's doing

Kailash — mountain where Shiva resides, but in these stories, residence of the Gods, creating awful congestion problems, smog, etc.

Kali — lit. 'black', the fierce and bloody consort of Shiva whom it is wiser to propitiate than question

kali — the fourth of the four ages (*yuga*) of this creation, when the topsy really turns to turvy

Kalidasa — a poet-dramatist of the 5th century A.D. who gave *natya* new life with his heart-throbbing plays

Kamasutra — an apologetic treatise on erotica that gave a big boost to contortionology

Kannaki — a lovely Goddess who elevated herself from the deepest bog of despair to become the only expert in the sixty-four arts and sciences in Heaven

karma — the doctrine of transmigration of souls; all good and proper, but what moves them to move from this to that, here to there, and especially, up to down? *see 'dharma'*

Karttikeya — son of Shiva; God of War and incidentally also called Skanda, *which see*

karuna — the pathetic sentiment *(rasa)* — sad, but quite Indian

Kovalan — quartered and martyred, his greatest claim to fame, apart from rescuing a Brahmin from a raging elephant, is his wife, Kannaki, who nearly made it as a *devadasi* here

Krishna — eighth incarnation of Vishnu and amorous beyond compare; loved by both men and women — true emanci- and ewomanci-pation

krita — the first of the four ages (*yuga*) of this creation; good but dull and only one way to go — DOWN

Kshatriya — the second of the four classes of Indian society who, emulating the Gods, specialized in killing and kingship

kusha — sacred grass that might do well in So Cal's dry climate

lasya — feminine dance, invented by Shiva for drama after he received a bunch of feminist complaints that his male *tandava* dance was hogging the whole show

lila — game or play that Gods and Goddesses like to watch in which humans writhe about trying to overcome the miseries inflicted on them

Madhavi — a beautiful courtesan with too much heart and love for anything but a Buddhist nunnery

Mahabharata — a grand old saga that made a life-stopping Sunday nine to ten a.m. endless Indian TV series and a controversial eclectic production in the West

Maharajji — lit. 'respected great king'; often used in reference to mystics, Brahmins, and virtually anyone else whom one wants to supplicate or adulate for one reason or another

Mahatma — lit. 'great soul'; name by which the late spiritual and political leader Mohandas Gandhi is commonly known — one of DRIP's greatest successes

Mahishasura — lit. 'great Asura'. A Demon destroyed by: a) the God Skanda, or b) the Goddess Durga, which is the more bloody and usually preferred

Marut — Storm God, but only found in a group of seven scatterbrains whose erratic behavior provides sustenance to weather channels and forecasters

maya — elusive illusion

Meenakshi — Dravidian Goddess born with three breasts and a predicated future as the divine housewife of Shiva which retarded the feminist movement by about one thousand and seven hundred plus years

Mohini — the alluring feminine form adopted by God Vishnu, firstly to steal the nectar away from the underworld, and later to seduce Shiva in order to beget Skanda who had to be born without female intervention in order to destroy the Demoness, Taraka — what a plot!

nachnevali — why does this always have to be translated by the derogatory expression 'dancing girl' ? They don't have to be girls, and most of them are not, except in the beginning

Nat — community of actors, acrobats, puppeteers, and whatever else will get them a buck, and who can blame them?

natya — a computer program for Sanskrit drama invented by the Supreme God Brahma and passed on to Bharata; nevertheless, it had a few bugs in it

Natyashastra — Bharata's *Companion* for the programs called Natya ™ 1.0 and Natya™ 1.01, copyrighted in the 2nd century A.D.

nirgun bhajan — a devotional, philosophical or moral song dealing with abstractions of nothing

Parvati — Goddess 'of the mountain' and lovely wife of Shiva who liked to go snowshoeing when she wasn't housewifeing

Purusha — primeval man of the Vedas; the metaphorical lamb sacrificed by the Gods to create the present universe and these stories

raga — melodic takeoff point for *rasa,* mystifying to the uninitiated

Ramarajya — the good old times before inflation and devaluation

Ramayana — the story of Rama, seventh incarnation of Vishnu, and the good old times (*see above*) including wife-napping and eventual destruction of the Demon wife-napper, Ravana

rasa — sentiment, of which there were initially eight, with a ninth added later to complete Brahma's penchant for symmetry

raudra — the furious sentiment *(rasa)* best avoided except when umpires are blind

Ravana — ten-headed Demon and wife-napper who got his just deserts when the forces of good de-napped Rama's wife, Sita

RIP — Real Intellectual Pursuits; Vishnu's put-down of DRIP

rishi — seven sagacious characters who (over?)heard the Vedas

ROR —Representations of Reality; committee proposed by Shiva to counter the RIP roar tactics of Vishnu

Rudra — Vedic God of the Terrible who is equated with Shiva on purely circumstantial grounds

sadhu — a holy man usually unkempt, often mistaken for a faker

salaam — a polite greeting with bent body and a one-handed movement, as though splashing water on one's own face; better in the plural because it tends to go on and on

sanyasi — an ascetic who generally abandons wife and children for hermitage food

sarangi — a fiddle with so many sympathetic strings that it takes hours to tune and can more easily be played badly than well

Sarasvati — wife of Brahma, the Creator, and Goddess of learning and the arts; her ventures into the publications world are generally unknown and unheralded

Sati — Shiva's wife who got burned up at his sloppy appearance

SHIT — Sincerity, Honesty, Integrity, and Truth

Shiva — One of the three principal members of the Hindu Trinity, known especially as THE DESTROYER, but also as a computer manufacturer and nuclear reactor designer; he is also, in these stories, an intrepid fieldworker whose methodology is frequently questioned

shringara — the erotic sentiment *(rasa)* that sends goose bumps up and down wherever it counts most

Shudra — the fourth and lowest class in Aryan lore, who theoretically have nothing better to do in terms of *dharma* than to run around after the others — for how much longer?

Silappadikaram — the story of an ankle bracelet and a triangle — Kannaki, Kovalan, and Madhavi — concocted by 'Prince' (talk about putting it on!) Ilango Adikal nearly two thousand years ago

Skanda — also known as Kumara and Karttikeya; a six-headed Vedic God of war and slayer of Taraka whose newest ambition is to become a Prosecution Attorney but he collects celestial unemployment benefits as he waits for his next case

Soma — a climbing plant of some kind, the juice of which did some pretty fantastic things for Gods and Brahmins; would that we knew exactly just what it was in his juice that made him such an important God in Vedic times

Surya — effulgence personified, the Sun God; having had a spotty career, was now making his way back into the limelight with an idea — his first for quite a while

tabla — a pair of hand drums quite unlike the doldrums

tandava — a vigorous, masculine form of dance designed by Shiva to wear out recalcitrant dancers who ignore Director's commands

Taraka — a Demon belonging to a community that opposed sacrifices to the Gods and thus had to be destroyed; being a formidable foe it took the non-woman-born Skanda to do it

tawa'if — quite a lot like *ganika* courtesans, but wearing floppy pants while dancing and singing

treta — the second of the four ages *(yuga)* of this creation when the rot begins to set in

Triple Oh Seven — the false avatar that Vishnu claims to have disclaimed

Vach — Goddess of Speech who bestows the gift of gab, not to mention gag, to those who please or displease her — a pretty important lady for storytellers to woo

Vaishya — the third of the Aryan classes without whom shopping malls and motels would have to close down

Varuna — one of the old, old Vedic Gods and once King of the Universe; with the passage of the waters of time his role is diluted so that he becomes the God of Seas and Rivers

Vatsyayana — a quaint writer who spent much of his life dreaming up impossible sex positions to describe in his *Kamasutra*

Vayu — of 'breeze-dried' fame, the blustering God of Wind

Veda — lit. 'knowledge,' perhaps even 'true knowledge,' certainly out-of-date knowledge; curiously composed in 'books' by the Aryan Gods long before they were written down and preserved by Brahmins for thousands of years aurally and orally, involving prodigious feats of memory

vimana — seven-storied temple tower — designed to out-do six-storied towers?

vira — the heroic sentiment *(rasa)* without which the Gods would have little to brag about

Vishnu — the middle member of the Trinity, THE PRESERVER, and leader of the Opposition Party; not in the upper echelon of Gods in the Vedas, he rapidly gained advancement in the ranks by his miraculous abilities of reincarnation which drained him both physically and mentally, as a result of which he is, in these stories, mostly recuperating and only occasionally finding the energy to let his RIP roar

Vishvakarma — not to be mistaken for the chap below; Mr. V., or rather the God V. is the very thoughtful Designer of the Universe and loves to provoke thought by posing puzzles, which are manifest in all his creations; he is also known for leaving windows open

Vishvanathan — not to be mistaken for the God above, nor the cricketer, is a plain chap, in fact a chopper of wood who has his biggest thrills buzzing the world of the Gods, Mount Kailash

wah wah — substitute for applause practised by Indians whose hands and ears are too sensitive for clapping

Yama — He may have been the first mortal to die and enter the celestial world, thereby establishing his rights over death; the only celestial CPA and a thoroughly efficient deity who watches over everyone with an eager eye, ready to pounce at the slightest wavering of the life force

yuga — periods of the universe, of which there are said to be four, excluding dawns and sundowns; the numbers of years involved are mind-boggling, until we get down to what's left

Zeenat — first name of a famous Bombollywood Goddess everyone should know; it is perhaps prophetic that this book ends with her name